HIS FIR[illegible]ITH JEAN-LU[illegible]ARD SHATTERED BEN SISKO'S LIFE FOREVER . . .

Lt. Commander Benjamin Sisko, first officer of the USS *Saratoga,* watched as the Borg ship on the viewscreen disappeared and was replaced by a human face . . . No, not human, but a monstrous marriage of metal and flesh. Sisko recognized the face, which belonged to one of the best-known captains in the fleet.

"Picard," Captain Storil intoned softly.

"I am Locutus," it said. The voice was Picard's, but lifeless, grating, devoid of intonation. "You will be assimilated. Resistance is futile."

"Load all torpedo bays," Captain Storil ordered. "Ready phasers."

Sisko watched the screen as *Saratoga's* phasers and torpedoes streaked through the void and flared briefly against the leaden, layered surface of the Borg vessel. Simultaneously, the Borg ship fired at the nearby USS *Melbourne,* which exploded with a painful brightness on the viewscreen.

That's it, Sisko thought before he could stop himself. And we're next.

Look for STAR TREK Fiction from Pocket Books

Star Trek: The Original Series

Probe
Prime Directive
The Lost Years
Star Trek VI: The Undiscovered Country
Star Trek V: The Final Frontier
Star Trek IV: The Voyage Home
Spock's World
Enterprise
Strangers from the Sky
Final Frontier
#1 *Star Trek: The Motion Picture*
#2 *The Entropy Effect*
#3 *The Klingon Gambit*
#4 *The Covenant of the Crown*
#5 *The Prometheus Design*
#6 *The Abode of Life*
#7 *Star Trek II: The Wrath of Khan*
#8 *Black Fire*
#9 *Triangle*
#10 *Web of the Romulans*
#11 *Yesterday's Son*
#12 *Mutiny on the Enterprise*
#13 *The Wounded Sky*
#14 *The Trellisane Confrontation*
#15 *Corona*
#16 *The Final Reflection*
#17 *Star Trek III: The Search for Spock*
#18 *My Enemy, My Ally*
#19 *The Tears of the Singers*
#20 *The Vulcan Academy Murders*
#21 *Uhura's Song*
#22 *Shadow Lord*
#23 *Ishmael*
#24 *Killing Time*
#25 *Dwellers in the Crucible*
#26 *Pawns and Symbols*
#27 *Mindshadow*
#28 *Crisis on Centaurus*
#29 *Dreadnought!*
#30 *Demons*
#31 *Battlestations!*
#32 *Chain of Attack*
#33 *Deep Domain*
#34 *Dreams of the Raven*
#35 *The Romulan Way*
#36 *How Much for Just the Planet?*
#37 *Bloodthirst*
#38 *The IDIC Epidemic*
#39 *Time for Yesterday*
#40 *Timetrap*
#41 *The Three-Minute Universe*
#42 *Memory Prime*
#43 *The Final Nexus*
#44 *Vulcan's Glory*
#45 *Double, Double*
#46 *The Cry of the Onlies*
#47 *The Kobayashi Maru*
#48 *Rules of Engagement*
#49 *The Pandora Principle*
#50 *Doctor's Orders*
#51 *Enemy Unseen*
#52 *Home Is the Hunter*
#53 *Ghost Walker*
#54 *A Flag Full of Stars*
#55 *Renegade*
#56 *Legacy*
#57 *The Rift*
#58 *Faces of Fire*
#59 *The Disinherited*
#60 *Ice Trap*
#61 *Sanctuary*
#62 *Death Count*
#63 *Shell Game*

Star Trek: The Next Generation

Relics
Imzadi
Reunion
Unification
Metamorphosis
Vendetta
Encounter at Farpoint
#1 Ghost Ship
#2 The Peacekeepers
#3 The Children of Hamlin
#4 Survivors
#5 Strike Zone
#6 Power Hungry
#7 Masks
#8 The Captains' Honor
#9 A Call to Darkness
#10 A Rock and a Hard Place
#11 Gulliver's Fugitives
#12 Doomsday World
#13 The Eyes of the Beholders
#14 Exiles
#15 Fortune's Light
#16 Contamination
#17 Boogeymen
#18 Q-in-Law
#19 Perchance to Dream
#20 Spartacus
#21 Chains of Command
#22 Imbalance
#23 War Drums
#24 Nightshade

EMISSARY

The Novel by J.M.DILLARD
Based on the Teleplay by MICHAEL PILLER
Story by RICK BERMAN & MICHAEL PILLER

POCKET STAR BOOKS
New York London Toronto Sydney Tokyo Singapore

This book is a work of fiction. Names, characters, places and incidents are either products of the author's imagination or are used fictitiously. Any resemblance to actual events or locales or persons, living or dead, is entirely coincidental.

An *Original* Publication of POCKET BOOKS

A Pocket Star Book published by
POCKET BOOKS, a division of Simon & Schuster Inc.
1230 Avenue of the Americas, New York, NY 10020

ISBN: 0-671-79858-8

First Pocket Books printing February 1993

10 9 8 7 6 5 4 3 2 1

Printed in the U.S.A.

For Dave Stern,
with heartfelt thanks

EMISSARY

CHAPTER 1

HIS FIRST ENCOUNTER with Jean-Luc Picard shattered Ben Sisko's life forever.

On stardate 44002.3, a fleet of forty Federation starships received orders to proceed to Wolf 359 to intercept a Borg vessel on its way to Earth. The *Saratoga* was the first to arrive.

Lieutenant Commander Benjamin Sisko served as the *Saratoga*'s first officer. Like the rest of the crew, Sisko had never seen a Borg and knew little of the race save that Starfleet Command deemed them a grave threat. He knew they were considered even more treacherous, more dangerous, than the Romulans; he knew that most others who had engaged them perished. Sisko was not afraid. He had absolute faith in himself, his captain, his ship, the Fleet.

But he had not been prepared for the *size* of the thing.

On *Saratoga*'s main bridge viewscreen, the Borg ship hung gray and motionless against a backdrop of stars, dwarfing the Federation vessel with its vastness. To Sisko's eyes it wasn't even a proper ship, but a huge ungainly cube of spaceborne metal layered with thousands upon thousands of randomly placed conduits, piping and tiny compartments. There was no sleekness to it, no grace, no suggestion its builders had taken any care or pride or pleasure in its design. It looked as if some mindless force, some instinct, had driven them to add on each scrap of metal, each honeycomb, bit by bit. Like a bird building a nest, Sisko thought.

Or a hive. Insects building a gigantic metal hive.

At the sight, Captain Storil leaned forward in his chair and frowned, a faint crease appearing between his dark upswept brows.

Sisko took note of the gesture. For the captain, it was the equivalent of a gasp, a muttered curse, a reaction of resounding surprise. Storil was a Vulcan, dedicated to the repression of feeling in the pursuit of pure reason. Like most of his race, he possessed an astonishing intelligence and a degree of mastery over his emotions that made him, by human standards, seem cold and calculating. Sisko had at first worried that the Vulcan's decisions would not take into account the morale of his mostly human command; that was before he learned that Storil's devotion to logic was nothing compared to his devotion and loyalty to his crew.

"Ensign Delaney." Storil tilted his head in her direction. "Attempt to establish—"

The screen flickered and went dark. In place of the Borg ship, a face appeared. A human face, Sisko thought, in the first millisecond before the image coalesced, but even before the features formed completely he knew something was terribly *wrong.*

"Picard," Storil whispered beside him.

Sisko returned his gaze to the screen. It was indeed Jean-Luc Picard who stood on the bridge of the Borg vessel. Sisko had seen a Fleet missive when Picard assumed command of the *Enterprise* several years before—Picard was one of the best-known captains and *Enterprise* one of the best-known ships in the Fleet. The impression Sisko'd gotten was of a dignified, confident man, but there had been warmth beneath the dignity. This was indeed the famous captain of the *Enterprise.*

And yet . . . it was not. Not human, not machine, but a monstrous marriage of metal and flesh. One of Picard's arms had been extended with an intricate mechanical prosthesis, his eyes augmented with a sensor-scope protruding from one temple; his pale face was utterly, frighteningly blank. The dignity and the warmth were gone. Behind him, Borg stood motionless, thoughtless, in their individual honeycomb compartments. Sisko got a fleeting mental image of mindless hive insects excreting skeins of metal, wrapping Picard in a cocoon of machinery.

If any part of Jean-Luc Picard remained, the man-machine hybrid gave no sign. The sensor-scope flashed red, whirred softly, and angled forward, studying the humans with an intelligence as empty, as infinite, as cold, as space.

If that was what the Borg intended for the *Saratoga's* crew, Sisko intended to go down fighting.

"I am Locutus," it said. The voice was Picard's, but lifeless, grating, devoid of intonation. "You will be assimilated. Resistance is futile."

Sisko's lips parted, half in astonishment, half in outrage at the forthright arrogance of this proclamation; his gaze caught the captain's. Storil's face remained impassive, composed, but Sisko had served with him enough years to recognize the faint glimmer of defiance in the captain's dark slanting eyes.

Assimilate? Sisko's look said. Like hell we will.

The Vulcan's gaze serenely affirmed the sentiment.

"You will disarm all weapons and escort us to sector zero-zero-one," Locutus continued. "If you attempt to intervene, we will destroy you."

Zero-zero-one: Earth. Hranok, the Bolian tactical officer, moved pale blue hands over his console, then lifted his chin and made a small sound of indignation.

Sisko stared down at his viewer and saw a schematic display of three starships gliding silently into formation around the *Saratoga;* now four Davids challenged Goliath. "Sir, Admiral Hanson has deployed the *Gage,* the *Kyushu,* and the *Melbourne.*"

Captain Storil's attention did not waver from the screen. "Move us to position alpha, Ensign."

"Aye, sir," Ensign Tamamota replied, eyes wide as she forced her attention away from Picard on viewscreen. Tamamota was young, a bit green, but her hands were steady on the controls; the Vulcan's stolid, quiet presence had a calming effect.

"Load all torpedo bays," Storil ordered in the same tone he might have used to order a routine tactical check, but Sisko fancied he detected a faint heaviness there; the captain deplored the use of weaponry, relied on it only as a last resort. "Ready phasers."

Picard's mutated image disappeared abruptly, indicating he had understood Captain Storil's reply, and was replaced once more by that of the Borg ship.

Hranok's muscular torso leaned over his console. "The Borg ship is attempting to lock on to the *Melbourne* with its tractor beam."

"Target the origin point of that beam, Lieutenant," Storil said smoothly. "Fire when ready."

Sisko watched the screen as *Saratoga*'s phasers and torpedoes streaked through the void, flared briefly against the surface of the Borg vessel, then dimmed.

Simultaneously the Borg ship fired a bright, searing beam, striking the *Melbourne.*

That's it, Sisko thought before he could stop himself. And we're next.

For an instant the *Melbourne* trembled, illuminated against the blackness by a deadly corona of light. Sisko squinted against the painful brightness on the screen, forced himself not to look away as the *Melbourne's* hull exploded into scorched, hurtling fragments, forced himself not to think of those dead and dying on a bridge very like this one.

Sisko prided himself on being unshakable and efficient during emergencies. In his first year at the Academy he had failed an unannounced emergency drill miserably because of an attack of nerves. Since then he had trained himself so that, even now in the face of certain attack, he felt the overlay of calm descend, felt his brain shut off the capacity for emotion until he became as impassive and detached as his captain. A part of his mind screamed that they were all certainly about to die, that he should leave his post, find his wife and son, spend his last few seconds with them—but the rational part knew that Jennifer and Jake's best chance lay in his ability to perform his duty efficiently now.

Time slowed. Sisko became hyperaware of his breathing, of the beating of his heart. He faced his captain, calmly waiting, not thinking at all as the Borg ship turned, ominous and implacable, to face the *Saratoga.*

The deck lurched, Sisko staggered, regained his footing as Lieutenant Hranok called: "The Borg are attempting to lock on to us."

"Evasive maneuvers," Storil said evenly, clutching the arms of his chair for balance. "Delta pattern."

At the navigation console, Tamamota's fingers swiftly manipulated the controls. "Delta pattern initiated." She glanced down at her readout, recoiled slightly from what she saw, swiveled her head toward the captain. "We're not moving."

From Ops, Delaney confirmed what Sisko already knew: "They've locked on."

Sisko watched the screen as the *Gage* and *Kyushu* opened fire on the Borg vessel, trying in vain to save the *Saratoga,* just as *Saratoga* had done for the *Melbourne.*

And the outcome would be the same, Sisko realized, with terrible, cold certainty, yet he permitted himself to feel nothing, only to concentrate on the task at hand as Delaney tersely reported, "Our shields are being drained. Sixty-four percent . . . forty-two—"

"Recalibrate shield nutation," Storil ordered patiently, as if they were not seconds away from death.

Feverishly, Hranok worked his console. "Modulation is having no effect."

"Shields are going," Delaney called, and this time there was a clear, strident note of panic in her voice. "We're going—"

Darkness. With a roar, the bridge erupted in flame. Sisko was slammed to the deck. When *Saratoga* righted herself, he drew in a lungful of smoke, coughed, and pushed himself to his knees. The billowing smoke clutched at his throat, stung his eyes; he wiped away the sweat trickling down his forehead, refusing to be alarmed when his sleeve came away soaked dark red.

No time to be frightened, no time to think. Time to *act.*

The bridge lay dark and smoldering, illumined only by the sparks raining from damaged consoles. Sisko strained to hear his captain's calm voice. Being a Vulcan and stronger than most of his crew, Storil would be the first to recover—if he was alive.

Silence.

"Damage report," Sisko shouted hoarsely, and coughed again.

No answer. The emergency lights flickered once, then came on.

"Damage report," Sisko insisted, as if by sheer determination he could will other survivors. He pushed himself unsteadily to his feet.

Movement nearby in the dim light. Hranok, wounded, bleeding, pulled himself up on his console while Sisko moved quickly from body to warm body, feeling for pulses, finding none: first Garcia, then Delaney. Dead. Dead. Tamamota, dead.

Don't feel, act. Don't think, just act.

Captain Storil, the hardest of all, unseeing eyes open and staring serenely, matter-of-factly through the haze at him.

Don't feel. Just act.

Sisko drew his hand away from the Vulcan and rose slowly to face Lieutenant Hranok, who hunched over his console in obvious pain, though Sisko could not see his wounds.

"Direct hit," Hranok croaked. "Decks one through four."

Decks one through four. Jennifer and Jake. Don't feel. Don't think. Just act.

Sisko touched his comm insignia and said, "Engineering, your status."

Silence. Sisko and Hranok exchanged grim looks.

"Warning," the computer said, in a loud, overriding voice that echoed on the silent, haze-filled bridge. "Damage to warp core. Containment failure in four minutes."

Don't think.

Sisko hit his insignia again. "All hands, prepare to abandon ship." He moved toward the lift, turned as he realized Hranok was still huddled over the console, trying to work the controls. "Let's get the civilians"—

(*Jennifer and Jake*)

Don't feel—

"to the escape pods, Lieutenant," he said firmly, not allowing himself to hear his perfect imitation of Storil's calm, reassuring intonation.

Don't think—

Just act.

Hranok nodded and followed.

The turbolift doors opened onto a surrealistic vision of hell. The air was filled with smoke and a cacophony of despair: the wails of children, the cries of the wounded, muffled weeping.

Don't think. Don't feel. . . .

In the dim emergency light, shadowy forms emerged from the ghostly haze, dark silhouettes against a glowing red background of flame. Sisko smelled seared flesh, felt heat on his face. He and Hranok stepped onto the deck and staggered to the left. The deck was tilting; stabilizers were failing. Life support would be next—if they had time. Sisko's mind steadily ticked off the seconds, calmly reasoned that he would be able to make it to his quarters, see if Jennifer—

Don't think. Don't feel. . . .

Fire leapt at them from a side corridor, singeing the shoulder of Sisko's uniform; he grabbed Hranok's arm, and together they fought their way past the flames toward a group of frantic civilians struggling with armloads of personal possessions. One woman, her hair singed, her face severely burned, stopped in her flight to retrieve a holo she'd dropped on the deck and began to weep in panic as other items tumbled from her trembling arms.

"Leave everything," Sisko shouted over the roar of flames, with such confidence, such authority, that the woman immediately straightened, leaving the holo where it had fallen. "Go to your assigned evacuation area *now.*"

The woman let her treasured possessions clatter to the deck; those with her followed suit, began moving swiftly, purposefully.

Sisko moved forward, passing other civilians, searching despite himself for two faces, fighting against panic when he failed to find them.

The computer's unfeeling voice blotted out all other sounds: "Warning. Damage to warp core. Containment failure in three minutes."

Three minutes. Enough time. There might still be enough time. They were nearing Sisko's quarters. . . .

A slumped, unsteady form emerged from the haze; Sisko started in recognition, then swallowed disappointment that this familiar face was not the one he sought. "Doran!"

Jennifer's closest friend. Doran's family occupied the quarters next to theirs.

He caught her as she staggered, exhausted, into his arms.

Hranok had already forgotten his wounds; he scooped her up in his muscular arms easily. "I'll take care of her. Go on."

Sisko shot him a grateful look, paused to ask Doran: "Have you seen Jennifer?"

Doran turned her smoke-smudged face toward him, looked at him with mournful eyes, opened her mouth to speak, and began to weep instead.

Sisko felt a purely physical pain in the center of his chest. He turned and broke into a half run, no longer seeing those who passed, no longer seeing the flames, not seeing anything at all until he arrived at his quarters.

The door was jammed open. Thick, dark smoke billowed out. Sisko stepped into it without hesitation, not even noticing its effect on his lungs, his throat, his eyes.

An explosion had ripped a large hole in the deck, allowing fire to leap up from the level below. Sisko's quarters and a lifetime of accumulated possessions had been destroyed.

He did not care. He pushed his way through scorched debris and shouted, "Jennifer!"

Silence.

"Computer," Sisko ordered. "Locate Jennifer Sisko."

Silence. He pushed aside smoldering fragments of furniture and twisted metal bulkhead, searching.

At the edge of the largest pile of collapsed bulkhead and wreckage he uncovered her hand, limp and smudged with soot from the smoke.

He set to work with a strength and intensity that bordered on insanity. The edge of the bulkhead was jagged, sharp; his hands became bloody and blistered by the heated metal. Sisko did not notice.

Don't think. Don't feel. Just act. . . .

Within seconds he had uncovered Jennifer's twisted upper torso and discovered Jake's small, dark body beside her; she had shielded the child with her body and taken the brunt of the blow. He could see no blood, but in the darkness and the smoke, it was difficult to be sure. And he could not see her breathing, but his mind refused to acknowledge the fact.

No blood. Then she'll be all right. Just knocked unconscious by the fall, that's all. . . .

"It's going to be okay," Sisko told his family in the same calm, confident tone—Captain Storil's tone—he had used to soothe the civilians in the corridor, not for a moment allowing himself to think that his words went unheard. "I'll get you out of there. You're going to be okay."

He strained, letting the sharp, hot metal cut into

his palms, letting it sear his flesh, but he could not lift the wreckage that crushed his wife's lower body. He strained again. And again. And again.

Don't panic. Don't feel.

In desperation, he circled, cleared away more debris, found a way to reach underneath the wreckage and pull Jake free. The boy was unconscious and badly bruised but breathing; without a scanner, Sisko could only guess at his internal injuries. When the boy moved slightly in his grasp, Sisko felt a surge of relief so intense it verged on tears.

Don't feel. . . .

"Okay, Jake," he said, in the same cheerful voice he used to comfort the boy after a nightmare, "we'll just get your mom now and get outta here."

But Jennifer was pinned too tightly. Sisko was struggling to lift the wreckage again when Hranok's silhouette appeared in the doorway.

"Commander . . ." It was a plea, an urgent summons.

Sisko turned to him. "Help me."

Hranok took a tentative step into the smoke-filled quarters, reached for his tricorder and scanned Jennifer. Sisko did not look at him, only pushed harder against the bulkhead as Hranok replaced the tricorder without a word.

"Sir." Hranok's tone was unusually gentle. "We have to get to the—"

At his abrupt silence, Sisko stopped pushing and met the Bolian's startled gaze, followed it to where it rested: on the commander's charred, bloodied hands.

Sisko stared down at them numbly, not understanding the significance. His hands were unimportant now; the only thing that mattered was Jennifer. He felt a surge of irritation at Hranok's hesitancy.

"Just help me get her free."

Hranok reached down and scooped Jake up in his strong arms, then lingered awkwardly beside his commander. "Sir . . ."

Furious, Sisko grasped the jagged edge of the bulkhead, not even flinching as the heated metal sliced deep into his flesh, and pushed with all his strength. "That's an order!" he shouted at Hranok, then turned to see the Bolian staring in mute horror, Jake in his arms.

For a moment Hranok and he gazed at each other in silence, and then the Bolian said simply, "She's gone. There's nothing we can do."

Sisko stared at Hranok and did not understand. Did not let himself understand; he could not let her go so easily. "Transporters?"

"None of them are functional, sir." Hranok swung himself and Jake toward the exit. "We have to go."

"Warning," the computer said. "Damage to warp core. Containment failure in two minutes."

Sisko shook his head. He knelt beside Jennifer and took her cool, limp hand in his bloody one. He could not leave her to die alone. In his mind there was no other possible choice; death with his wife seemed a far better fate than life without her. "You go ahead, Lieutenant. Take the boy."

His voice was deceptively rational, reassuring;

another might have left him behind. But when a security officer appeared in the doorway, Hranok handed the boy to him, then grasped Sisko's arm and yanked him to his feet.

"Now, sir."

With a calm tinged with madness,

(*Don't feel. Don't feel . . .*)

Sisko said, "No. I can't leave without her."

Hranok pulled with all his might. Powerless against the Bolian's greater strength, Sisko was propelled toward the door; he struggled to turn his head, to keep his gaze on Jennifer as long as possible, unable to feel, unable to grasp the reality of what was happening.

"Dammit," he told Hranok, with the same strange, numbed calm, "we can't leave her here."

Hranok replied by pushing Sisko out the door. Sisko held up his wounded hands—hands that had failed him, had failed Jennifer—and stared dully at them.

He did not remember running through the burning corridors, did not remember joining the dozen others in the cramped escape pod. Sisko remembered only two things: the sight of Jake, still unconscious in the security officer's arms, and the sight of the dying *Saratoga* as other tiny pods sailed free.

Sisko made his way to the porthole and stared at the receding wreckage, its scorched and twisted hull gleaming with the reflected glow of the continuing battle, the area of space lit up like a summer sky with heat lightning. The *Kyushu* was gone now, and the *Gage* would be next, and so it would continue until all of them were gone.

To Sisko it was meaningless. Irrelevant, just as Picard had said. The Borg were right: resistance *was* futile. All was destroyed.

Feelings were the most irrelevant of all; Sisko was beyond emotion. In his mind he lay dead beside Jennifer, their bodies consumed by flame.

He watched as *Saratoga* exploded like a small sun, and let himself be blinded by the light.

CHAPTER 2

THREE YEARS AFTER the incident at Wolf 359, Commander Benjamin Sisko stood in the soft grass, fondly watching his twelve-year-old son. In the shade of a large old oak Jake sat fishing on a large rock, trousers rolled up to his knees, bare feet dangling in the water. Sisko smiled at the bucolic sight. Lately Jake had become enamored of Twain and his tales of the lazy, simple life of a boy on the Mississippi.

"Hey there, Huckleberry."

Jake turned at the sound of his father's voice, lips stretched in a reluctant grin; a shaft of sunlight pierced the branches and gleamed in his dark, curly hair. The smile so increased his resemblance to Jennifer that Sisko drew in a silent, painful breath as he crossed over and perched beside his son on the rock. With each passing day Jake grew to look more like his mother and less like his father; at least to Sisko's mind. Time had not dulled the memories of his wife. Sisko returned to the horrors of the *Saratoga* each night in his dreams; each waking day his mind wandered undistracted. At least Jake was there each day to remind him of the small things, the good things that he might otherwise have forgotten: Jennifer's same shy, crooked grin, Jennifer's gestures, Jennifer's good nature and complete inability to stay angry about anything for more than a full minute.

Jake was angry now. And like his mother, doing a miserable job of hiding it.

"How're they biting?" Sisko asked.

Jake shrugged and returned his attention to the placid blue water, its smooth surface broken by the red and white bobbing cork. "Small fries. Threw 'em back. You want to go for a swim?"

"Don't have time," Sisko replied gently. "We've got to get ready."

A sullen look came over the boy's face. Sisko experienced a pang of guilt.

"It won't bc so bad, Jakc. I'vc hcard Dajor is a beautiful world." Or rather it *had been* beautiful before the Cardassian conquerors departed, leaving massive devastation in their wake.

Jake stared down at the water, at the reflection of the young barefoot boy frowning back at him. "So why can't we live on the planet instead of in some old space station?"

Sisko couldn't blame him. Since the death of his mother, Jake had associated living in space with danger, had dreamed of a safe, quiet life on Earth, the planet of his mother's birth. For the past three years Sisko had tried without success to land an Earthside assignment; the closest he'd come was shore duty on Mars, helping to reconstruct the fleet at the Utopia Planitia yards. Jake had settled into life there, had felt comfortable there. But few Starfleet families stayed long at Planitia. The duty was considered dull, a temporary stop between more exciting, career-furthering opportunities. Jake would make a friend his own age, become close, then be crushed when the child's parents were transferred out after a few months. The third time it happened, Jake simply gave up trying to make close friends, for fear of being hurt; the boy's loneliness tugged at his father's heart.

When Sisko heard he had been assigned to the space station, he protested—to no avail. Starfleet obviously felt his career had stalled at Utopia Planitia and so presented him with a challenge: Deep Space Nine.

Sisko did not want a challenge; he no longer gave a damn whether his career stagnated or not. The promotion to full commander had seemed meaningless. Before Jennifer's death, he had been unrelentingly ambitious, his career second in importance only to his family, but now nothing mattered except Jake. Sisko was seriously considering leaving the Fleet, not because he wanted to but for the boy's sake. He'd even been looking into some civilian job possibilities on Earth. Thus far none had panned out. Much to Sisko's surprise, he felt a secret guilty relief at the fact.

"Well, it's what Starfleet decided," he told Jake.

"You promised we'd stay on shore duty." The boy's tone grew dangerously close to a whine.

Sisko tensed a bit, fought to keep the defensiveness from his words, his posture. "The station is in orbit of Bajor, Jake. It'll be just like shore duty."

"Will there be kids there?"

"Absolutely," Sisko assured him, hoping like hell he was telling the truth. "Lots of kids."

A feminine voice filtered through the comm insignia on the breast of his uniform. "Bridge to Sisko."

Sisko straightened, touched the insignia. "Yes, Captain?"

"We're approaching Deep Space Nine, Commander. We'll be docking in seven minutes."

"Acknowledged." Sisko pressed his communicator again, then put an arm around his son's stiff shoulders. "C'mon, Huckleberry. We'll take the pond with us."

Unsmiling, unresponsive, Jake rose and began reeling in the line.

"Computer, end program," Sisko ordered as he pushed himself to his feet. The yellow grid of the holodeck walls replaced the grass, water, trees. Jake slung the pole over his shoulder as they exited. He kept his sullen expression and avoided Sisko's eyes as they strode down the corridor, but at an observation window he paused, wide-eyed with curiosity, his anger abruptly and utterly forgotten. "Is that it?"

Sisko followed his son's gaze. On the viewscreen the space station hung amid the stars, the planet Bajor hovering nearby. A handful of ships were docked at the station, including one Sisko recognized as the *Enterprise.* He nodded in reply as he stared at Deep Space Nine's gothically ornate alien beauty. The Cardassians were master architects, but their sweeping, angular style was dark and brooding.

And there was something else about the station's design that vaguely disturbed Sisko; it was the almost organic look to the metal, the way the outer docking ring had long, arching projections, like ribs sticking out from a circular spine. For no reason he could fathom, the observation made him think of the Borg and Locutus, and from there he was in his quarters aboard the *Saratoga* again, struggling vainly to free Jennifer's trapped, lifeless body. . . .

The scene aboard the *Saratoga* was obliterated by the sudden flash of an image: a strange middle-aged woman extending long, gentle fingers toward his face.

And light. Not the painful blinding light of the ship's explosion but a radiant, beautiful light, so brilliant that in his dream Sisko had closed his eyes and still seen it clearly.

Welcome . . .

And seen the woman's eyes, dark, unfathomably wise, beautiful eyes, full of peace and knowing and pain—a pain Sisko understood all too well. The woman's face metamorphosed, grew younger, became Jennifer's face.

Breathe, Jennifer said.

A forgotten dream from the night before. Sisko tried to remember more, but could retrieve only the image of the woman and the light and a strangely emotional sense of deep mystery, of coming home.

Welcome . . .

The dream image faded, sank into elusive forgetfulness. The horrors of the *Saratoga* faded, and the sense of paternal guilt eased, replaced for a fleeting instant by an inexplicable surge of hope.

Jake looked questioningly at his father with a slight, curious Jennifer-frown.

Sisko pulled himself out of the strange reverie and patted the boy on the shoulder. "C'mon, Jake. Let's go."

The door slid slowly open with a distinct unreassuring groan. With Jake beside him, Sisko stepped inside the airlock and drew in a lungful of stale, unpleasantly warm air. Nearby, a uniformed Starfleet ensign lay on his back beside an open console panel, reaching up inside the panel to manually work the controls. Ruddy-faced, sweating, he glanced over at Sisko and Jake to make sure they were clear of the door.

"Sorry about that, Commander," he apologized, with a faint trace of Irish brogue. His face was broad, pleasant, open; damp golden brown curls clung to his forehead. Sisko liked him immediately, though he couldn't say the same for the surroundings. A glance at the primitive gears and levers inside the open panel confirmed that this was far from Starfleet technology. "All the interlock servos in this airlock were stripped by the Cardassians."

"We would have transported aboard if we'd known you were having problems," Sisko replied.

The ensign grimaced as he struggled once more with the lever; the door began to close. "That wouldn't have been possible either, sir. We've got some stray nucleonic emissions that have to be tracked down before we can safely reinstate transporter operations. It's a junkyard the bloody Cardies left us with, if you ask me."

Sisko grunted his understanding as he surveyed the damage. Although the Federation and the Cardassians had ceased hostilities and Sisko was not a man given to prejudice, he was less than kindly disposed toward the culture, which embraced treachery, vindictiveness, and racism, looking on the more spiritual Bajorans as inferior chattels. Sisko realized he was bigoted against bigots, but it was one bias he did not strive to transcend.

The door clanked shut. The ensign wriggled out from under the console and got to his feet. "Miles O'Brien, your chief operations officer."

With an honest smile he extended his hand to Sisko, then drew it back in dismay when he realized it was covered with black grease.

Sisko grinned. "Ben Sisko." He caught Jake's eye

and saw the boy was smiling, too; Miles O'Brien was impossible to dislike. "My son, Jake."

"Hi," Jake said shyly.

O'Brien gave him a smile, then turned back to Sisko. "Can I show you to your quarters, Commander?"

Sisko nodded, hoping the quarters were in better shape than the airlock. He and Jake followed O'Brien into an overheated corridor. Sisko drew the back of his hand across his sweaty forehead. "Is it my imagination or is this station unusually warm?"

O'Brien glanced over his shoulder with an apologetic expression. "The environmental controls are all stuck at thirty-two C. We're working on it."

Sisko was not reassured. Apparently, neither was Jake; he stared glumly down the gloomy, deserted corridor. "Are there any kids here?"

"Kids?" O'Brien reacted with surprise, then studied Sisko and seemed to pick up on the parental guilt triggered by Jake's innocent question. "Well . . . sure, some. I have a two-year-old"—and at Jake's disappointed expression, he quickly added—"but she's a little young for you. I think I've seen a Ferengi boy about your age. If he hasn't left with the others."

"A Ferengi," Jake repeated, clearly intrigued by the notion.

A set of doors opened, and O'Brien ushered them forward. Sisko took a step and stopped.

"The Promenade," O'Brien said. "Or at least

what remains of it. During their occupation, the Cardies sold commercial concessions to the highest bidder. Kept the mining crews entertained."

Sisko swiveled his head to more fully take in the extraordinary sight. The place had obviously served as a combination free port and flea market. It was crammed full of kiosks, restaurants, bars with secluded upstairs areas that Sisko suspected housed sexual holosuites, conventional ship's stores, gambling casinos, even a Bajoran temple. The combination of simple, mystical Bajoran design and ethereal, ornate Cardassian style produced a striking and exotic effect. The place had no doubt been bustling during the Cardassian occupation, but now it appeared almost deserted and looked as if it had been ravaged by vandals. Storefronts had been broken out, walls scorched from phaser blasts. Sisko picked his way over the wreckage littering the thoroughfare and felt his jaw muscles tense. Beside him, Jake had fallen utterly silent.

Sisko had known something about the destruction inflicted on Bajor's surface. After a century of occupation the Cardassians' extensive mining operations had exhausted the planet's resources, and the conquerors had wearied of the decades-long struggle against Bajoran terrorists. They had departed—but not without first poisoning the wells and scorching the ground, leaving behind a wasteland whose inhabitants were forced to turn to the Federation for help.

It had not occurred to Sisko that the Cardassians

would also have destroyed their own space station out of spite, to prevent locals from getting any use out of it.

O'Brien's expression was grim; Sisko suspected that this man, like him, harbored no great love for the invaders. "I'm told the Cardassians decided to have some fun the day they left," the ensign said quietly as they moved through the devastation. A Bajoran woman sifting through the debris of a ruined storefront glanced up as they passed. "Four Bajorans were killed trying to protect their shops."

They passed by a bar-casino where three Ferengi were packing up equipment.

"Why hasn't anybody cleaned this up?" Sisko asked tightly. He thought of Jake, alone and forlorn, playing amid the rubble, and felt a surge of anger toward Starfleet. If Command had informed him of the damage to Deep Space Nine, he would never have accepted the assignment, would never have brought his son here. . . .

"We've got all available personnel assigned to repairing primary systems, sir." O'Brien stepped carefully over a broken piece of toppled Bajoran religious statuary. "The Cardassians took every component of value. We have virtually no defenses. Major Kira, the Bajoran attaché, and I decided—"

Sisko cut him off. "Understood. But what about the civilians who operated these shops?"

"A lot of them lost everything. A few are trying to rebuild, but most are packing up to leave."

They walked in silence for a few moments, Sisko growing guiltier and more apprehensive about what he had brought Jake to with each step. The boy's eyes were somber and wide, his mouth a small, tight line.

Ahead of them, a Bajoran temple, simple and elegant compared to the surrounding Cardassian structures, caught Sisko's eye. As they approached it, someone stirred in the arched, shadowed entryway: an elderly Bajoran monk dressed in traditional robes, his eyes large and compelling beneath thick white brows. His odd hypnotic gaze met Sisko's.

"Welcome, Commander."

Sisko hesitated

(*Welcome*)

remembering the dream from the night before, the dream of the wise woman with the all-knowing eyes. For the first time, he realized she was an alien, a Bajoran.

(*Breathe,* Jennifer said.)

Sisko shifted uncomfortably. He wanted to ask O'Brien how the locals had learned of his coming, whether they had seen his holo, but he could not bring himself to look away from the Bajoran's omniscient gaze—could not, at the moment, bring himself to speak.

The monk wore a faint beatific smile. "Please enter. The prophets await you."

(*Breathe,* Jennifer said again.)

Sisko flashed suddenly on a memory: the

Saratoga's darkened bridge, the smell of smoke, the greater than human warmth of Captain Storil's pulseless flesh against his hand. Then he remembered struggling in vain to raise the flaming bulkhead, the sight of Jennifer's motionless torso, trapped . . . a frustration beyond sanity, beyond grief. . . .

He shook the memory off, blinked, managed to find his voice. "Another time, perhaps."

The Bajoran did not reply, merely watched placidly as the three continued past. They were a meter away, barely within earshot, when Sisko heard the monk say softly, knowingly, "Another time."

Sisko was not the only one who had been devastated by his first sight of the ruined Promenade. Miles O'Brien had stared at it several times in the past few days and was still convinced he would never get used to the sight of it. He had made the foolish mistake of assuming he was completely over his anger at the Cardassians, but each viewing of the Promenade brought the memories of Setlik back full force.

As he led the new commander and his son to their quarters, O'Brien knew precisely what Commander Sisko was thinking: that he had made a terrible mistake in accepting the assignment, in bringing his son here. O'Brien knew because he had thought the very same thing. He had been sorry to leave the *Enterprise,* but he was a trained officer and an optimist by nature, and he had made his choice.

Besides, the promotion from noncom to an ensign had been too great an opportunity to turn down. He would do his duty, and for Keiko and Molly's sake, he would put the very best face on things. If he had to, he would reassemble the entire bloody station with his own two hands and turn it into something to be proud of.

Now he felt a surge of empathy for the commander and his young son: hard enough to come into such a strange new environment, but he'd heard Sisko was a widower. O'Brien tried to imagine what it would be like bringing Molly into this place after losing Keiko—and stopped quickly when the thought became too painful. He watched as father and son took a few tentative steps inside their new quarters. The room was typically Cardassian—all in shades of gray and black, forbidding-looking, with a huge, outrageously ornate bed in its center. The whole station had the same depressing color scheme, and O'Brien wondered if he would ever become used to it.

The boy's expression grew noticeably glum, and Sisko seemed to fare no better. O'Brien began to suspect that the commander had been less than enthusiastic about the assignment even before the disheartening tour.

O'Brien forced a smile and said cheerfully, "When my wife, Keiko, saw our quarters, she started talking about visiting her mother in Kumomoto. . . . The Cardassians aren't much for bright colors. Perhaps Starfleet would see clear to letting us do a bit of redecorating."

Sisko did not reply, simply walked to the bed and examined it as the boy wandered off into the adjacent bedroom.

O'Brien took advantage of his absence to sidle alongside the commander and speak quietly. "Sir, I wouldn't allow the boy to go roaming. We're still having some security problems—"

"Dad!" O'Brien and Sisko both looked up as an indignant shout came from the next room.

Jake appeared in the doorway, thin dark brows knitted together in disapproval. "There's nothing to sleep on in here except a cushion on the *floor!*"

"We can get you a real bunk off the *Enterprise,*" O'Brien soothed quickly, then turned to the commander. "Oh, and I almost forgot, Captain Picard wants to see you as soon as possible."

Sisko averted his eyes. A shadow seemed to pass over his face at the mention of Picard. Just coincidence, O'Brien decided—Sisko was still probably distracted by the condition of the space station.

Oddly, the commander changed the subject, as if he hadn't registered O'Brien's statement. "Any word on our science and medical officers?"

"They're expected tomorrow," O'Brien answered.

Sisko turned toward the disconsolate boy. "Jake, I want you to stay here until I come back."

"Where's the food replicator?" the boy asked instantly.

O'Brien repressed a grin. Jake looked to be twelve or thirteen, right at the age, Keiko said, when they begin to eat you out of house and home.

"I'm afraid they're all off-line," he answered, and added, at Jake's expression of utter dismay, "There's plenty of emergency rations. I could send some down."

"Dad," Jake wailed, in a tone that clearly said, *I hate this place!*

Sisko's expression of forced optimism matched O'Brien's. The commander's tone was gentle but brooked no argument. "We're just going to have to rough it until we get things up and running, Jake. Okay?"

"Okay," Jake said feebly, in a manner that indicated it was definitely *not.*

"Okay," Sisko affirmed, and smiled.

O'Brien and the new commander took the turbolift to Ops. "The heart of the station," he said with first stirrings of pride, as Sisko tilted his head back to take in the multi-tiered facility where a handful of Bajorans and Starfleet personnel were already busily at work.

High above them were almond-shaped observation windows, some revealing a view of Bajor, some of docking bays, others of stars. O'Brien thought they resembled Cardassian eyes staring out into space. Ops bore the same grim, muted color scheme as the rest of the station. Despite the disarray—open panels from which conduits hung, gaps where the Cardassians had torn out machinery before their flight—O'Brien could see the potential.

"Operations houses computer and life support,

tactical controls, master communications, and the transporter pad," he explained, absently wiping beads of perspiration from his forehead. "Obviously we've got a bit of work to do, but once we're up and running . . ."

Commander Sisko nodded, still gazing up appreciatively at the different levels. "Impressive design." His tone was pleasant but detached. O'Brien got the impression that this was a man who did not want to be here and had already made up his mind he would not remain long. A shame; he already liked Benjamin Sisko. A more casual command style than Captain Picard, perhaps, but O'Brien saw a capable officer who would no doubt command loyalty.

O'Brien folded his arms and tilted back his head to take in the view. "I'd like to ask the designer what he was thinking about when they built this place. I still haven't been able to find an ODN access." He pointed at the metal-grid mezzanine and the steps that led to the small balcony just off the commander's office. "That's the prefect's office up there."

Sisko shook his head and said, with irony, "So all others have to look up with respect. Cardassian architecture."

"Yes, sir." O'Brien paused awkwardly. "Major Kira has been using it."

Sisko glanced around, searching, then said with faint dismay, "The only office in Ops?"

O'Brien gave an apologetic nod.

Sisko exchanged an amused glance with him and said lightly, "I guess it's time to meet Major Kira."

O'Brien hesitated. He believed in going by the book, and although he figured he could find a way to get along with the major well enough, he was more than a little concerned about her attitude toward authority. "Sir . . . have you ever served with any Bajoran women?"

Sisko's gaze was blankly innocent. "No. Why?"

O'Brien barely succeeded in repressing a grin. No point in talking about it; the commander would find out for himself soon enough. "Just wondering, sir."

Sisko made it up the rattling metal stairs in two swift steps. The tour of the Promenade and his gloomy quarters had brought him close to a decision to apply immediately for a transfer—he hated to think of Jake alone and friendless in those dark Cardassian rooms—but the sight of Ops had been encouraging, and O'Brien certainly seemed capable.

And then there was the strange dream about the wise Bajoran woman, and the oddly troubling encounter with the monk. . . .

Welcome, Commander.

The Bajora themselves were an intriguing people, deeply religious, and Sisko looked forward to learning more about them, despite O'Brien's whimsical expression when he mentioned Major Kira; Sisko had no clue as to what that was supposed to mean.

"Just wondering, sir," O'Brien had said, but Sisko had clearly heard the subtext: Don't say I didn't warn you.

He got a clue to O'Brien's unspoken warning when he arrived at the top of the staircase and approached the office entrance. A feminine voice came booming through the wall. Judging by a glance over his shoulder at O'Brien's bemused grin, Sisko was sure it could be clearly heard in Ops.

"You're *throwing* it *away! All* of you!"

A second voice, male, spoke through a comm link; Sisko had to strain to hear this one: "You're being a fool."

"Then *don't* ask for my *opinion* next time!"

Sisko winced faintly at the sound of a forceful palm being slammed against a comm terminal, then carefully removed any trace of amusement from his expression as he pressed the buzzer by the door.

It slid open almost immediately. A Bajoran woman, her short auburn hair swinging forward against her cheeks, leaned aggressively forward in the doorway.

Not leaned, Sisko decided. Blazed. Rained sparks.

"Yes?" The woman demanded, narrowing her large eyes at him. As she straightened, her hair swung back, revealing several silver ornaments in one ear. Decidedly nonregulation. She caught Sisko's disapproving gaze and returned his look with one that was a clear challenge.

Better to mention the earrings another time.

"I'm Benjamin Sisko," he stated firmly.

"I suppose you want the office." She stepped back to allow him passage, folded her arms, and scrutinized him coldly.

He fought to repress an incredulous smile at her attitude as he entered. "Well, actually I thought I'd say hello first and *then* take the office . . . but we could do it in any order you'd like."

She swept her arm back in welcome and said with exaggerated warmth, "Hello."

Sisko's amusement faded. He was confident enough in his own ability to command not to mind a little informality, even a little testing of the boundaries, but he'd be damned if he'd tolerate any unearned hostility.

Relax, he told himself. You're not staying, remember?

He folded his arms and looked directly, unflinchingly, into her eyes. "Is something bothering you, Major?"

She scowled. "You don't want to ask me that, Commander."

"Why not?" Sisko asked evenly.

"Because I have a bad habit of telling the truth, even when people don't want to hear it."

Sisko kept his tone pleasant. "Perhaps I want to hear it."

She considered this for a moment; the anger eased briefly, then returned. "I don't believe the Federation has any business being here."

Sisko nodded thoughtfully, reminding himself once again that he would leave soon, so none of this mattered. "The provisional government disagrees with you."

She turned away, moved toward the desk, then leaned against it, facing him with eyes full of mistrust. "The provisional government and I don't agree on a lot of things . . . which is probably why they sent me to this godforsaken place." She sighed; her tone grew calmer. "Commander, I have been fighting for Bajoran independence since I was old enough to pick up a phaser. Finally we drove out the Cardassians, and what do our new leaders do? Call up the Federation and invite them in. What sort of independence is that?"

Sisko lifted his chin. "How can you make a comparison between the two? The Cardassians were invaders who ravaged your planet and your people. The Federation is only here to—"

"Help you," Kira chorused with him. "Yes, I know. The Cardassians said the same thing sixty years ago."

"Major," he said, struggling to keep his tone civil, "when I was ordered here, I requested a Bajoran national as my first officer, because unlike the Cardassians, I believe the Bajora should have the right to rule their own planet. I believe my request made sense. It still does. At least to me. Now, you and I are going to have to—"

He broke off as an alarm sounded on a nearby comm panel.

Kira whirled toward it, pressed a control, then squinted at the schematic of the station that appeared on the monitor. A location on the map flashed red—a warning. The major hit another control, and the map metamorphosed into the image of a humanoid who was not Bajoran.

A middle-aged man, Sisko thought at first, but there was something wrong with the monitor: the man's features seemed slightly blurred, unfinished, almost two-dimensional.

Palms flat on the console, Kira leaned toward the image. "Odo, are you reading something at A-fourteen?"

The man shook his head. With a start, Sisko realized that Kira's monitor was in perfect working order; it was Odo's features that were blurred.

"My security array has been down for two hours," Odo replied crisply. "I'll meet you there."

His image disappeared; the monitor resumed its standard feeds. Kira pushed herself up and strode toward the door, all business, any resentment abruptly forgotten. "We've been having a lot of break-ins lately. No need to come along, Commander."

Sisko ignored her and followed.

CHAPTER 3

On A-fourteen, Nog peered around the doorway and squinted, his tiny golden eyes trying to penetrate the dimness. He saw nothing, but that gave him little reassurance. By human standards, he was exceedingly myopic, but his oversized pinna caught sound quite well; for now the hallway remained silent.

Nog was Ferengi, very young and, at the moment, very nervous. He was ashamed of his nervousness, ashamed to be afraid—not that the Ferengi race approved of courage. Uncle Quark always said that courage and honor and altruism were the worst sort of stupidity, and there was nothing worse by Ferengi standards than stupidity. It was fine to be afraid, so long as your fear didn't cause you to get caught or lose profit.

Nog was terribly afraid of getting caught, of being stupid and disappointing Uncle Quark once again, of being a failure as a Ferengi.

Behind him, huddled over a safe, Jas-qal used the shield damper to neutralize the forcefield surrounding the safe. It surrendered with a slight crackle.

Nog turned at the sound, in time to see Jas-qal's huge paws scoop a handful of valuable mineral samples out of the open safe. Jas-qal was a B'kaazi, twice Nog's size, huge and ponderous and hideous by any standards, Ferengi or human. Nog resented and disliked the B'kaazi, but there was nothing to be done: Jas-qal could easily have crushed Nog into pulp and had indicated that he would most certainly do so if the adolescent Ferengi did not watch his sharp little tongue.

"Hurry up," Nog hissed. There were no sibilants in the phrase, but it was impossible for Nog to speak without emitting a slight hiss of air with each syllable, due to the gaps between his stubby, pointed teeth. He fidgeted, wiping perspiration from his tiny clawed hands onto the thighs of his pants; he did not want to get caught this time. He wanted to prove to his father and uncle that he was as capable as they of committing a successful crime. He had hoped they would trust him to perform the act alone and had been indignant at their insistence that Jas-qal perform the actual deed.

With agonizing deliberateness, Jas-qal dropped the mineral samples into the pouch, then at last turned and joined Nog at the door. As they hurried out into the Promenade, Nog's Ferengi heart beat with wild exhilaration. They were going to make it! Uncle Quark would be pleased, and perhaps next time trust his nephew enough to let Nog perform such challenging missions alone. . . .

Jas-qal stopped abruptly in his flight; Nog paused beside him and squinted as he followed the B'kaazi's gaze. A humanoid was coming toward them across the Promenade at top speed, the strange one called Odo, who wasn't really humanoid at all, and in fact wasn't anything that anyone had ever heard of.

"All right," Odo called in his intimidating voice. "Just stand where you are."

Nog began to tremble as he and Jas-qal wheeled around and stumbled clumsily in the opposite direction. Of all the Starfleet people, Odo frightened Nog the most, but perhaps if he ran quickly . . .

Two other Starfleet officers—a Bajoran and a human Nog had never seen before—appeared in front of the two fleeing criminals.

Nog stopped in his tracks. Jas-qal was not so cooperative; he pulled a dagger from his waistband and faced Odo menacingly. Nog sighed; he could have told Jas-qal it would do no good. One could try to outrun the strange security officer, but there was no point in trying to fight.

The B'kaazi hurled the dagger; the weapon whipped through the air.

In the millisecond it took for the knife to approach, Odo's torso became fluid, twisted, reshaped itself to move aside, out of danger's way . . . then sprang back. With a resounding *thunk* the dagger embedded itself in the wall behind the security officer.

Jas-qal recovered, tried to charge past Odo before he had a chance to re-form, but too late: Odo grappled with him, trying to contain him. The B'kaazi's bulk was formidable; a long struggle was sure to ensue. Nog braced himself for an escape attempt—

Until a phaser blast scorched the wall over the fighters' heads.

"That's enough," the unfamiliar human male said, keeping the phaser leveled at the B'kaazi's chest.

Odo slowly released his hold on Jas-qal and turned his unfinished, flattened features toward the new Starfleet officer with contempt. "Who the hell are you?"

"This is our new Starfleet commander, Odo," the Bajoran woman said.

Odo studied the new human, completely unimpressed by this revelation. "I don't allow weapons on the Promenade. That includes phasers."

The human drew back at this, apparently on the verge of replying when an all too familiar voice interrupted: "Nog? What's going on?"

The young Ferengi repressed a bleat of despair.

As he hurried toward the Starfleet officers surrounding his young nephew, the Ferengi named Quark was in anything but a charitable mood.

"Surly" was the best word for it. After all, he had suffered enormous business losses, first from the rampaging Cardassians, then from the loss of customers, and he had been furious to learn that the Federation intended to occupy Bajor—the crowning blow that led to Quark's decision to evacuate.

Quark did not mind Bajorans. They were an odd people who filled their minds with mystical mumbo jumbo, but at least they left him alone to do his business. And he rather liked the Cardassians. True, they were violent, but Quark understood violence, and they were treacherous and deceitful, traits Quark greatly admired. He knew how to deal with the Cardassians and their straightforward cruelty, but the Federation—especially the humans—puzzled and irritated him no end. They utterly lacked any sort of common sense, as illustrated by their bizarre, silly notions of ethics and honesty, which to Quark proved their stupidity.

Then there was the overeager Nog, who had fouled up yet another assignment; Quark's patience with his nephew was wearing thin. He had sent Jas-qal along as insurance, since the boy could not be trusted to complete even the simplest task that called for stealth and deviousness. He had expected to have the mineral samples in hand and be gone hours before Starfleet detected their absence. Now even Jas-qal had failed him, and Quark's bad mood increased tenfold. The valuable mineral samples would have more than compensated for the business loss and the cost of moving his operation.

Yet despite his evil humor, he approached the Starfleet officers with an innocent, simpering demeanor; at least he would not miss the opportunity to teach Nog something about dealing with a human, like this commander. Perhaps there might still be a chance of getting his hands on those samples. . . .

The three officers looked askance at Quark as he approached.

"The boy's in a lot of trouble," Odo said. Quark kept his expression polite and repressed the urge to curl his lip at the shapeshifter; Odo had an especially obnoxious concept of justice and a perverse notion of what constituted wrongdoing.

Quark turned his attention to the commander, a tall—but then, most entities were taller than he—dark-skinned human. "Commander, my name is Quark. I used to run the local gambling establishment." He shot a disapproving glance at Nog, who reacted with an appropriately shamefaced expression; perhaps there was hope for the boy yet. "This is my brother's boy. Surely you can see that he has only a peripheral involvement in this. We're scheduled to depart tomorrow." He shot a sidelong glance at Nog that was intended to seem stern to the human but that said to Nog, You see? Watch how easily this stupid human can be deceived by a swift tongue. "If we could be permitted to take him, I promise you he will be severely—"

"That won't be possible," the human interrupted, his dark features as unreadable as stone. He turned to Odo with a nod at the young Ferengi and Jas-qal. "Take them to the brig."

Odo acknowledged the order with an expression of pleasure and led Nog and the hulking B'kaazi away as Quark stared bitterly at the human for a few seconds.

This was going to be far more difficult than he had expected. This human seemed to follow human rules, but he was as crafty as any Ferengi.

He released a sigh of disappointment and hurried on stumpy little legs to follow the prisoners.

Kira watched them go and shook her head. "Quark probably sent the two of them here to steal the ore samples in the first place."

She turned to study the new commander, who wore a thoughtful expression. She still did not trust Starfleet, or Sisko for that matter, but she had been impressed by his willingness to listen and by his refusal to be angered by her bluntness, and she approved of his swift, stern handling of Nog and Quark. Clearly he was more creative than she had anticipated; he was obviously plotting something.

The memory of her dream attempted to resurface, but Kira pushed it firmly away, last night the dream had seemed important, relevant—but that had only been wishful thinking. She would not allow her hopes to intrude on reality. The reality was that Sisko was better than she had expected—but he was only a Starfleet officer, nothing more.

"Major," Sisko replied slowly, "there's a Ferengi legal tradition. It's called plea bargaining. I might let the boy go, but I want something in exchange from Mr. Quark. Something very important."

Kira had just opened her mouth to ask exactly what that something was when Sisko's communicator signaled.

"O'Brien to Commander Sisko."

Sisko pressed his comm badge with an air of resignation, as if he knew precisely what the ensign was going to say. "Go ahead."

"Sir," O'Brien's voice said, "the *Enterprise* hailed us again. Captain Picard is waiting to see you."

"Acknowledged," Sisko said with a frown. He terminated the comm link and glanced at Kira. "This won't take long."

Kira tilted her head, intrigued, and watched as Sisko headed toward the airlock. This Starfleet commander was a far more complicated person than she had expected; she had noticed the very subtle change in the commander's expression at the mention of Picard's name and had read the emotion hidden there. It was one Kira had learned as a child from the Cardassians, one with which she was all too familiar: hatred.

She stood watching for a few seconds after the door closed over him.

Ben Sisko stood for a time at an observation window in the airlock and stared at the *Enterprise*. Impossible to admire from a distance her beauty, her grace, her sleekness, without thinking of the *Saratoga*.

Impossible to step through the airlock into her corridors, and not see Hranok beside him as they stepped from the turbolift onto the civilians' deck. Impossible not to smell smoke, hear wailing, see the dark, shadowed outlines of the wounded staggering toward him through the haze. . . .

As he made his way to the *Enterprise*'s main observation lounge, Sisko reminded himself that he had no right to harbor any hatred toward Picard. The human was not responsible for the crimes of the Borg. Not responsible. No right.

And yet by the time he arrived at his destination, by the time he pressed the chime and heard the voice, the strictly human voice, that bade him enter, Sisko was blinded by rage.

He had no right to hate. Yet he was as helpless to resist his own fury as Picard had been to resist the Borg group mind.

The door opened. Sisko entered.

Captain Picard sat at the end of the table, reviewing information on a padd. At the sight of his visitor, he smiled and rose, extending a hand. His appearance should not have been at all striking: he was a physically unimposing man, bald, with a white fringe of hair at the back of his head. Even so, he emanated a strength, a grace, a presence that were impressive.

"Commander," he said with sincere warmth. "Come in. Welcome to Bajor."

(*You will be assimilated*)

Sisko took the proffered hand, could not quite

bring himself to match the firmness of its grip. He did not know what he had intended to say to Picard at their first real meeting; he did not intend to say what he did.

"It's been a long time, Captain."

Picard tilted his lean, sculpted face and studied Sisko with two very puzzled, very hazel eyes. Very human eyes, but Sisko saw only flashing red, heard the whirr of an optical sensor-scope.

Picard sat. Sisko sat. Picard asked curiously, "Have we met before?"

Sisko told himself that he did not hate Jean-Luc Picard, that he had nothing against the man. But he was consumed with hatred for the Borg; he answered not Picard but Locutus.

"Yes, sir. We met in battle. I was on the *Saratoga* at Wolf 359."

(*Resistance is futile*)

Picard's face went slack; the warmth fled his eyes—entirely human eyes now—and in its place Sisko saw the flaming wreckage of the *Saratoga.* The *Kyushu.* The *Gage.*

(*Jennifer's lifeless hand*)

And then Picard banished the specters with a blink and composed himself. When he spoke again, his tone was cool, infinitely remote. "I assume you've been briefed on the political situation on Bajor."

Sisko tried to keep the chill and the anger from his own eyes and failed. "I know the Cardassians ravaged the planet before they left."

(*Hranok dragging him to the escape pod. Hurtling past the scorched, smoldering hulls of starship after starship, watching as the* Saratoga*—as Jennifer—dissolved into blinding supernova white . . .*)

Ben Sisko blinked to clear away the afterimage of the past, forced himself to pay attention to the captain's words.

". . . retribution for the years of Bajoran terrorism," Picard was saying. "The relief efforts we've been coordinating are barely adequate." He rose and moved over to the observation window, deliberately putting distance between himself and Sisko, clasping his hands behind him as he stared out at the planet. "I've come to know the Bajora. I'm one of the strongest proponents for their entry into the Federation."

"Is it going to happen?" Sisko asked.

The captain turned a distant chiseled profile toward him. "Not easily. The ruling parties are at each other's throats. Factions that were united against the Cardassians have resumed old conflicts."

"Sounds like they're not ready." Sisko heard Kira's angry, impatient tone in his own voice.

Picard wheeled around to glance at him sharply. "Your job is to do everything short of violating the Prime Directive to make sure they *are* ready."

Sisko gave a short defensive nod. The comment rankled, renewed his anger; he did not need to have his job explained to him. Despite his reluctance to accept the assignment, he was a Starfleet officer. He would do his duty to the utmost of his ability regardless of the personal cost.

(*She's gone, Hranok said*)

Captain Picard took a step toward him; his tone became candid, inviting confession. "Starfleet has made me aware of your objections to this assignment, Commander. I would think that after three years at the Utopia Planitia yards you'd be ready for a change."

Sisko stiffened, thought of Jake by himself in the dark, dismal Cardassian quarters. "I have a son that I'm raising alone, Captain. This is hardly the ideal environment. As I said, I knew of the devastation on Bajor, but no one mentioned that the station itself—"

Picard cut him off. "Unfortunately, as Starfleet officers we do not always have the luxury of serving in an ideal environment."

Sisko did not back down from the polite rebuke. "I realize that, sir. And I'm investigating the possibility of returning to Earth for civilian service." It was almost the truth. He *had* investigated the possibility and had found nothing as yet; he resolved to renew the search immediately.

Picard drew back from him with disapproval. "Perhaps Starfleet Command should begin to consider a replacement for you."

"That's probably a good idea," Sisko said flatly.

Seconds passed as the two regarded each other with veiled hostility. And then Picard replied slowly, "I'll look into it. In the meantime . . ." The coldness faded from his eyes and voice, replaced by muted pain. Sisko knew that the captain was struggling to find the right words to broach the subject of Wolf 359.

Sisko rose abruptly. When he entered the room, he had wanted nothing more than to tell the captain how he had suffered at Locutus's hands. Now he wanted nothing more than to leave, to let each man confront his own ghosts alone, in peace. "In the meantime," he said quietly, "I'll do the job I've been ordered to do to the best of my ability, sir. Thank you for the briefing."

He locked eyes with Picard and waited to be dismissed.

Picard studied him for a long time, clearly not wishing to end the conversation. The captain's expression was taut, controlled, but Ben Sisko detected a faint, fleeting glimmer of anguish in his eyes and knew Picard saw the same in Sisko's own.

"Dismissed," Picard said at last.

As the doors closed behind Ben Sisko, Jean-Luc Picard sank back into his seat and stared distractedly at his padd for a few seconds, then lifted his gaze to the planet Bajor.

Nearly two years had passed since his last nightmare—more recollection, really, than creative dream—about the experience with the Borg. He did not allow such memories often. In fact, he had repressed them so successfully that, as he had studied Ben Sisko's service record before their meeting, he had ignored the slight subconscious unease he felt at the mention of the *Saratoga.*

How could he have forgotten, failed to make the connection? He had been at Wolf 359 in full consciousness as Locutus. And as Picard, trapped and helpless while his knowledge was stripped from him and used to annihilate his fellow officers, a reality far worse than any terror met in dreams.

He closed his eyes and heard the voice of the Borg, a thousand thundering voices that spoke as one:

Captain Jean-Luc Picard, you lead the strongest ship of the Federation fleet. You speak for your people . . .

And his own reply, confident and utterly naive: *I have nothing to say to you! And I will resist you with my last ounce of strength!*

Strength is irrelevant, the Borg had replied. *Resistance is futile. We wish to improve ourselves. We will add your biological and technological distinctiveness to our own. Your culture will adapt to service ours.*

He had been human then, prideful and strong, or so he had thought, and he had been outraged by his abduction and by the Borg's mindless arrogance. *Impossible!* he had cried. *My culture is based on freedom and self-determination!*

Freedom is irrelevant, the Borg had answered implacably. *Self-determination is irrelevant. You must comply.*

We would rather die, Picard had said. He had

been foolish enough to think that death was the worst fate the Borg could inflict upon him, upon all of humankind, but the chilling answer had come:

Death is irrelevant. Your archaic cultures are authority-driven. To facilitate our introduction into your societies, it has been decided that a human voice will speak for us in all communications. You have been chosen to be that voice . . .

And so he had been Changed, his brain and body mechanically and surgically altered so that his consciousness was embraced and absorbed by the Borg group mind. And in their infinite disregard for suffering, the Borg did not do him the kindness of blotting out the consciousness that was Picard; he had been forced to experience it all, to hear himself speak as Locotus at the Borg's prompting, unable to control his body, his voice, unable to hide his knowledge of Starfleet strategy and weapons from them. Picard had been there and had watched in horror as first the *Melbourne* was destroyed, and then the *Saratoga* and the *Kyushu* and the *Tolstoi* and the *Gage* and thirty-five other starships. . . .

How could he have forgotten the *Saratoga?*

Picard's memory moved to a time, weeks later, when he had returned to Earth to recuperate from the trauma. He shuddered at the recollection of his confession to his brother, Robert: *They used me to kill and destroy. And I could not stop them. I tried so hard . . . but I just wasn't strong enough. Not good enough . . .*

They had been sitting in the dirt in the family

vineyard, both of them covered with mud after an all-out fistfight; it was the first time in years that Picard had wept openly, tears streaming down his cheeks, the taste of salt mingling with that of earth.

Robert had regarded him in solemn silence for a moment and then said: *So. My brother is a human being after all. This is going to be with you a long time, Jean-Luc, a long time . . .*

A long time, three years. He had been fortunate to pass them without being forced to confront a survivor of Wolf 359; but then, there had been so few.

So few . . .

With a sudden chill he recalled Sisko's mention of raising a son alone. Picard opened his eyes.

"Computer," he ordered hoarsely, focusing his gaze on Bajor. "Personal file on Benjamin Sisko, commander. The name of his deceased wife and the cause of her death."

A pause, and then the uninflected response: "Jennifer Sisko, lieutenant. Expired Stardate 44002.3 aboard the *Saratoga*—"

"That will be sufficient," Picard whispered, staring at the space station hub through the window. He drew a hand across his forehead.

Jennifer Sisko, lieutenant. Wife of Benjamin, mother of Jacob. And how many others?

Remember: The Borg, not you, committed the crimes. You wanted to stop them. You tried . . .

Yes. I tried. And I failed. And it was my knowl-

edge they used to help them kill so quickly, so efficiently.

The helplessness—that had been the most horrifying part of it all. He had always possessed a strong, confident personality, always been in control of himself, had known since boyhood that he wanted to command a starship and had never let anything stop him from achieving his goal. But he had been forced to watch with mute rage and pain as the Borg used his body, his voice, to threaten and his mind to kill. The helplessness had been the worst of all.

Yet, as Counselor Troi had reminded him gently three years ago, he was not helpless now. He could not change the facts of his mental violation by the Borg, could not bring Jennifer Sisko and all the others back from the dead.

But he could find a way to help Benjamin Sisko and his motherless son.

Picard stood. His experience with the Borg had been different from Sisko's, but he understood something of what the man was going through. He had wrestled with some of the same demons, had come very close to resigning his commission in an effort to retreat from past horrors.

He hoped that Sisko managed to overcome those demons; otherwise, Starfleet would lose a fine officer.

Yet whether Sisko decided to leave or stay, he would find his way smoothed by an anonymous benefactor; and as long as Picard lived, young

Jacob Sisko would be given every possible assistance in his chosen career. He would help them both however he could.

Picard gazed at the exotic Cardassian design of the space station for a full minute, then turned his back on it and left.

CHAPTER 4

IN THE SECURITY OFFICE at the space station, Odo settled himself at his desk and gave his attention to the work on his data pad, actively ignoring the little Ferengi, Quark, who sat fidgeting nearby.

Odo disliked Quark. Odo disliked Ferengis in general. They approved of dishonesty and thievery, and Quark was especially obnoxious because of his simpering demeanor when Odo knew very well that the Ferengi would slip a dagger into his back, given the opportunity. Odo believed very strongly in justice and honesty; it was a part of his being, like breathing or eating or shifting shape. He knew the Ferengi mocked such beliefs, another good reason to dislike them.

But then, Odo disliked everyone.

Except Major Kira. He got along well with her because, like him, she believed in total, blunt honesty and refused to waste time with empty, polite words and protocol. One always knew where one stood with Kira.

He was not sure what to make of this Sisko. He had seen how the Starfleet commander looked at him after the brief demonstration of his shape-shifting ability, knew that Sisko had wondered about his unfinished face, but hadn't asked. Odo hadn't decided whether to be insulted or grateful at the human's polite silence, but he knew Sisko wondered what sort of a being his new security officer was.

Odo wondered himself; he had no memory whatsoever of his origin or of his people. Fifty years ago he had been discovered alone in an alien spacecraft near the Denorios Asteroid Belt. The Bajora had taken him in and treated him like one of their own.

His true form, to which he returned each night, was that of a shapeless gelatinous mass, but to assimilate, he had been obliged to take on the form of a Bajoran. He had never been able to get the humanoid appearance quite right; his features seemed flattened, two-dimensional. Something about the cheekbones and the nose—especially the Bajoran scrollwork on the bridge, between the brows—always eluded him. Or perhaps his deep resentment at constantly living in a humanoid form made the change more difficult.

He knew only one thing about his people: justice was such a significant part of them that it existed in his racial memory. Odo could not conceive of doing any work other than security; he had been the Bajoran law enforcement officer for Deep Space Nine under the Cardassians. Starfleet had allowed him to continue in that role, since no one else was so familiar with the station, especially the Promenade and those who frequented it. He had been grateful to keep his job, but he had been more than a little disgruntled at the thought of a Starfleet officer coming here to tell him what to do; even the Cardassians had been intelligent enough to allow him free rein.

Odo had little regard for regulations. After all, laws came and went, were adapted and then discarded, but the *spirit* of justice was eternal. Major Kira had warned him about the regulation-crazy Starfleet types, and Odo had assumed that Commander Sisko would fit into this mold. He had been prepared to thoroughly dislike him.

But Sisko had surprised him. The commander apparently had a brain and a sense of justice and knew how to use both. Odo knew he was planning something creative for the Ferengi, and approved.

He glanced up as Sisko entered the room.

"You wanted to see me?" the commander asked. His manner was curt, tense, as if he had just gone through a very difficult experience and was trying to mentally shake himself free from it, but then he caught sight of the Ferengi and the mood lifted. A glint of humor came into his eyes as he casually folded his arms and leaned against the bulkhead.

Quark was on his feet, facing Sisko plaintively. "Commander, about my nephew—"

"Well, well," Sisko interrupted. "Mr. Quark. It's good to see you're still here." He gestured broadly with exaggerated politeness.

Odo repressed a smile as he pretended to return his attention to his datapad; Sisko was giving Quark some of his own smarmy medicine.

"Have a seat, please," the commander said.

Quark swiveled his large rectangular head to glance at the chair behind him, then crawled back into it reluctantly. "Of course I'm still here, Commander. We're not leaving until tomorrow, which is why it's vital that we—"

"I don't think so," Sisko said cheerfully.

Quark's wide mouth dropped open, revealing a row of wideset pointed teeth. "Wh-what?"

"It's really quite simple, Quark. You're not going to leave."

Odo gave up all pretense of working and stared up at Sisko with surprised amusement.

The Ferengi emitted a hiss. "Not going to leave . . . ? But we're all packed and ready to—"

"Unpack." Sisko's tone brooked no argument.

Quark leaned forward, mouth still gaping in disbelief. "Why would you want *me* to stay?"

Odo could resist no longer. "I'm curious myself," he admitted to the human. "The man is a gambler and a thief."

"I am not a thief," Quark said in a comical attempt at wounded dignity.

Odo gazed steadily at him. "You are a thief."

"If I am," Quark said, "you haven't been able to prove it in four years." He smiled a sharp-toothed little smile that made Odo think of a hungry Bajoran sand dragon and of the holo he'd once seen of a Terran crocodile.

Sisko did not return the smile; his voice became earnest. "My officers, the Bajoran engineers, and all their families depend on the shops and services of this Promenade. But if people like you abandon it, this is going to become a ghost town. We need someone to step forward and say, 'I'm staying, I'm rebuilding.' We need a community leader. And it's going to be you, Quark."

"Me?" Quark marveled. "A community leader?" He glanced helplessly at Odo as if seeking reassurance that the commander was entirely mad.

Odo settled back in his chair and grinned. Shrewd, this Benjamin Sisko, and not afraid to bend the rules creatively. To the Ferengi, he said, playing along, "You seem to have all the character references of a politician."

Quark failed to appreciate the humor; he spread his clawed hands and shook his head at Sisko. "How could I possibly operate my establishment under Starfleet rules of conduct?"

Good question; Odo turned to Sisko for the answer.

Sisko gave a little shrug. "This is still a Bajoran station. We're not here to administrate. You run honest games, you won't have any problems from me."

"*Honest* games?" Quark growled with a disdain that offended Odo. "Hmph." He folded his stubby arms in unconscious imitation of Sisko and fell silent.

Sisko and Odo waited.

At last the Ferengi shook his head. "Commander, I've made a career out of knowing when to leave. This Bajoran provisional government is far too provisional for my taste. And when governments fall, people like me are lined up and shot."

Sisko nodded with a bit too much sympathy and understanding, Odo thought; the commander turned to leave, stopped, paused thoughtfully in the doorway. "That poor kid," he said softly, "is about to spend the best years of his life in a Bajoran prison. I'm a father myself. I know what your brother must be going through. The boy should be with his family, not in a cold jail cell." He eyed the speechless Ferengi for an instant, then added, "Think about it."

And he turned and exited. Quark sat in his chair, stunned and gaping as the door closed behind Sisko's retreating back.

Odo smiled and turned conversationally toward the Ferengi. "You know, at first I didn't think I was gonna like him."

Inside the Promenade, Kira shoveled rubble from the walkway into a nearby receptacle and stopped struggling to repress the memory of the dream. Physical labor always freed her mind to roam, but now it returned, as it had been fighting to all day, to the previous night's dream. The more she worked, the more she began to recall.

The rational part of her mind was convinced that none of them belonged here on the Cardassian space station . . . yet when she thought with her *pagh*—or rather, when she simply didn't think—she knew otherwise.

Just as she had known in the dream last night, the same one she had been having for the past several nights. The dream about Sisko.

Or perhaps she was only trying to convince herself it had been about Sisko. It had been about a man, a brown-skinned human with dark eyes and hair, a man who would become very important to her people. The Bajora needed help so desperately that many were claiming to have received knowledge that one would come to help, to bring hope: the stranger whose appearance had been predicted by the prophets.

But Kira was by nature a cynic, and now she feared her people's desperation and her own were clouding her judgment, making her believe in things that did not exist but were much desired. Where are the prophets now that we need them? she thought bitterly, thrusting the shovel into the ruins.

And yet . . . when she thought with her *pagh,* not her mind, she could sense such amazing things in Sisko's *pagh* that she almost believed, almost dared to hope . . .

Sometimes she felt that her mind housed two

different personas—the mystic and the skeptic—that were always at odds. No wonder her planet was in such a mess.

If only Opaka would agree to see her; there were many things Kira wished to speak to her about. The dream was one of them. There had been another face in the dream, a Bajoran one, ancient and wise, haloed in silver-white.

"Major?"

The sound of her commander's voice startled her. She turned at the questioning tone, realized he was curious about the shovel, probably wondering whether such a task was appropriate for an officer. She shrugged, and the dream and the *pagh* were once again reduced to irrelevance; Sisko was no longer the prophesied stranger but a regulation-worshiping Starfleet type who irritated her.

"Everyone else is busy repairing the primary systems," Kira said, straightening to empty the shovel into the receptacle. She allowed her tone to become challenging. "I suppose Starfleet officers aren't used to getting their hands dirty."

Sisko raised an eyebrow, then located a shovel, picked it up, and set to work.

Kira turned her face away from him and pretended to be unimpressed, but she found herself trusting him enough to mention her past, a compliment she had thus far reserved for Odo. "In the refugee camps," she said, "we learned to do whatever had to be done. It didn't matter who you were."

They worked silently for a time; then Sisko spoke. "I was just talking to our good neighbor, Quark. He's laying odds the provisional government's going to fall."

Kira acknowledged the comment with a nod. "Quark knows a sure bet when he sees it." Sisko turned his head sharply to stare at her. She shrugged. "This government will be gone in a week. And so will you." So her common sense said; but hadn't the dream said otherwise?

Sisko hurled a shovelful of trash into the receptacle. "What happens to Bajor then?"

"Civil war," Kira said, trying to ignore the emotions, the horror, evoked by those two words. The thought filled her with bitterness; now that the Cardassians had gone, after ransacking the planet, her own people would start fighting in the ruins, destroying what little was left. "The politicians are too busy drawing their maps to see what has to be done."

"And what's that?"

"Nothing Starfleet can help us with." She hesitated, wondering how much information she should impart to this stranger, dream or no dream. At his sincerely interested gaze, she said at last, "The only one who can prevent a civil war is Opaka."

"Opaka?"

"Our spiritual leader. She's known as the Kai. Our religion is the only thing that holds my people together. If *she* would call for unity, they would listen." She set down the shovel and bent over to pick up some small fragments from the walkway; Sisko knelt beside her to help.

"Leaders of all the factions have been trying to get to her," Kira said softly, "but she lives in seclusion and rarely sees anyone."

Sisko considered this, tilting his angular face. "Perhaps she would be more receptive if someone from the Federation asked to meet with her."

Kira looked up at him. "You?" She made a soft sound of disbelief. "Believe me, she has no more use for the Federation than I do."

A shadow fell over both of them; Kira glanced up, startled, into a face haloed by silver—the wise, ancient face from her dream.

Ben Sisko stared up, thinking he had fallen back into the dream in which the omniscient Bajoran woman extended her long, gentle fingers toward his cheek.

(*Breathe,* Jennifer said)

But the face that hovered above him and Kira was male, older, familiar—that of the white-haired monk who had welcomed him to the Bajoran temple.

"Commander." The aged Bajoran's countenance was placid, his voice full of the knowledge that Sisko had been aware for some time of the inevitability of this encounter, and of what would follow. "It is time." He turned his robed back, trusting the human to follow, and began to stride through the wreckage.

Sisko's heart beat faster. He stood up, mesmerized, and for a second, no more, stared after the old monk. Odd emotions tugged at him, emotions he had thought were long buried, emotions that had surfaced during the dream.

(*Breathe*)

He glanced down to see Kira staring up at him in frank amazement; her face flickered, became Jennifer's. Sisko blinked and the apparition vanished.

He would talk to the Kai in order to help the Bajorans, he told himself. In order to do his duty as a Starfleet officer, and nothing more. These were rational reasons: then why did the monk's appearance and Kira's mention of Kai Opaka tug so at his heart?

Sisko drew a breath, set down his shovel, and followed.

They transported planetside, where a bright midday sun shone on the ruins: scorched earth, dead and dying foliage, the burned-out shells of buildings.

As Sisko walked along the rubble-strewn streets, the sights made him flash on a memory: himself in the *Saratoga*'s escape pod, staring out at the burned-out hulls of dead starships. But this was devastation on an even greater scale; Sisko had never personally witnessed such destruction. He felt a pang of guilt at his outrage over the comparatively minor damage to the station.

A few buildings had been spared—all of them

rounded, spherical, soft, and graceful, more harmonious with the natural surroundings than the harsher, outrageous angles of the Cardassian structures. The monk led Sisko to one of them, a temple or monastery, Sisko guessed, from the elaborate stone carvings at the entryway.

The massive stone structure's interior was dim, shadowed, illuminated only by the sunlight that streamed through cracks and holes in the walls. Sisko was shocked by the damage, the desecration of what was clearly one of the holiest places to the Bajora: windows had been smashed, interior walls knocked out, religious statues beheaded.

Yet the Cardassians had not succeeded in destroying the aura of serene contemplation, of sanctuary, that permeated the site. His guide led him past one monk who chanted mournfully amid the ruins and another who, hobbled by injuries, painstakingly patched an exterior wall.

"Commander Sisko."

A feminine voice. He turned toward the sound, toward the shadowed form of a woman. Sunlight filtered between them, glittering with airborne dust. Sisko held his breath as the woman from his dream stepped forward, emerging from the darkness like the ghostly figures of the *Saratoga*'s wounded.

She was Bajoran, middle-aged, dressed in a bright sheath, and she was injured. She limped, supporting herself on a cane as she moved toward her visitor, and her face was badly bruised; Sisko saw the pain of the entire Bajoran race carried there. Yet this woman's face shone with an interior radiance, an inner peace that no enemy could violate.

Sisko understood the sadness and envied the calm.

Kai Opaka smiled faintly, gesturing at the ruins surrounding them. "I apologize for the conditions in which we greet you."

"The Cardassians?" Sisko asked. It was not really a question.

Kai Opaka answered with a knowing gaze as she moved haltingly across the stone floor. Sisko repressed an urge to offer a hand in support—the Kai's dignity discouraged it—and followed her deeper into the monastery.

"Desecrating the center of our spiritual life was a way to strike at the heart of the Bajoran people," Opaka said.

She led him to a contemplation area, where carved wooden benches formed a semicircle around a reflecting pool. Above it, windows looked out onto a distant range of mountains, serene and inviolate, their images shimmering across the still surface of the pool.

Opaka settled herself carefully onto one of the benches; Sisko sat beside her. She turned to him with a small smile. "Your arrival has been greatly anticipated."

Sisko forced himself to recover from the strange surge of emotion caused by the memory of the dream, forced himself to react strictly as a representative of the Federation. "I'm glad to hear that," he said, all Starfleet business. "If Bajor can join the Federation it will bring stability—"

"I do not speak of the Federation," the Kai interrupted firmly. "I speak of *your* arrival."

"Mine?" Sisko felt a ripple of fear; he suddenly wanted to flee this mysterious woman.

Opaka reached out with long, gentle fingers and cupped one side of Sisko's face, studying him as an old woman might admire the face of a beloved grandchild. "Have you ever explored your *pagh,* Commander?"

"Pagh?" Sisko wanted to pull back, flee from her touch; he wanted to draw closer, to trust.

Her hand moved delicately, firmly, to Sisko's ear; one finger slowly traced the outer rim. "Bajorans draw courage from their spiritual life. Our life-force, our *pagh,* is replenished by the prophets."

The radiance in her eyes grew as her finger moved. She stared in frank wonder at Sisko, as if she had just witnessed the most amazing of miracles. With a sudden move, she squeezed Sisko's earlobe. He jerked his head, startled at the intense pain.

"Breathe," Opaka said.

(*Jennifer*)

Sisko drew back, suddenly uncomfortable, frightened because of the emotion evoked by that simple touch: grief.

(*Jennifer*)

(*She's gone, Hranok said*)

He wanted the Kai to learn no more of him, Ben Sisko the man; he tried to return the conversation to political matters. "Kai Opaka, if we could discuss your role in the post-Cardassian transition . . ."

"Breathe," Opaka insisted.

Sisko gasped in a lungful air and realized he had been holding his breath.

Opaka ran her fingers back up the outer rim of Sisko's ear. "Ironic," she said thoughtfully, more to herself than to Sisko. "One who does not wish to be among us is to be the emissary."

Sisko stiffened. Was his lack of interest, his desire to leave Deep Space Nine, so obvious?

The Kai leaned closer, studying each millimeter of his face. After a full minute of silence, she drew back. "There is much to be learned from your *pagh,* Commander." She leaned on her cane and pushed herself to a standing position. "Please come with me."

Sisko rose as Opaka removed a tiny control from the folds of her robe and touched it.

The reflecting pool disappeared—a hologram—revealing a carved stone stairwell leading downward. Sisko followed her down into a secret cavern, untouched by the Cardassians, primitively illumined by rows of flickering candles nestled in hollowed-out stone shelves.

The cavern evoked a sense of déjà vu in Sisko; he tried to remember whether he had been here before, in the dream.

At the base of the stairs, Opaka turned to him, balancing her weight on the cane. "You are correct that Bajor is in grave jeopardy . . . as grave as any crisis in our history. But the threat to our spiritual life far outweighs any other."

"Perhaps," Sisko responded, "but I'm powerless unless I have a unified—"

Opaka cut him off. "I cannot give you what you deny yourself."

Sisko frowned, mystified. "I'm sorry . . . ?"

"Look for solutions from within, Commander." At Sisko's puzzled expression, the Kai limped across the stone floor to a carved box that reminded him strongly of holos he'd seen of the Hebrew Ark of the Covenant. With a skillful touch she removed the lid and stepped back so that Sisko could see.

He moved closer, feeling the strange pull of the contents of the ark. Suspended inside a forcefield, a shimmering double orb of pure radiant energy floated; Opaka's face glowed green with reflected light as she stared down reverently at it. It looked like a revolving hourglass, Sisko thought, or the mathematical symbol for infinity. Forever.

"What is it?" Sisko asked softly, swiveling his head to see that Opaka had retreated even farther from him; she stood now with her hand on a wall panel.

"The tear of the prophet," Opaka said. She pressed the panel, and a passageway opened in the stone. She stepped inside; the passageway disappeared. Alone in the cavern now, Sisko turned, startled, ready to cry out her name. . . .

The cavern dimmed, then brightened with a strange greenish light.

Sisko returned his gaze to the ark. The forcefield

surrounding the glowing infinity orb had vanished. The orb itself had brightened, increased in size, started to spin. As Sisko stared in amazement, it began to spin faster, all the while growing larger, larger, until the ark could no longer contain it and it spun out into the room, enveloping him with a force more fearsomely powerful than that of a cyclone. The light brightened to blinding intensity, blotting out the sight of the ark, the cavern, everything except itself. Sisko cried out and closed his eyes, but still the light increased to a level beyond physical pain. . . .

And then it faded. He opened his eyes tentatively, expecting to see the shadows of blindness or, at the very least, a green afterimage imposed on the walls of the cavern.

No shadows. No afterimage. No cavern. Sisko blinked, stared out at a vast expanse of white sand framing blue water and blue sky, drew in a lungful of air and tasted brine. He stared down at himself and saw not a Starfleet uniform but his own body, younger, leaner, clad in a bathing suit he had long ago forgotten owning.

He nearly dropped the tray of drinks in his hand—three glasses of lemonade.

"What the hell . . . *Opaka?*"

Two bathing suit–clad passersby shot him an odd look. Sisko fell silent, meditating on the strange sense of familiarity, of déjà vu, that he was experiencing now, the same feeling he'd had upon meeting Opaka.

His meditation was interrupted by the swift, certain conviction that his feet were being scalded by hot sand. Hologram or not, the sensation was real.

"Ahh . . . *aaaahhhh!*" Sisko pranced on tiptoe, eyeing the area around him. The water was too distant, but he spied a nearby beach blanket. Sisko leapt for it, inadvertently kicking sand on the supine sunbather who lay there.

"Hey!" The woman rolled over onto her side, clutching an unfastened bathing suit top to her breasts, dark brows knit tightly above her sunglasses.

"I'm sorry," Sisko said, feeling completely confused and ridiculous. "It's just that the sand was burning my—"

At the sight of her face, he broke off and sank slowly, slowly to his knees, pierced to the heart. He had forgotten how utterly beautiful she had been.

"Jen . . . Jennifer?" he whispered. He stretched out his free hand toward her. The woman recoiled, uncertain, as Sisko gently removed the sunglasses. Jennifer's gold-flecked brown eyes squinted at him in the harsh light without a glimmer of recognition.

"Yes? I'm sorry . . . Did we meet last night at George's party?"

"George?" Sisko repeated dully, too numbed to make sense of her words. "*Jennifer* . . . wait a minute. This is impossible." He struggled to his feet, sloshing lemonade onto the tray.

Jennifer's mistrust had turned to concern. "Are you okay?"

Sisko swiveled his head, looking in nightmarish confusion for Opaka, the cavern, the glowing green orb. . . . "What are you doing here? What am *I* doing here?"

Jennifer sat up, still clutching the bathing suit top. "You really should wear a cap when you're out in the sun."

"I *know* this place," Sisko told himself in amazement. "This is Gilgo Beach, where we met."

Now it was Jennifer's turn to grow confused. "We've met here . . . before?"

"I was carrying"—Sisko looked down at the tray—"three glasses of lemonade. . . ."

Her forehead puckered; she maneuvered the suit top into place and fastened it.

"My feet were burning," Sisko continued, growing excited as everything came rushing back in memory. "I stopped here. Do you understand how incredible this is? No, of course you don't. *Jennifer.*"

He stared at her, overwhelmed by her nearness, wanting to touch her, to explain everything to her, to tell her how tall Jake had grown in the last three years, how much like his mother the boy had become. . . .

But she would not understand. In fact, she would think him insane. Sisko contented himself with staring at her face, her beautiful face, and struggled not to be swept away by a tide of emotion. After a time the silence grew awkward; she shifted, clearly uncomfortable. If he did not reassure her, she would ask him to leave. Sisko cast about for something, anything, to say. The best he could come up with was "Have a lemonade." He shoved the tray at her.

She drew back, mistrustful, but the undercurrent of amusement in her tone gave him hope. "Sorry. I don't accept drinks from strange men on the beach." She pushed herself up onto graceful legs and strode out to the water's edge. Sisko set the tray on the blanket and followed.

She ignored him at first, but did not protest as he walked beside her. The cool water foamed as tiny waves broke over their feet. The beach stretched out before them, a white arc of sand disappearing into an infinite horizon of sea.

Jennifer spoke at last. "Tell me the truth. Did we really meet before?"

Sisko studied her. How could he tell her the truth—that she was some sort of hallucination or holographic projection? How could he tell her about their marriage, their son, her death aboard the *Saratoga?*

He told the truth as it had been, that first meeting on Gilgo Beach. "No."

She shook her head and flashed him a big shy Jennifer-smile. "So how did you know my name?"

"I . . ." Sisko foundered, then made up a lie, then remembered with amazement that the lie had actually been the truth in the past. "George told me."

"Then you *were* at the party last night."

"Late . . ." He paused, remembering. "I got there late . . . and you were just leaving . . ."

The Jennifer-smile widened. "Are you going to tell me your name?"

"Oh." He returned the grin, allowed himself to slip into that long-ago conversation, into the rhythm of the past, allowed himself to enjoy Jennifer as she had been, young and strong and beautiful. Did it really matter that she was not real? She was *here.* "Ben Sisko. I . . . I just graduated from Starfleet Academy. I'm waiting for my first posting."

"A junior officer?" Jennifer's eyes narrowed; her tone grew teasing. "My mother warned me to watch out for junior officers."

"Your mother's going to adore me," Sisko said without thinking.

She threw her head back, grinning at his impudence. "You're awfully sure of yourself."

"It's not every day you meet the girl you're going to marry."

She stopped in her tracks, surf breaking around her ankles, and laughed out loud; overhead, a seabird cried. "Do you use this routine with a lot of women?"

"No," Sisko answered truthfully. "Never before. And never again."

"Sure," Jennifer said, her tone still teasing; she glanced away, but he caught the glimmer of a deeper emotion in her eyes and knew that he had touched her, that she believed him.

"How about letting me cook dinner for you tonight?" Sisko asked impulsively, yet knowing with hidden astonishment that he was speaking the very same words he had uttered fifteen years before. "My father was a gourmet chef. I'll make his famous aubergine stew."

A flicker of uncertainty, of mistrust, crossed her features as she stared out at the horizon. "I don't know . . ."

"You're supposed to say yes," Sisko prompted, smiling; the thought of reliving that first dinner with Jennifer filled him with lightness. If he could only remain here forever, in the past . . .

Behind them, above Jennifer's head, the air shimmered, filled with greenish light: the orb. Sisko's hope became tainted with grief. This was not real. This was illusion, a hologram, a trick of Opaka's; Jennifer was dead and he was speaking with a shadow, a ghost of memory. He would be forced to return to the empty present.

He wanted to clutch her, to take her with him and never let her go, but he could not bring himself to touch her for fear of grasping only nothingness and salt-scented air. . . .

Jennifer's voice drew him back to unreality. "I'll probably be sorry." She shook her head and grinned.

The orb began to spin, bathing the beach in light.

"Jennifer—" Sisko began urgently, struggling to reach out for her, but the glowing force surrounded him. "No . . . wait!"

Jennifer, the sand, the water, disappeared in a blaze of green that was brighter and more painful to Sisko's eyes than the explosion that had torn the *Saratoga* apart. He felt himself enveloped by the orb's mysterious energy, swept back into the present.

He opened his eyes and found himself once again in the dim candlelit cavern, Opaka beside him. They stared down at the infinity-orb, nestled safely inside the ark.

"Is it some sort of holographic device?" he asked unevenly. His legs trembled, threatened to give out beneath him.

"No," Opaka said, her eyes shining with reflected light. "What you experienced barely begins to reveal its powers." She closed the lid of the ark, blotting out the glow, and turned to him in the dimness. "This orb appeared in the skies over a thousand years ago. Eight others have been discovered since. They have been studied and documented for a millennium. Tradition says they were sent from the Celestial Temple. What they have taught us has shaped our theology."

She lifted the ark and gently handed it to Sisko, then said in a voice laced with meaning and emotion, "I entrust this to you."

Sisko stiffened. "Why?"

"It will lead you to the Temple."

"Excuse me?" He felt suddenly foolish; he had been hypnotized, that was all, and Opaka was taking advantage of his deepest emotions in order to persuade him to fulfill some ridiculous Bajoran prophecy.

She must have sensed his fear. She straightened, her wounded leg forgotten, and repeated firmly, "It must lead you to the Celestial Temple so that you can warn the prophets."

Sisko eyed her skeptically. "Warn them about what?"

"The Cardassians took the other eight orbs. They will stop at nothing to decipher their powers, even if it means discovering where they came from. If they do, they might destroy the Celestial Temple itself . . . which could mean the spiritual disintegration of Bajor."

He shook his head, took a step backward. "To expect me to go off on some sort of . . . of quest?"

Opaka leaned toward him, her tone and posture emphatic. "I cannot unite my people until I know that the prophets have been forewarned."

Her gaze was unyielding; Sisko heard the message loud and clear: *Do this or I will not help you.* And then a small sympathetic smile softened her features.

"You will seek the prophets," she said knowingly. "In the end, not for Bajor and not for the Federation . . . but for yourself. For your own *pagh.* It is, Commander, the journey you have always been destined to take."

CHAPTER 5

Miles O'Brien walked into his quarters aboard the *Enterprise* for the last time. The outer room had been stripped of all of his and Keiko's belongings; out of habit, O'Brien stared down at his feet, to avoid tripping over any of Molly's toys, but the deck was clean, and echoed uncomfortably beneath his heels.

"Keiko?"

No reply. O'Brien passed through the empty living room into the bedroom, where Keiko sat on the bed in the dark, Molly asleep in her arms. She did not look up as he approached; as he neared, the light from the living room glistened off the tears streaming down her cheeks.

"What's this?" O'Brien asked softly, with a pang of guilt. "Aw, honey, don't." He sat down beside her on the bed; she did not react. "We talked about this."

Keiko stared down at her sleeping child. O'Brien heard the guilt, the fear of being selfish, in her hushed reply. "I'm still wondering what a botanist is going to do on a Bajoran space station."

He tried to cheer her up with humor. "From the looks of the place, the Cardassians must think sterility is an art form. You could turn it into a garden." The thought had occurred to him earlier, when he had stood inside the grim quarters assigned them; Keiko would find a way to make the place warm and livable—a formidable challenge.

His attempt at humor didn't work. She gazed up at him in the darkness, all seriousness. "I don't need busywork, Miles. I have a career on the *Enterprise.* I'm happy here. We met each other here. . . ." Her voice trailed off.

O'Brien sighed, unable to think of anything else to say to comfort her. It was Keiko who had insisted that he take the promotion and the transfer to Deep Space Nine, and Miles who had worried that Keiko would be unhappy there. Now that the deed was done, their positions were reversed: O'Brien was looking forward to the challenge of bringing the station back to working order, and Keiko was having second thoughts—but nothing could be done to change the situation now.

"I love you," O'Brien said simply.

It was the right thing to say. Keiko smiled sadly and placed a hand on his, carefully so as not to disturb the child. "I'll be fine once we get settled."

O'Brien nodded sympathetically. "Are you all packed?"

"Everything's been sent over."

"Why don't you take the baby?" O'Brien said. "I'll be along in a couple of minutes. There are a few things I still need to do."

The bridge was still on the night-watch shift. O'Brien stepped out of the turbolift and walked along the aft station, feeling awkward, thinking he had made a mistake to come there. But he could not bring himself to leave without saying good-bye to the *Enterprise.*

The lieutenant in charge, Suarez, noticed and seemed to understand. "The captain's in the ready room, Chief. Should I tell him you're here?"

O'Brien hesitated. He felt he should say good-bye to the captain, but the meeting would be painful; better he should simply slip out unnoticed. He shook his head. "That's okay. Thanks."

He took one last look around the bridge, then retreated to the turbolift and took it down to Transporter Room Three.

"Transport me to the Ops pad, Maggie," he said, with false cheerfulness, to the new transporter chief.

"Yes, sir." Maggie smiled her farewell as O'Brien moved toward the pad.

A voice spoke behind him. "Mr. O'Brien."

O'Brien turned to face Captain Picard.

"I believe I just missed you on the bridge," Picard said.

"Yes, sir," O'Brien admitted guiltily. "I didn't want to disturb you."

Picard motioned for the transporter chief to leave; once the doors had closed behind Maggie, his demeanor became more relaxed. "Your favorite transporter room, isn't it?" he asked softly.

O'Brien nodded, glad to see the captain once more, but anxious for the uncomfortable encounter to be over. "Number three, yes, sir."

Picard did not quite smile. "You know, yesterday I called down here and asked for you without thinking. It won't be quite the same."

O'Brien shrugged. "It's just a transporter room, sir."

Picard finally smiled at that, and O'Brien had to grin, too, at his pathetic attempt to avoid admitting how he felt about leaving his old station, about leaving the *Enterprise.*

An awkward pause followed, and then O'Brien asked, "Permission to disembark, Captain?"

Picard straightened. "Permission granted."

O'Brien stepped onto the pad; Picard moved to the console. They exchanged a look.

"Energize," O'Brien said, when he could bear it no more. Picard pressed the control.

O'Brien watched his past dissolve in a shimmer of light.

After securing the Bajoran ark and its mysterious contents in the science lab, Sisko stepped inside his quarters, dark save for starlight filtering through the portholes.

His experience with Opaka and the orb had left him with a sense of wonder that was still undimmed. The relived memory of that first encounter with Jennifer on Gilgo Beach had been as wonderful as it was painful; he could not shake the feeling that it had been *more* than a memory, that he had really *been* there, with Jennifer, in the past.

And he could not shake the feeling that the experience and the Kai's prophecy were somehow related, somehow deeply meaningful.

You will seek the prophets . . . not for Bajor and not for the Federation, but for yourself. It is the journey you have always been destined to take.

It was foolish, he knew, to give any credence to such religious ravings, to attach anything other than purely scientific significance to the orb and to the strange experience it was capable of evoking; but for the first time since his arrival, he felt a sense of purpose, a sense of being where he was supposed to be. . . .

Correction. Make that for the first time since Jennifer's death.

Sisko groped his way in the darkness through the vast outer quarters toward the smaller inner room, taking care to make no sound; Jake was a notoriously light sleeper, waking at the slightest sound. He stole into the inner room, where his son lay, fully clothed, on his stomach, sound asleep on the floor cushion—head to one side, dark brows furrowed, full lips parted.

Sisko knelt beside him, smiling at the soft, regular sighing sound, not quite a snore. The recent sight of Jennifer, fifteen years younger, brought home the resemblance between the two resoundingly; the realization brought more wistful fondness than pain. And it brought guilt as well. Had Opaka's insistence that he was Bajor's long-awaited savior appealed to his ego? Was that the real reason he was suddenly considering staying? Ego or not, he had to put Jake's interests first.

Sisko gently untangled the blanket from around the boy's feet and pulled it up to Jake's shoulders.

True to form, Jake opened big, sleepy eyes and frowned up at his father, not really awake. "What?"

"I was just thinking," Sisko said softly, smiling down at his son, "how much you look like your mom."

The frown melted into a shy Jennifer-smile, then faded altogether as Jake's eyelids closed. Sisko rose and headed for the outer room.

In the archway his comm badge signaled. "Kira to Sisko."

He closed the door softly behind him before responding. "Go ahead, Major."

Her voice held a clear note of amusement. "Sorry to disturb you, Commander. But there's something on the Promenade you might want to see."

The lift opened to the strains of raucous alien music. Sisko took one step forward, stopped . . . and let a grin spread slowly over his features.

On the darkened Promenade, one kiosk shone

like a beacon: Quark's casino. Sisko ambled down the freshly swept walkway watching the handful of pedestrians—a few Bajora, a few other shopkeepers, a few spacefarers from docked vessels—hurry toward their bright destination.

Inside, the casino showed few signs of Cardassian devastation. A huge spinning vertical wheel—the Ferengi version of roulette, Sisko guessed—whirled under the guidance of Quark's Ferengi pit boss.

"Fortune's fates are with you today, friends," the pit boss announced in an amusingly unctuous nasal voice. "Prompt wagers, please." He leaned forward to hear the whispered question of a Bajoran officer, then straightened up. "I'm sorry, madam, Quark's casino does not accept travelers' vouchers. Gold or hard currency, please. Final wagers . . ."

Sisko shook his head, still grinning, and elbowed his way through the smoke-filled room, past crowded gaming tables. As he passed one table, a voice cried, "Dabo!" followed by a chorus of groans. Sisko craned his neck, searching for Quark and simply taking in the sights. On a central podium, a musician played a triple keyboard; nearby, a giggling couple was being escorted up the stairs to a sexual holosuite. Sisko made his way to the bar and started slightly when Quark appeared on the other side.

The Ferengi offered up a snaggle-toothed smile. "What'll you have, Commander?"

Sisko placed a hand on the polished bar and

glanced approvingly over his shoulder at the crowd, then back at Quark. "How's the local synthale?"

Quark added new wrinkles to his already generously creased nose. "You won't like it." The Ferengi reached for a glass and began drawing a drink from beneath the bar. At Sisko's mildly quizzical reaction, he lowered his voice conspiratorially and added, "I love the Bajorans. Such a deeply spiritual culture. But they make a dreadful ale. Don't ever trust an ale from a God-fearing people." He slammed the glass on the bar in front of Sisko. "Or a Starfleet commander who has one of your relatives in jail."

Quark leaned forward over the bar and wrinkled his brow ridge as he examined Sisko's face closely. "Are you sure you have no Ferengi blood?"

"None I'll admit to." Sisko permitted himself a slight smile. "All right, Quark, you've kept your part of the bargain. Let's talk."

Inside the vast dark quarters, Jake lay awake for some time after his father left. He stared out at the stars through observation windows shaped like strange alien eyes.

The mention of his mother had surprised him. Dad didn't speak about her often, though Jake knew that he, like his son, thought about her all the time. At times, the past three years seemed like three days, as if Mom had simply been away on a long trip. Sometimes when Jake couldn't sleep, he would close his eyes and imagine his mother walking into the room, antigrav suitcase slung over one shoulder, arms spread, smiling. He could almost hear her voice: *Miss me?*

Yeah, Mom. Missed you awful . . .

Sometimes he dreamed that she really did come back, suitcase over her shoulder, smiling and laughing, kneeling down so that he could run into her open arms and hug her tight and never let go.

With Dad beside her, laughing and grinning the way he never had in the past three years, she would explain how it had all been a mistake, how she had not died on the *Saratoga;* that was someone else. After all, Jake had not actually seen her die; he hadn't seen the body, right? The dream was so clear, so simple, so wonderful. Then he would wake, sobbing and giggling with relief that quickly turned to sorrow.

At other times, the past three years seemed like an eternity, especially when he thought about Dad. Their grief over Mom's death seemed to both separate and unite them. Dad had grown fiercer in his love for Jake, and yet at the same time he had changed, become quieter, more distant. In three years Jake had not seen his father cry over his wife's death, had not heard him speak of what actually happened that day on the *Saratoga.*

He remembered very little of that day, only that Mom had been off duty, classes had been canceled, and the children were all sent to their quarters because of the Borg. The teacher had been nervous, actually afraid, Jake had realized with wonder, but he hadn't been frightened himself, until he hurried to his quarters and found Mom waiting for him there, wide-eyed with fear.

He had been too stupid to be scared. . . .

And then the firing began, and the ship started to shake like it was going to fly apart, and he had only the briefest memory of Mom putting her arms around him, holding him, telling him everything would be all right.

And then the explosion to end all explosions deafened him, threw him and Mom to the deck, and there was only a split second before consciousness winked out when he was aware the room was collapsing around them and a flaming bulkhead was bearing down on them. . . .

He came to in a starbase hospital room, Dad sitting woodenly beside him. He asked about Mom the minute he was able to speak.

Dad wasn't able to answer . . . and in his father's grief-stricken silence, Jake heard his worst fear confirmed. And he cried and cried and cried, more tears than he had ever thought himself capable of shedding during his entire life.

Dad had never wept. He just sat, mute and expressionless, and held Jake's hand, and for the next three years he was never again the same. It was as if someone had drained all the life, all the joy, all the happiness, out of him, as if Dad had died, too, and an empty shell of a man had stayed behind to make sure Jake was fed and bathed and did his homework. He had tried to make his dad laugh, feel better, talk about what happened the day Mom died, but no matter what he did, there was no piercing that shell of grief.

Sometimes Jake felt he had lost both parents that day aboard the *Saratoga.*

The fear of Dad *really* dying, though, consumed Jake. If they could just go to someplace *safe,* someplace far away from Starfleet and the Borg and aliens and hidden danger . . . someplace like Earth. Mom and Dad were both from Earth; maybe being there again would cheer Dad up, make him the way he used to be.

Any place, even Planitia, would be better than this strange, awful space station.

Besides, the simple, awful truth was: if they hadn't been in space, Mom would still be alive.

In his darker moments, the thought made Jake crazy with anger. He wanted to strike out, to hurt someone . . . and the nearest someone was Dad. After all, even though Dad kept promising to get an Earthside assignment, it hadn't happened in *three years.* He obviously wasn't trying hard enough. After Mom's death, Dad didn't care enough about anything to try hard. At times the sheer frustration of it made Jake cry like a little kid.

Dad wouldn't do anything to save himself, protect himself, and now here they were in this dangerous place where there had just been a lot of fighting. Jake knew something awful was going to happen to Dad here; he *knew* it, and he knew there was nothing he could do to keep it from happening.

Or was there?

He had spent the day bored and restless in the gloomy quarters. Dad had brought along some instructional holos from Dr. Lamerson, Jake's teacher on Planitia, so that Jake could finish his courses without interruption. But that wasn't the same as being in the classroom in person. The other students weren't there, and the Dr. Lamerson holo wasn't programmed to answer all of Jake's questions; the computer could, of course, but it didn't know how to make its explanations sound as interesting as Dr. Lamerson's.

So he'd finished up the day's lesson and played some games with the computer, but then he'd grown terribly, terribly bored and sorry for himself. He had no one to play with and nothing to do; Dad was miserably unhappy and there was nothing Jake could do to cheer him up.

He didn't want to be on this crummy old space station the Cardassians had trashed; he wanted to be on Earth, in a real class with kids his own age instead of with a brooding, grief-stricken father who had no time for him, but Starfleet and Dad just simply didn't care about him, and the thought made him angry.

He wanted to get even, somehow, wanted to strike out and hurt someone, anyone, even Dad. If he'd been on a planet he would have run away, but there wasn't anywhere to run to on this stupid station.

Jake sighed and tossed restlessly in the strange

bed, kicking the covers down around his ankles, then sat up abruptly, frowning at the stars as a thought occurred to him.

The Ferengi. There was a Ferengi his age, maybe a little older, right? He might know where to run to escape from trouble . . . or where to find some. Maybe he could show Jake how to get down to Bajor, and from there, Jake could find his way onto a shuttle and go all the way to Earth. Dad would *have* to listen then; he would have to come and get his son, and Jake would just refuse to let him leave.

In the quiet dark, it all seemed so simple.

Jake lay back down on the bed with a sigh, and resolved to find the Ferengi no later than tomorrow.

"Wake up, Miles," Keiko said. "You're having a dream."

O'Brien lurched forward with a start and opened his eyes to find himself lying in his wife's arms.

"Easy." She drew back to avoid a collision, then leaned slowly forward again as he stilled. Even in the darkness, he could make out her face, soft and limned with starlight filtering down from the observation windows. The door to Molly's room was open; he could hear the child's gentle, sighing breath in the quiet.

He exhaled harshly and settled back against the pillows, his heart still beating rapidly from the adrenaline inspired by the dream. He did not want to recall it; he wanted only to orient himself, to know that he was with Keiko in the strange Cardassian bed, the one they had laughed about earlier that afternoon.

It looks like a sleigh, Keiko had said skeptically, as they stood looking down at it. *An obnoxious canopied sleigh without legs . . .*

Well, perhaps we'd better test it to be sure it works, O'Brien had said in his serious-engineer voice, and she had fallen for it, as she always did, raising her head to look at him in surprise, only to break into giggles at the gleam in his eye.

He had been happy at that moment; the quarters still needed work to look like a home, but they already looked better, warmer, almost welcoming despite their alienness, simply because Keiko was in them. It was even better now that her things were here, silent reassurance that she would stay.

Soft, cool fingers stroked his forehead, easing the heat there. "Do you want to talk about it?" Keiko murmured drowsily.

"Did I . . ." Still mildly confused, O'Brien let his head loll against his pillow and her arm as he looked about him at the strange room. "Did I—I woke you. I'm sorry. I didn't kick you, did I?"

Keiko snuggled against his shoulder and shook her head, making a negative sound that ended in a small yawn. "You were singing, I think. And then you cried out. Did you have a nightmare?"

"Singing?" O'Brien asked, then fell silent, remembering. In the dream he had been on Setlik Three again. Captain Maxwell was there, and

Keiko and Molly, and somehow Deep Space Nine and these very quarters were there, too. He and his former captain were having a wonderful reunion, drinking ale and singing: *The minstrel boy to the war is gone, in the ranks of death you'll find him . . .*

Suddenly a dream-Cardassian appeared from nowhere, phaser aimed directly at Keiko, who was holding the screaming Molly.

No! O'Brien shouted. Captain Maxwell threw him a phaser, and O'Brien fired without thought. He had no time to make sure it was set on stun and not kill. He watched in disbelief as the Cardassian was incinerated before his eyes. But Captain Maxwell was still smiling and lustily singing: *His father's sword he has girded on, and his wild harp slung behind him . . .*

In the bed, O'Brien ran his palm over his eyes. "Setlik," he told Keiko hoarsely. He said no more; he did not want to frighten her by admitting to the sudden urgent fear he felt for her sake and Molly's, stemming from a ridiculous conviction that the station was in great danger from the Cardassians and that she and Molly were in imminent danger of death. He thought of Commander Sisko lying alone in his quarters without his wife and wondered if he, O'Brien, would be able to bear settling into this bed alone, without Keiko.

He shivered; she tightened her arms about him, and they were silent for a moment.

"It's the station, of course," Keiko said finally, firmly, in the same tone he had heard her use to soothe Molly after a nightmare. "Everywhere you look, you're constantly reminded of the Cardassians. It's little wonder you're dreaming about them, Miles. I mean, look at you: you're even sleeping in a Cardassian bed."

"Well, then," he said, pulling her to him, "we'd better do something to make it more our own and less the Cardassians'," and she kissed him, giggling softly.

An hour later, as O'Brien fought to surrender to sleep, the song began silently repeating itself in his tired mind:

The minstrel boy to the war is gone,
In the ranks of death you'll find him.
His father's sword he has girded on,
And his wild harp slung behind him.

And the voice changed from O'Brien's to Stompie's. Technician Will Kayden, his name had been, but to O'Brien and his peers he was known as Stompie, a nickname derived from his enthusiastic, percussive way of accompanying himself on the Celtic harp.

Against O'Brien's closed eyelids, Stompie's image coalesced and became as clear, as detailed, as a holograph, as if he were a breathing flesh-and-blood man standing before O'Brien instead of a shade with an existence confined to memory. Stompie was tall but slight of build, with hair as orange as a carrot and a grin as wide as a starship. He was also young—awkwardly so—and so relieved to find a fellow Irishman aboard his very first starship that, as Captain Maxwell had so aptly put it, he hung on O'Brien like an eager puppy.

Miles didn't mind. After all, he was glad at the sight of a countryman, too, and he appreciated the young man's enthusiasm and warmth and passion for music. He and Stompie became loyal friends immediately; as Stompie said, true friends are recognized, not made.

In O'Brien's memory, Stompie closed his freckled eyelids and began plucking his harp as he sang in his clear, emotion-laden tenor:

> *"Land of song," said the warrior bard,*
> *"Though all the world betrays thee,*
> *One sword at least thy rights shall guard,*
> *One faithful harp shall praise thee."*

Stompie had sung that song in the rec lounge the night before Setlik, with O'Brien and Captain Maxwell and a cheerful group in attendance. O'Brien had been happy that night and had, along with Maxwell, raised his glass of ale and joined in the singing. The tune had been Stompie's particular favorite, and so became O'Brien's, too; but it was not until after the minstrel was gone that O'Brien found meaning in the lyrics.

That was two hours before they learned of Setlik, two hours before the *Rutledge* had been diverted from her course to attempt a rescue mission. It was a sleepless night for them all, knowing, as they did, that innocents would be slaughtered before the *Rutledge* could arrive, and knowing also that facing the Cardassians meant facing death. Worst of all, there was the knowledge—for O'Brien and a select few—that Captain Maxwell's wife and children were stationed on Setlik, and that all attempts at communication with them had failed.

By the time the *Rutledge* arrived, all communications with Setlik were out. Sensors indicated heavy casualties; the survivors had escaped to an outlying district and were still fleeing the Cardassians.

O'Brien read the faintest glimmer of hope and terror in his captain's taut expression; Maxwell's family lived in the outlying district.

They had to abandon their plan to scan for survivors and beam them to safety; without communications it was impossible to get a fix on them. Reluctantly, Maxwell handpicked a small squadron to beam down.

O'Brien was not surprised when Captain Maxwell insisted on beaming down to Setlik along with the other volunteers. It was irregular as hell, and the first officer registered her obligatory protest, but the halfhearted effort to stop him ended there. O'Brien and Stompie Will Kayden and Maxwell and a handful of others beamed down to Setlik.

Dawn at the outpost was beautiful; a bright orange sun rose up out of the mists into a purple sky. The air was cool and heavy with dew, and for an instant after they materialized in the deserted street, O'Brien heard only the early-morning quiet of a civilian neighborhood.

And then, in the distance, phasers whined. Captain Maxwell stiffened at the sound and turned toward Will Kayden, who lowered his somber freckled face toward his tricorder.

"Cardies," Stompie said, stretching a long, thin arm to indicate the direction. "Less than a kilometer away. Moving in this direction." He turned the tricorder on the multifamily dwellings behind him and confirmed what the ship's scans had already reported. "Civilians inside each one, sir."

"Break up," Maxwell said, and gestured toward the buildings. "Round up as many as you can and get them transported out of here. Volodzhe, Meier, Tsao, cover this block. Rendell, Lind, Garcia, take the next block. Stompie and O'Brien, come with me."

The entrance to the building had been secured; O'Brien had to use his phaser to gain access. As they entered, they kept shouting reassurances that they were Starfleet—and hoping like hell the civilians believed them. The entrance opened onto a central living area and kitchen that serviced a dozen or so families and that led back to separate private apartments.

Maxwell gestured swiftly to the left, center, then right. "I'll round them up from this direction. Chief, you go that way. Stompie, that way. Bring the civilians back to this central area on the double, and we'll get them beamed to safety."

Outside, the sound of phaser fire drew closer.

Beyond thought, O'Brien propelled himself down the hallway toward the apartment entrances, phaser at the ready. All too aware that those he was trying to save might mistake him for a Cardassian and fire at him, he kept shouting, "Starfleet! USS *Rutledge.* We're here to evacuate you. Move quickly!"

A young woman, her eyes wide with fright, appeared in the doorway of the first apartment, a two-year-old boy in her arms. "The *Rutledge?* Captain Maxwell?"

O'Brien glanced at her over his shoulder as he hurried down the corridor. "Maxwell, yes."

"Maria Huxley's husband," the woman said, breathless as she jogged behind him. "She's here, in this building."

Maxwell had known, then. O'Brien continued his search. In less than a minute he had assembled a group of three women and four children and returned with them to the living area. Stompie was just reappearing with his group, also women and children, and they listened for a moment to the drone of phasers growing closer, until it was just outside in the street. The woman who had asked about Captain Maxwell tightened her grip on her son, who began crying.

O'Brien allowed himself an impatient glance in the direction Maxwell had gone. "We can't wait," he said, tightening his grip on his phaser, and Stompie nodded, his expression calm as he smiled and reached forward to stroke the crying boy's hair. The mother returned the smile uncertainly; the boy ceased weeping. O'Brien did not quite smile himself he pressed his comm insignia.

A sudden sound: metal slamming against metal. The sound, O'Brien knew, of the Cardassians kicking down the entryway at the far end of the building.

Stompie gazed up knowingly at O'Brien at the sound. *Time to hurry, Miles,* his eyes said, but there was not the faintest trace of fear of them.

As cool under fire as a mountain lake, Maxwell had said of him—years later, after Stompie was gone, years after the horrifying seconds that followed.

Cardassian voices, growing nearer; cries that might have been human. The whine of phaser fire moving through the wing into which Maxwell had gone. The three youngest children in the group began to weep softly.

Miles spoke into his comm badge: "O'Brien to Transporter Room Two. Thirteen civ—"

A beam of red light streaked by in his peripheral vision and hurled Stompie against the wall, illuminating his torso with a dark red glow. The two-year-old beside him shrieked.

What happened next occupied the space of less than a second; in O'Brien's memory, it seemed like an eternity.

Suspended, his back against the wall, Stompie trembled in agony, blue eyes wide as he beheld the face of his killer. A small puff of smoke escaped from his chest, filling the air with the scent of burned flesh. His mouth opened, but he did not cry out, only released a final soft sigh as he slid to the floor and died sitting up, eyes open.

O'Brien whirled on the killer, the faceless, inhuman enemy, and stunned him without a thought, without being consciously aware of anything, anyone, except his friend. The Cardassian dropped.

Movement: a black-sleeved arm sweeping across his field of vision, knocking the phaser from his hand. O'Brien reached out blindly, seeing nothing now but rage and hate, and caught one of the Cardassian's wrists, then the other, roaring as he slammed the alien into the wall. The air rushed from the Cardassian's lungs with a loud gasp. O'Brien seized the hand that held the phaser, pinned it against the wall and then slammed it again and again, until the weapon clattered to the floor.

With a surge of strength, the Cardassian pushed. O'Brien staggered backwards, stumbled over a wailing child, and lost his footing. The Cardassian scrabbled for his weapon.

This is it, then, O'Brien thought glumly, suddenly numb, unable to digest it all, unable to comprehend that Stompie was dead and that he, Miles, would now join him.

And then something arced at him through the air. Instinctively he reached for it, caught it before his conscious mind realized that it was the Cardassian's phaser and that the woman who had asked about Captain Maxwell had thrown it to him.

He fired.

He knew—had to have known—that it was set on kill; he had just witnessed his friend's death. And yet, as the Cardassian fell to the floor, writhing and screaming in the throes of a painful death, Miles gaped in utter disbelief, his rage evaporating.

He had never before taken a life. Now the faceless enemy suddenly took on a countenance not so dissimilar from O'Brien's own—a face that contorted in final agony and remained distorted even after the eyes had dimmed.

Stompie was dead. Yet O'Brien found no solace in the fact that he had avenged his friend; Stompie's death served only to underscore the horror of what Miles had done. He was now, like the Cardassian, a murderer.

He did not remember contacting the *Enterprise* and beaming up the civilians, but apparently he had done so with complete efficiency. He had even thought to inquire after the captain, and learned that Maxwell was not responding to comm signals.

Fearing that the captain was dead, O'Brien made his way cautiously through the seemingly deserted building until at last he found two Cardassians lying stunned in a corridor beside the captain. Maxwell stood, unharmed, in a doorway, one hand against the jamb; he did not bother to turn as O'Brien approached behind him.

"Captain?" O'Brien said softly. Maxwell finally turned his face toward him. "Stompie . . ."

O'Brien faltered, then fell silent as he followed his captain's gaze to the scene inside the apartment. A table had been overturned, an abstract sculpture shattered; above it, a painting of Earth as viewed from Luna hung askew, its beauty marred by an ugly diagonal scorch mark that extended across the wall. In the midst of the destruction, a slender dark-haired woman lay facedown across a six-year-old girl. Clearly the mother had turned her back to the attackers at the moment of her death in a futile effort to shield her daughter from the blast. Nearby, a teenage boy lay sprawled, his chest scorched and torn, his face locked in an expression of rage. He had seen his mother killed and had leapt fearlessly at his attackers, O'Brien decided.

He turned away and closed his eyes. He wanted to comfort Maxwell, but the horror of the past few moments had left him without words.

"It happened so quickly," Maxwell said softly behind him. There was no anger, no rage, only disbelief and the first hint of dulled pain in his voice. "A second, two seconds before I got here." He faced O'Brien, who opened his eyes and was frightened, not by the sound of advancing phaser fire but by the utter lack of emotion in his captain's expression. "They never even saw me, Chief. They never knew I had come for them. I was this close—*this* close—and I couldn't save them."

O'Brien shifted restlessly in his Cardassian bed at the memory of Maxwell's frighteningly blank expression. Upon their return from Setlik, the captain had retired to his quarters, but the following day he was on duty, showing no outward display of grief—as if he had not lost his family, as if Stompie Will Kayden had not died. In the years that followed, while O'Brien served with him, he never saw Captain Maxwell show a single sign of sorrow, never heard him mention Setlik or his wife and children or Stompie.

As if they had never existed. As if Setlik had never happened at all.

No mention until years later, when Captain Maxwell of the starship *Phoenix,* without provocation or orders, destroyed a warship with six hundred fifty Cardassians aboard.

O'Brien had never spoken to anyone, not even his wife, about Setlik before that time. But when he saw what the silence had done to Captain Maxwell, he told Keiko everything: about Stompie, about the murdered Cardassian.

In his bed, he opened his eyes and stared at the stars through the eerily shaped observation window. Beside him, his wife sighed in her sleep and rolled toward him. O'Brien stared at her in the dimness, overwhelmed by her fragility, afraid to take his eyes off her for fear she might disappear, might fade, like Stompie, into a memory.

What would happen to him if he lost Keiko and Molly? Would he deny his grief, only to go mad one day and destroy everything in his path?

How did Ben Sisko bear it?

He turned and put an arm around his wife and let the feel of her heartbeat lull him to sleep.

Station log. Stardate 46452.2 The *Enterprise* has been ordered to the Lapolis system. They're scheduled to depart at zero five hundred hours after offloading three runabouts. Meanwhile, our medical and science officers are about to arrive and I'm looking forward to a reunion with a very old friend.

Ben Sisko stood beside Major Kira and strained to pick out two blue Starfleet uniforms amid the sea of non-Fleet civilians coming through the airlock gate. Word had come that the new science officer and the chief medical officer had arrived at the station.

Sisko knew little about the medical officer except that his name was Julian Bashir, he was absurdly young, fresh out of Starfleet Medical, and he was a specialist in multi-species medicine, which made him well suited for the assignment.

But Ben Sisko and the science officer, Lieutenant Jadzia Dax, were very old, very dear friends. In fact, Dax had been his mentor and fatherly adviser. But these facts were causing Sisko more than a bit of discomfort at the moment. The two friends had not set eyes on each other since Dax, then an aging white-haired male, left Utopia Planitia. Sisko had no idea what he looked like now.

What *she* looked like.

He caught a glimpse of blue; Dax and Bashir had seen the two Starfleet officers and headed toward them. Dr. Bashir, broad-shouldered and olive-skinned with brown hair and warm brown eyes, looked every bit as young and green as his personnel record indicated, and then some. And Dax . . .

Sisko fought hard not to gape; his lips parted slightly despite his efforts.

Dax was definitely female, definitely beautiful, and every bit as young as Bashir. She was long-limbed and tall, with a pale, delicate beauty that reminded Sisko of ancient daguerreotypes he had seen of Victorian-era women; her honey-brown hair was drawn into a kind of pony tail, revealing a long white neck. From her temples down, she had a series of small, crescent-shaped spots running along her hair line and down her neck. At the sight of Sisko, she smiled broadly in recognition, a serene smile uncannily like that of her predecessor.

Ghosts, Sisko thought, as he returned the smile awkwardly. Inwardly he felt a strange sorrow: the outer Dax, the old man, was gone; a part of his friend had died, never to return. Everywhere I turn, ghosts and memories . . .

With Kira accompanying him, Sisko strode toward the new officers, intending to take Dax's outstretched hand. He was not at all prepared when she pulled him to her and firmly planted a maternal kiss on his cheek; he jerked back slightly, caught off guard.

Kira watched with badly hidden amusement, Bashir with a faint trace of jealousy.

Sisko felt the warmth rushing to his cheeks and was grateful his dark complexion hid the blush from his second-in-command. No point in saying anything to Dax; after a few hundred years of life, he—that is, *she*—did whatever she wanted to do, and protocol be damned. She never intentionally flouted regulations, but she felt she understood the spirit of the law and was beyond the letter.

Dax held on to Sisko's hand but pulled back to fondly gaze at him with a young woman's eyes, eyes that held the accumulated wisdom of centuries. "Hello, Benjamin."

Sisko allowed himself a smile at last. Strange, to look down and see Dax as a woman; he and the old man had been the same height. "This . . . *this* is going to take some getting used to."

"Don't be ridiculous. I'm still the same Dax," she said with the what-the-hell directness of advanced age, but there was a bright, youthful energy in her voice, her posture, her eyes, that the old man had lacked. She directed her smile at Kira.

"Major Kira Nerys." The Bajoran extended her hand formally.

"Jadzia Dax. And this is Dr. Julian Bashir." She gestured warmly toward the young man as if the two were already fast friends.

Bashir took Sisko's hand a little too eagerly, squeezed a little too firmly—nervous, Sisko realized. This was Bashir's first assignment, and he was Bashir's very first commanding officer.

Dax noticed the younger man's tension and took Bashir's arm with reassuring maternal warmth.

Sisko repressed a chuckle; Bashir obviously misinterpreted Dax's innocent parental concern as something entirely different. Sisko decided to explain to her when they were alone that she was no longer in an old man's body, and her habit of touching people now had an unintended effect on the male population.

"Julian's been a wonderful traveling companion," Dax was saying enthusiastically. "Did you know he finished second in last year's graduating class at Starfleet Medical?"

Bashir shrugged, obviously no good at being modest. "I mistook a preganglionic fiber for a postganglionic nerve during the orals or I would have been first."

Kira's eyes narrowed slightly in disapproval. Sisko expected her to come up with an insult to put the young doctor in his place, but instead she said, with surprisingly perfect decorum, "Commander, if you'd like me to give them a tour of the station—"

"You and Dr. Bashir go ahead," Sisko replied. And God help Bashir, he thought, once Kira gets him alone. "I'm afraid I have to put Lieutenant Dax right to work."

Kira nodded and briskly gestured Bashir toward the Promenade.

The young doctor hesitated awkwardly and turned toward Dax in an unsuccessful effort to sound casual. "Maybe we could get together later, Jadzia, for dinner or a drink?"

Dax smiled. "I'd be delighted."

Kira pressed her lips together tightly.

Sisko lifted a brow in surprised amusement at Dax's acceptance. Did she really have any idea what sort of "friendship" the young doctor was interested in cultivating?

He waited until he and Dax reached an interior corridor, well beyond earshot of Kira and Bashir before he raised the issue.

Half jokingly he said, "He's a little young for you, isn't he?"

Dax did not quite smile, but she was clearly amused by the situation, as if she was all too well aware of the effect this new body had on others. "He's twenty-seven. I'm twenty-eight."

"Three *hundred* and twenty-eight, maybe," Sisko corrected her. "Did you tell him about that slug inside you?" He could never quite bring himself to refer to the symbiont by its proper name.

She looked at him fondly, receiving the affectionate insult with good grace. "Yes, Benjamin, he knows I'm a Trill. He finds it fascinating. He's never met a joined species before." Her tone grew slightly professional. "And it's *we.* You know that. You're speaking to both of us all the time; it's not as if you're speaking just with the outer host. Symbionts have feelings, too." Her lips curved wryly.

"I wonder if Bashir would be as fascinated if you still looked the way you did the last time I saw you," Sisko teased.

She laughed. "Perhaps not."

"I don't really know this new host," Sisko said suddenly. "I miss Curzon." He had not meant to voice the thought, and fell silent, abashed.

"I know." Dax's voice and eyes softened. She laid a hand on Sisko's arm. "I miss him, too, Benjamin. If it makes you feel any better, a part of him, all his memories, will always be with me."

They stepped aboard the lift and rode up in silence.

Kira did not like Bashir; she did not like him at all, but for the commander's sake she was civil as she led him to the damaged infirmary. Sisko had won her cooperation—as much as anyone in Starfleet could hope to, that is—and her respect by returning from Kai Opaka's with the ark. Kira was keenly curious about what had transpired at the monastery, but Sisko had been subdued since his return. She only knew that something very deep, very spiritual, had happened to him. She could sense it in his *pagh*—at least, when she wasn't feeling too cynical. She knew that technicians were going to examine the ark, and that was another matter altogether. She feared that scientific inquiry might reduce the religion of the Bajora to foolishness. Sometimes Kira felt it *was* the greatest sort of foolishness, but at other times she knew it was the greatest of all wisdom.

She wanted to keep both options open. Examining the orb too closely might close off one of them.

She ushered Bashir into sickbay and narrowed her eyes at the tiny examining room. It seemed to her entirely inadequate for a station this size, with only one table, a few life-support panels, and a paucity of equipment, most of which had been smashed by Cardassian vandals.

"I'm afraid we've had some security problems," she said curtly. "Looks like some looters got in here."

Bashir took in the room with a sweeping gaze, then faced Kira—not with the disappointment she expected from someone who had been spoiled by training at a state-of-the-art medical facility, but with something akin to awe.

"This will be perfect!" Bashir's eyes blazed with excitement. "Real"—he groped for the word—"frontier medicine."

"Frontier medicine?" Kira snapped. She'd had just about enough of Bashir's disgusting display of naïveté.

Bashir stopped at her icy tone and leveled his overconfident gaze at her. "Major, I had my choice of any job in the Fleet."

"*Did* you." she said flatly, folding her arms at his arrogance.

Bashir went on in a rush of enthusiasm. "I didn't want a cushy job or a research grant." He waved his arms at the pathetic surroundings. "I wanted *this*—the farthest reaches of the galaxy, one of the most remote outposts available. *This* is where the adventure is. *This* is where heroes are made. Right here. In the wilderness."

Kira fought the smile that played at her lips. She disliked this human, but his utter naïveté, and his gung-ho enthusiasm were pushing her toward the verge of laughter; she and Odo would be able to entertain themselves at innocent young Dr. Bashir's expense for a long time to come. She managed a fearsome scowl and replied tightly, "This *wilderness* is my *home.*"

Bashir reacted with comical embarrassment at the realization that he had offended her. "I didn't mean—"

"The Cardassians left behind a lot of injured people, *Doctor,*" Kira said sharply, with a nasty emphasis on his title. "You can make yourself useful by bringing some of your Federation medicine to the 'natives.' You'll find them a friendly, simple folk."

She turned on her heel and left him to stare quizzically after her.

Julian Bashir moved to the door of the tiny sickbay and watched as Kira strode down the corridor, bootheels ringing against the deck. Her remarks had dampened his enthusiasm and left him perplexed; he honestly did not understand the antagonism he so often elicited from people.

Bashir had been born confident. He had always known what he wanted and had no patience with those who could not make up their minds.

All his life he had been brighter, faster, and more talented than his peers. As a result, in any given group he was always the youngest and always an outsider resented by the others, which meant he was often alone. He had never learned to underrepresent his genius and skill in order to be accepted. After all, he saw no virtue in false modesty; he believed in honesty, even if it made him seem arrogant. All through the Academy, he had told himself that his isolation didn't matter. Once he made it through, got his degree, and finished his training, he would find a place where he'd fit in, where his intelligence and abilities would be appreciated.

He had thought Deep Space Nine would be such a place. After all, they so clearly needed him here. But Kira's response bothered him. Despite his rationalization that it was not *his* fault if others could not deal with his genius, he wanted to be liked. And it was painfully clear that the major despised him.

He glanced up and smiled as the security constable, Odo, passed by in the hall. They had been introduced very briefly on the way to sickbay, Odo responding with an uninterested grunt, and Bashir was intensely curious about the constable's background. Kira had volunteered no information, and there had been no appropriate pause in the tour during which he could ask. Odo was certainly not Bajoran, from the looks of him—even the Bajora possessed the skill to surgically correct such facial disfigurement—so Julian had concluded that Odo was of another species altogether, a species with which Bashir was entirely unfamiliar. And since his specialty was multi-species medicine, he could scarcely allow the opportunity for education to slip by.

Odo acknowledged Bashir's smile with a barely perceptible nod—perhaps, Julian told himself, the constable's species did not smile—and made as if to hurry down the corridor after Kira.

Bashir did not let him escape. Still smiling, he stepped forward into the corridor, half blocking Odo's path, and said conversationally, with a jerk of his head in the direction the major had gone: "Are they all like Major Kira?"

Odo stopped awkwardly and blinked at him. "Are who all like Major Kira?"

Bashir folded his arms and leaned against the cool bulkhead. "Bajoran women."

Odo surveyed him expressionlessly for a moment, then replied coolly, "I wouldn't know, Doctor. I don't know all Bajoran women." His tone grew sarcastic. "If you mean, however, are they all female like Major Kira, I suppose I would have to answer affirmatively."

"I didn't mean . . ." Bashir straightened, suddenly awkward as he realized he had unintentionally offended yet another person within the space of five minutes. "I didn't mean to generalize hastily. I just . . . well, she seemed so *hostile.*"

"Major Kira is hostile only when she's given cause."

He flushed. "I didn't give her cause. I didn't say anything that should have made her angry—"

"Doctor," Odo interrupted sharply. When Bashir broke off to stare angrily at him, the constable's tone softened. "The major has good reason to indulge in a bit of free-floating hostility. She grew up in the camps. I doubt that someone from your pampered, Academy-educated background can understand that." Bashir started to protest, but Odo waved his hand for silence. "Kira saw her family and her planet destroyed by the Cardassians. She doesn't trust or like people unless she's given good reason."

"But I didn't give her any reason to be angry," Bashir said. He had met a Bajoran at the Academy, a young woman who was soft-spoken and entirely pleasant, but Odo and Kira were making him wonder if bluntness and sarcasm were the norm for the culture. "All I did was refer to Bajor as the frontier, and she took it the wrong way."

Odo tilted his oddly angled face and said, "Hm. I

suppose Kira never learned to appreciate condescension. Neither did I. We both got enough of it from the Cardassians."

Bashir felt warmth rush to his cheeks again. "Look . . . I'm sorry. I didn't mean to sound condescending. I have a bad habit of putting my foot in my mouth. I was just trying to say that I was glad and excited to be assigned to Bajor. I look forward to contributing in some small way to its reconstruction. That's all."

"I'll be sure to explain that to her when I see her," Odo said dryly, but he sounded faintly mollified.

He moved as if to leave, but Bashir stepped into his way again and said, "Constable, I hope it wouldn't seem . . . condescending to ask a few questions about you—from a strictly medical standpoint."

Odo stared silently at him; Bashir wished he knew how to interpret the constable's odd features. For all he knew, Odo could have been overwhelmed with either joy or rage at the idea.

He continued awkwardly. "You say you grew up on Bajor. But . . . you're not Bajoran."

Odo stiffened slightly. "How very clinically observant of you, Doctor."

Bashir had never been good at detecting irony; he had no clue as to whether he was encountering it now. He decided to take Odo's comment at face value and forge ahead. "Would you mind if I asked—"

Odo interrupted him with a long-suffering sigh. "I am a shapeshifter, Doctor, and as you can see,

I'm not particularly good at replicating humanoid bodies. As a matter of fact, I find it quite taxing to maintain this shape, but I am forced to do so because most humanoids are less than willing to accept my true form."

"Which is . . .?" Bashir asked, half grinning with scientific delight.

"An amorphous gelatinous semisolid. I must return to that form at least once every twenty-four hours."

"Amazing! My specialty is multi-species medicine, and yet I've never heard of a species like yours."

"Neither have I," Odo said softly, a comment that Bashir did not understand but glossed over in his excitement.

"Tell me, Constable, where are you from?"

"I haven't the faintest idea."

Now Bashir was certain that the constable was putting him on. "No, seriously . . ."

"I *am* being serious, Doctor. I was found as an infant on an abandoned spacecraft. I have no knowledge of my origins."

"This is wonderful," Bashir said excitedly. "I'd love to do a paper on you! Even if that's not possible, I'd appreciate any data you have from your physicians so that I would know how to treat you in case of an emergency."

"I have no data." Odo's tone hardened. "And I have no need of a doctor. I've managed to survive this long without one. Even if I *were* hurt, I doubt a humanoid doctor could do anything for me."

"You'd be surprised." Bashir's confidence remained unshaken. "Maybe the Bajoran doctors didn't know what to do for you, but I've had the latest training. You'd be surprised at the advances in technology—"

"Face it, Doctor," Odo interrupted, with a venom that made Bashir fall silent. "I don't need you. In fact, I have no use whatsoever for you *or* your technological advances."

Bashir stepped aside this time and let him go, but he stood watching after him for a long, long time.

CHAPTER 6

IN THE LABORATORY, Sisko showed Dax the infinity-shaped orb, freed from its ark and suspended now behind a forcefield.

She drew in a breath and glanced up at him, then back at the orb, her face illuminated by childlike awe and reflected greenish light. "Benjamin, it's *beautiful!*"

"Yes," Sisko said in a low voice. "And its effects are even more amazing."

Dax turned to him, suddenly transformed into the scientist Sisko remembered. "Have you had a chance to test its properties?"

He shifted uneasily, unable to bring himself to speak so soon of Jennifer and Gilgo Beach to this person who—in outward appearance, at least—was a stranger.

"I've been waiting for my science officer," he said evasively. "Your field, not mine. We do have one advantage. The Bajoran monks have been studying these things for a thousand years. I've had our computers set up to interface with their historical data banks."

She nodded approvingly before turning back to admire the orb. "Good. That should give us something."

"Soon as possible, Dax." Sisko paused. "The Cardassians stole whatever they could from the monasteries; according to Opaka, eight other orbs are missing. They're undoubtedly in some Cardassian laboratory, being turned upside down and inside out."

"Cardassians." Dax sighed. "I don't understand their mentality—to willfully desecrate another culture's religious items . . ." She gave Sisko an acknowledging nod.

He rose and headed for the exit, slightly ashamed of feeling grateful for an excuse to get away from his old friend.

Dax's presence brought home the loss of old Curzon. Occasionally she would make a remark or use a vocal inflection or an expression that he had associated with the old man, and that he realized now was the symbiont.

"Benjamin . . ."

He paused in the doorway, turned to gaze questioningly at her.

"I was happy when I heard you'd accepted this assignment," Dax said, her expression one of concern. "I'd been worried about you."

The words tugged at his emotions. Curzon had been worried about Sisko's stalled career, had nagged him constantly about getting himself transferred off Planitia. Sisko smiled sadly.

"A part of him, all his memories, will always be with me," Dax had said.

And with me, too, Sisko thought. To Dax he said quietly, "It's good to see you too, old man." Then he left before she could see the grief gathering in his eyes.

Dax watched him go. She had not been completely honest with Benjamin: she was still worried about him, despite the fact that he had at last taken a step to further his career. But that move had been forced upon him, and she sensed his heart was not in it; there was a reluctance in his every word, every gesture, that was hidden to all except those who knew him well. His wife's death had taken everything out of Benjamin—his drive, his ambition, his humor.

Dax understood his sense of loss: the centuries-old symbiont within her had experienced the death of many hosts. It had been only partly true that Curzon was in a sense immortal; his joined memories were accessible to Dax via the symbiont, since host and symbiont were truly one unit, inseparable. But in another sense, losing Curzon had been no less painful than feeling a part of oneself die in the agony of separation—a pain and a grief deeper than any member of an unjoined race could imagine.

Few species were as long-lived as the Trill; Dax had lost countless friends over her lifetime, and she knew that—barring an accident that might end her life prematurely—she would someday lose Benjamin Sisko too.

Because of the uniquely intimate experience of loss, and the perspective gained from centuries of life, Dax's race had come to accept death. She wished she could share that tolerance with Benjamin, help him to grieve and move on, but words were a poor substitute for experience. Benjamin would have to find his own way.

Besides, there was a new awkwardness between them now, because of the young female host; it would take time to reassure Benjamin that their relationship had not changed. True, this new host found males sexually attractive—a fact that the symbiont, who had only the most dispassionate interest in the procreation of the host species—found infinitely amusing. This new female found Sisko attractive, but Dax was used to adapting to new hosts; she could restrain this one successfully.

She smiled, remembering how nervous Benjamin had been when he first learned that Curzon was a Trill. It had taken a great deal of gentle explanation to convince Sisko that the symbiont was not a parasite, that the Trill race had evolved truly symbiotically, with each partner providing the other with benefits impossible to explain to an unjoined species. Benjamin had accepted that, finally, and Dax had faith he would quickly become accustomed to this new host, too.

She rose and moved over to a nearby console. "Computer: create a chronological data base for all historical references to the orbs, plus"—she frowned, thinking—"all reports of any unexplained phenomena in Bajoran space, including all supernatural occurrences recorded in Bajoran mythology."

"Time parameters?" the computer asked.

"Ten millennia."

"Initializing data base. Requested function will require two hours to complete."

Dax settled back in her chair and stretched, her gaze falling on the orb behind the forcefield. It truly was beautiful, much like the works of art she had seen on Garis Five, where the artists used light as a medium.

Symbiont and host shared a personality trait; both were overwhelmingly curious—hence the choice of science as a profession. Still staring at the orb, Dax rose and walked over to the field and, after a second's hesitation, pressed a control on the panel.

The forcefield disappeared. Dax stared into the green glow, squinting when the light intensified to a nearly unbearable radiance. She remained still and calm when the light spun out, enveloping her. She closed her eyes and still saw the bright green glow.

And then the light suddenly dimmed. Dax opened her eyes and saw that she was no longer standing in the space station's lab, but lying on a bed in a ceremonial medical chamber on her home planet. She looked down and saw that she wore not a Starfleet uniform but a host's robe.

Dax remembered the room—she had been here before—but to recall the past this sharply, in such detail, was startling. She turned her head and stared at the ancient white-haired man lying on the bed next to hers.

"Curzon?" she whispered.

He turned his wizened, gentle face toward her, reached feebly toward her with a frail, bony hand, and smiled.

For Dax, the memory was there: dying, struggling to breathe. Feeling regret, grief. Gladness that a part of oneself would continue. Hope for what was to come.

Dax smiled back at him, experiencing the memory from a double perspective—that of the young woman lying on the table, and that of the symbiont within the dying man. Jadzia the woman felt sorrow for the old man. And for herself she felt anticipation, nervousness, curiosity without bounds, gratitude that she had been chosen as host for such a brilliant scientist as Dax.

Around them, medical and religious attendants stood, waiting patiently, respectfully, for the ceremony of transition to begin.

Curzon's abdomen moved, bulged. Dax saw it through Jadzia's eyes, felt it from Curzon's perspective: a stirring, a withdrawal. Separation. Loss . . . unbearable loss, a part of one's mind suddenly gone, irretrievable. Pain. The struggle to accept . . .

Jadzia watched as a medical attendant drew the dripping symbiont—shapeless, wormlike—from the orifice in Curzon's abdomen and lifted it into the air. A second set of hands appeared, wielded ritual gold scissors, clipped the connection to Curzon.

Emptiness. Fading . . .

And then the attendant gently placed the symbiont on Jadzia's abdomen. She watched with sheer wonder as it found the orifice, gently burrowed its way inside, then . . .

Enlightenment. Joy. Excitement at the *knowledge,* the sheer centuries of *knowledge . . .*

The ceremonial chamber room began to glow, filled with green light until Dax was forced to close her eyes.

She opened them and was back in the lab, staring at the orb behind the forcefield.

In the commander's office, Ben Sisko surreptitiously watched a recorded transmission from Vasteras University. Beyond his console screen, Kira stood at the situation table, O'Brien at the engineering station.

Sisko had halfheartedly applied for a professorship at the university less than a week ago, before he had arrived at the station, and he was astounded by the swift reply; he assumed that indicated a rejection. Now he watched the screen with nothing less than amazement: the chancellor himself delivered the news: "It's not every day we have the chance to recruit someone with your experience, Ben. We hope you'll consider our offer seriously. I look forward to your response."

The recording ended. That was that; at long last, he had an opportunity to take Jake away from this terrible place and back to Earth. Home.

Sisko stared dully at the screen; he should have been delighted, not oddly disappointed. Instead he found himself thinking of Opaka and the infinity orb. It seemed somehow inappropriate to leave before he had helped solve the mystery of the orb, but he would have to make a decision quickly. The semester would be starting soon; the chancellor had to have his reply in a matter of days.

He started as his communicator signaled.

"Kira to Commander Sisko. A Cardassian warship has just entered Bajoran space."

"On screen." Sisko rose, stepped out onto his balcony, and looked down on his command. On the viewscreen, a huge Cardassian warship, dark and grim, glided toward the station.

"Message coming in from their commander, Gul Dukat," O'Brien reported.

Kira's eyes narrowed with recognition. "Dukat," she said in a voice filled with frank loathing. "He used to be the Cardassian prefect of Bajor."

"He's requesting permission to come aboard . . . to greet us." O'Brien's tone grew sarcastic. "It's surely a coincidence that the *Enterprise* has just left." He looked at his commander, awaiting orders.

Sisko glanced at his two officers. He had never met a Cardassian, but judging by the looks on Kira's and O'Brien's faces, he hadn't missed much. He sighed. "Mr. O'Brien, tell Gul Dukat I look forward to meeting him."

Jake wandered along the Promenade, occasionally glancing over his shoulder as if he expected to see his father behind him. He was more than a little nervous; he thought he had enough Federation credits in his account to buy passage from Bajor to Earth, or at least pretty close to Earth, and he'd figure out the rest of it when it happened. He just hoped there were shuttles leaving Bajor heading in the right direction.

He decided not to worry about running into his father; Dad was already too busy in Ops to pay much attention to him, and Jake could always lie and say he'd finished his lessons in record time this morning. Dad would never know, and there was no sign on Jake's forehead that said he'd sneaked out early before finishing his schoolwork.

Even so, he kept glancing guiltily behind him, expecting at any minute to see his father, arms crossed, a scowl on his face.

He didn't care. He just didn't care. Dad was unhappy, and that made Jake unhappy. He hated this broken-down place, and he could tell Dad did too. It would never seem like a home, the way Planitia did.

Sure, things weren't as bad as they had been:

Ensign O'Brien had finally fixed the temperature controls, and it looked like maybe they would get some working food replicators soon. But at Planitia at least there'd been real beds and real replicators and other kids his own age. Here there was a two-year-old girl and a teenage Ferengi that Dad said was bad news.

Bad news or not, the young Ferengi was the object of Jake's search now. The race both repelled and intrigued him. Repelled, because they were ugly, no two ways about it—ugly by human standards, Jake corrected himself; his dad was always reminding him that such judgments were never valid and changed depending on who was doing the judging. Jake guessed the Ferengi probably thought they looked okay, but he had no idea how they decided which individuals among them were the good-looking ones.

And he was intrigued by the Ferengi's absolute lack of morals.

Human morals, Dad had once corrected him. *We mustn't judge them by our standards, Jake. Their society evolved differently and developed different values. To them, stealing and cheating aren't bad—unless they're stupid enough to get caught. To them, cheating is a test of cunning, of skill, of bravery; and they feel no sympathy for the victims, who should have been intelligent enough to protect themselves, or at the very least, smart enough to figure out a way to get even.*

But Dad, Jake had protested, *that's* awful!

Dad had just grinned. *Then avoid any business dealings with them, son.*

And then Jake had asked about the rumor one of the kids at Planitia had told him, that the Ferengi had sharp teeth because they were cannibals, and Dad had thrown back his head and laughed.

But the more Jake thought about it, the less awful he thought the Ferengi attitude was. In fact, he decided it must be pretty exciting to be a Ferengi, and he resolved to try to make friends with one. And perhaps, if the opportunity for adventure presented itself . . .

He bet the Ferengi knew how to get off this crummy old station and onto the planet surface. Jake had made up his mind to get to Earth, no matter what.

The Promenade was almost crowded compared to the first time Jake had seen it; Quark's casino was open now, noisy and full of space traders and Bajora and aliens Jake had never seen before and could not name. Some of the shops had reopened, too, and many of those that were still closed had people inside, cleaning.

Jake walked close to the casino and peered inside. A couple of Ferengi eyed him curiously, but they looked to be adults, though Jake couldn't be sure, since they were almost as short as he was. One growled at him, "No children inside!"

Crestfallen, Jake turned and walked toward a cluster of food kiosks, drawn by the strange yet appealing aromas. The food here certainly smelled better than anything that came out of the replicators.

And there, buying some weird-looking glop-on-a-stick, was the object of Jake's search, the young Ferengi. Jake sidled up to him, trying not to stare, but Ferengis looked so *weird,* with their big bald square heads and huge elephant ears, and besides, Jake was impressed by the fact that this young creature was dangerous enough to have spent time in the station's brig. Jake gaped for a moment, unobserved, then summoned his voice and shyly said, "Hi."

The Ferengi turned, wrinkled his brow ridge at him, and snarled, in a nasal, unpleasant voice, "What do you want, hew-man?"

He was an intimidating sight, with his dirty, sharp-nailed hands and his huge skull and his pointed teeth. Maybe they're not cannibals, Jake thought wildly. Maybe they just eat humans.

The Ferengi studied Jake with tiny glittering eyes, then walked away contemptuously.

The boy followed, awkward and eager. "My name is Jake."

The Ferengi took a savage bite of his glop, swallowed after one chew, and said, with his mouth full, "I know who you are."

Jake felt a pang of disappointment. The Ferengi knew that he was the son of the Starfleet commander who had thrown him in jail. Even so, he persisted cheerfully. "What's yours?"

The Ferengi stopped, turned to Jake, and issued a

faint hissing sound, like an angry cat, that made the boy recoil slightly. "Why do you care?"

Jake felt himself flush, but he did not back down. "Not exactly a lot of friends to choose from here, you know what I mean?"

The Ferengi blinked; the contempt drained from his wrinkled features. He contemplated the human in silence for a good thirty seconds, and Jake fancied he saw a glimmer of understanding, of loneliness, there.

"Nog," the Ferengi said softly. "My name is Nog."

Jake smiled. Nog almost smiled, too, but the sound of the airlock made them both turn.

A dozen humanoids in dark uniforms stepped from the opening onto the Promenade. To Jake's human sensibilities, their faces were ugly, frightening. Thick cordlike ridges ran down their foreheads, circled beneath their dark eyes, and extended down their thick, bulky necks. There was something intimidating, sinister, about their posture and their expressions; something about the style of the severe black uniforms and the color of their dull, mottled skin reminded him very much of the space station itself.

They looked as if they *belonged* here; they blended into the very architecture and coloration of Deep Space Nine.

Cardassians, Jake realized, as the leader moved with the ease of familiarity toward a turbolift. The others headed toward Quark's.

Jake turned toward his newfound companion and saw that Nog's expression had grown stony with hate.

Gul Dukat entered Sisko's office without knocking. That was the first strike against him.

"Good day, Commander," Dukat said, with the unctuous, faintly hostile cordiality of a classic bully.

By Cardassian standards he was a middle-aged, medium-height, altogether bland, pleasant-looking male who did not appear capable of the cruelty he and others of his race had inflicted on the Bajora. To Sisko's human eyes Dukat's appearance was anything but pleasant, with all that ridged, mottled flesh disappearing inside a black uniform that looked armor-brittle, like the hard outer shell of an insect.

A dark, colorless insect. Against his will, Sisko was reminded of the Borg.

(Jennifer's lifeless hand)

He forced himself to shake off the memory at once. Dukat studied the office and the man behind his former desk as if he still owned the place and could not quite figure out what this interloper was doing here.

Sisko rose, nodded, but did not smile. "Gul Dukat."

He was trying very hard not to hate the Cardassian based on the destruction he had witnessed and the reports of atrocities he had heard, but for an instant he did not see Dukat at all; he saw

Opaka, bruised and leaning on her cane amid the ruins of the destroyed temple.

Remember, he told himself. *They are no longer the enemy. The Federation signed a treaty with them. As a representative of Starfleet, I am obliged to treat them with respect.*

"Excuse my presumption." Dukat smiled, showing a narrow strip of teeth. "But this was *my* office only two weeks ago." He sat down without waiting for an invitation. "So . . . have you been able to get the food replicators to work properly?"

"No."

"Neither could we," the Cardassian said merrily. "That's one technology you have over us. You know how to make a perfect onion soup." He stood suddenly, as if trying to startle Sisko, to get a reaction.

Mind games. Strike two.

"I'm not used to being on this side of the desk," Dukat explained. He walked over to the balcony and stared down at Ops with all of the imperiousness of a feudal lord surveying his domain. "I'll be honest with you, Commander. I miss this office. I wasn't happy about leaving it."

"Drop by any time you're feeling homesick."

Dukat wheeled around at the irony in Sisko's tone, acknowledged it with a humorless smile. "You are very gracious. And allow me to assure you that we only want to be helpful in this difficult transition. You are far from the Federation fleet, alone in this remote outpost, with poor defense systems. Your Cardassian neighbors will be quick to respond to any problems you might have."

A thinly veiled threat—strike three.

Sisko now officially admitted his hatred of Gul Dukat to himself, but kept his face and voice carefully neutral. With the *Enterprise* gone, the Cardassians could easily cause heavy damage to the station and leave the area long before Federation help could arrive. Dukat would not have bothered with the threat unless he wanted something from Sisko: But what? "We'll try to keep the dog off your lawn."

The Cardassian tilted his head quizzically, seemed to finally make sense of Sisko's words, and stared at him for a few seconds, measuring him.

"So what did you think of Kai Opaka?"

Dukat's abrupt change of subject caught Sisko off guard, but he kept his equilibrium; he looked evenly back at the Cardassian. So, he thought, now we know what you want, Dukat. And I'll be damned if you're going to get it.

"Oh, I stay informed," Dukat continued. "I know you went to the surface to see her. I understand you brought back one of the orbs. We thought we had them all. Perhaps we could have an exchange of information, pool our resources."

"I don't know anything about an orb."

Dukat smiled in disbelief, gave a little nod as if to say, All right, if you insist on playing the game this way . . . "We will be in close proximity should you wish to reconsider my suggestion. In the meantime,

I assume you have no objection to my men enjoying the hospitality of the Promenade." He bowed stiffly. "Commander . . ."

When the Cardassian was gone, Sisko sank into his chair with a sigh. Some instinct had said that Dukat must not get the orb, no matter what the cost of protecting it—but in his rational mind Sisko knew that that cost might be the lives of those on the station. Dukat had indicated that he was willing to wait . . . but only for a time.

Sisko drew a hand across his eyes. Was he letting Opaka's mysticism lead him into making a deadly mistake?

He rose and headed for the lab.

As Sisko entered the lab, Dax sat frowning at a monitor, thoroughly engrossed. Strange, to see his old friend suddenly metamorphosed into such a beautiful young woman; he doubted he would ever get used to the change. Even so, he was glad to have her here; at the moment he needed Dax's sage advice.

Sisko drew a breath and opened his mouth to speak, thinking she had not heard him enter, but she interrupted him without taking her gaze off the screen: "Benjamin, what do you know about the Denorios Asteroid Belt?"

Sisko stopped in his tracks and blinked. "Your basic charged plasma field. Nobody gets anywhere near it unless they have to."

Dax nodded, her eyes scanning the screen as she summarized for him: "In the latter part of the twenty-second century, a ship carrying Kai Taluno was disabled for several days in the Denorios Belt, where he claims to have had a vision."

Sisko walked up behind her to put a hand on the back of her chair—had it been Curzon, he would have clasped the old man's shoulder, but he felt shy around this beautiful young woman—and stared over her shoulder at the data scrolling by on the monitor. "Let me guess—he saw the Celestial Temple of the prophets."

Dax's lips curved upward slightly. "Not quite, but he did say the heavens opened up and nearly swallowed his ship."

He sighed; his mystical encounter with Opaka and the orb seemed meaningless, distant, in the face of the Gul Dukat's very real threat. "Are we reduced to chasing metaphors to solve this?"

She swiveled in the chair and rose, smiling at him. "Cynicism is not one of your attractive qualities, Benjamin." The timbre of her voice had changed, grown reedier, *older.* Sisko blinked, surprised at how very like Curzon she suddenly sounded.

Or was that the voice of the symbiont?

"As a matter of fact," Dax continued, with the authority of age and experience, "Kai Taluno was *not* a man prone to exaggeration."

Sisko raised a brow, repressed a smile. "I suppose you knew him."

"Just an acquaintance. I was a diplomatic apprentice at the time. We met at a peace conference. He was a rather dour, dogmatic man, actually—"

He interrupted. "You really think his 'vision' has anything to do with this?"

"Perhaps." Dax's voice became that of a young woman again; she sat back down at the console and keyed up more data. Figures began scrolling on the screen. "I've been able to confirm that at least five of the orbs were found in the Denorios Belt."

Sisko sat down beside her and squinted at the monitor as she worked the controls.

"There have also been twenty-three navigational reports over the years of unusually severe neutrino disturbances in that area." She pressed another panel, and more data wavered on the screen; she interpreted for Sisko faster than he could read it. "And thirty-two years ago a vessel of unknown origin appeared there, carrying a new life-form, an infant shapeshifter."

Sisko turned his head sharply to look at her. "A shapeshifter? There's a shapeshifter right here on DS Nine—the Bajoran security officer."

Dax took in this information thoughtfully. "I've been trying to correlate all these reports in one analysis grid."

She pressed another control. Sisko leaned forward to study the three-dimensional grid that appeared on the screen, brightly delineating a small area of space near the station.

"Our Celestial Temple?" Dax asked lightly.

Sisko shrugged. "It's worth a look." He stood up, rubbing his chin thoughtfully. "I just spoke with Gul Dukat; he made it very clear he's keeping an eye on us. So we've got Cardassians on our back doorstep. Somehow we need to get past them undetected."

Dax smiled up at him. "What were you just saying about that Bajoran security officer?"

O'Brien simply did not trust Major Kira.

Not that he disliked her personally, mind you—he was an easygoing sort who had difficulty disliking anyone—but her attitude toward authority in general and toward Starfleet in particular was often openly contemptuous, a fact that made him distinctly nervous about being her subordinate. He kept half expecting her to abuse her power.

Not an ideal situation for a newly commissioned ensign, to serve under such an ill-tempered, belligerent officer. Things were grim enough already, with Keiko trying to pretend she wasn't bored and discouraged in the strange new surroundings. Captain Picard—now *there* was an officer O'Brien trusted, was willing to risk his life for. But not Major Kira; he seriously doubted that she would appreciate such a gesture, and so it was that he set out with her and some others for Quark's with more than a few misgivings. What if somebody sneezed or hiccuped at the wrong time when they arrived at the casino and were all surrounded by Cardassians? Knowing the major, she would fire first and try diplomacy later.

Moments ago in Sisko's office, however, Kira had surprised him.

She had listened to Sisko's orders without question, then led O'Brien and a small contingent to Quark's with the cool competence of a born commander. O'Brien finally began to understand: this was something she *wanted* to do because it might help her people.

That was just as well, because when they arrived at the casino, the place was packed with dark-uniformed Cardies. The sight of them sent O'Brien spinning back into the past. He blinked, squeezing his eyelids tightly shut, trying to blot out the sudden graphic vision of the massacre he'd witnessed on Setlik Three. Trying to blot out the look on Stompie's face as he had died, and the look on Captain Maxwell's face as he stood over his dead family . . .

A roar came from one of the gaming tables, followed by raucous laughter; the Cardassians were winning. O'Brien opened his eyes and, for a fleeting instant, caught Major Kira's gaze, saw the hatred buried there beneath layers of cold determination. He hated them, too . . . when he allowed himself to forget that he had killed one, when he allowed himself to remember that they were people caught up in a culture that forbade compassion. He remembered his words to the Cardassian, Daro: *It's not you I hate, Cardassian. It's what I became because of you.*

Kira strode into the center of the crowd, snatched a mug away from one too inebriated to protest, and banged it on the bar.

"Can we have your attention, please?" Her strident tone silenced the jubilation to a hush. "This establishment is being closed."

A rumble of disapproval from the crowd; O'Brien tensed, reached for the phaser that was not there, once again cursed Odo's arbitrary rule banning phasers on the Promenade, and cursed Kira for backing him up.

"What do you mean?" A small bundle of fury, Quark pushed his way toward her, swiped at the air in front of her with a clawed hand. "You can't do this!"

Kira stared implacably down at him. O'Brien stepped forward at his cue, delivered his line smoothly, with just the right intonation, and wondered if perhaps he had missed his true calling. "If you have a problem, sir, you'll have to take it up with Commander Sisko."

Quark wheeled on him, trembling with rage. "I intend to. This is outrageous!" He softened his tone and addressed the crowd. "My apologies, friends. A minor misunderstanding that will be rectified shortly." He turned to his pit boss. "Give them something to put their winnings in."

The boss nodded, a little too knowingly, O'Brien thought, but the Cardies seemed to be buying it. They began scooping up their winnings and stuffing gold into the sack—quite a lot of gold. One of them hoisted the sack with difficulty; it was, O'Brien reflected, bound to be very heavy.

He glanced over at Kira to find her sharing a look

with Quark; O'Brien kept his expression grim, as the scenario demanded, but inwardly he smiled with relief.

Major Kira had her ways, but she could be counted on in a pinch. This just might work out. . . .

Odo fought panic. The weight of the gold pressed down on him, making breathing difficult—a purely mental symptom he had encountered before, one he knew how to deal with. He relaxed into a near-mindless state by focusing intensely on the sounds: the ring of three pairs of boots against a metal deck, the drone of self-satisfied drunken voices speaking Cardassian, a language he knew, unfortunately, too well. The sound was dampered by more metal—walls: they were inside the Cardassian ship now.

The panic eased; Odo tuned in completely, listening for the proper moment to make his transition.

". . . because we were winning too much, of course."

Laughter.

"Leave it to Starfleet to ruin a fine day," said another.

Footsteps stopped; the sound of a small door swinging on a hinge—a locker. Muffled footsteps again, filtered through metal; they had put the knapsack inside and were now walking away.

Odo waited for the footsteps to fade entirely,

then made the change, oozing out from underneath the gold, between the cracks of the locker, then down the bulkhead to the deck.

He drew a deep, unimpeded breath, then hurried down the corridor to his destination.

CHAPTER 7

AT HIS ENGINEERING control station in Ops, O'Brien studied the readout with a sense of victory and lifted his face toward Major Kira with something very close to a smile. For the first time since leaving the *Enterprise,* he felt a thrill of excitement tinged with honest camaraderie. "Major, scanners are picking up fluctuations in the Cardassians' energy distribution net."

Kira checked her panels and reacted with frank delight. "Their computer is crashing. Their shields and sensors are down. Odo's done it." She touched the comm control. "Ops to *Rio Grande* . . ."

"Go ahead," Sisko said. He and Dax had taken the turbolift to the landing pad on the station's inner ring, and now sat in the runabout's cockpit. The *Rio Grande* was a small vessel, sturdy, scarcely larger than the *Saratoga*'s escape pod—but he refused to let himself think about that.

Sisko felt a strange mixture of excitement and regret, felt as if he were teetering on the brink of a great precipice: on one side lay security, his responsibility to Jake, complete with the long-awaited planetside assignment; on the other lay the unknown, adventure, meaning, the hope that he could help Opaka and her people.

And the next few hours would determine which way he fell.

Kira's voice filtered through the comm grid on the runabout's control panel: "We're in business."

"Beginning launch sequence," Sisko said evenly, ignoring the fact that his heart had begun to beat faster, trying hard to ignore the sudden memory of Jennifer lying on a blanket, her skin glistening in the sun on Gilgo Beach.

Beside him, in the periphery of his vision, Dax worked the navigation panel with calm efficiency. As long as Sisko did not focus on her, he found it easy to imagine Curzon's bent, aged frame in the chair beside his. He allowed himself the mental image and drew reassurance from it.

O'Brien's voice now: "Cleared for departure."

Kira's followed. "Maintain visual blackout. Set audio to secure channel three-five-zero."

"Acknowledged," Sisko said.

Dax swiveled toward him, once again a beautiful young woman. "Course laid in," she said.

Sisko drew a breath as the runabout rose and sailed away from the station, into his future.

Back at the station, Kira looked down at the flashing signal on her master control panel and called over to O'Brien. "Odo's reached the transport site."

"Trying to lock on," O'Brien said, with more than a tinge of frustration. If Odo didn't make his exit without being detected, the entire operation would be in jeopardy. But the damnable Cardie technology refused to cooperate. O'Brien pressed the control that should have activated the transporter immediately—at least it would have on the *Enterprise.*

Nothing happened.

"I've never done this with a Cardassian transporter," he said, by way of explanation and apology. The major said nothing, merely scowled at him. O'Brien looked back down at his station with renewed aggravation and cursed the Cardie race silently but resoundingly—not for their atrocities but for their slipshod technology; he hated not being able to do his job properly. Swiftly he pressed another control to initiate an emergency backup sequence.

Nothing.

He put the damned thing on manual and tried to program the sequence in himself.

Nothing.

"Dammit!" O'Brien gave the panel a swift, solid kick. "What's the prob—"

The beam activated; the pad began to shimmer. O'Brien looked down at his foot, then at the panel, marveling at the connection. By the time he looked back up at the pad, Odo had fully materialized.

Major Kira grinned at the shapeshifter. "Nice work, Constable."

The runabout glided at impulse into the Denorios Belt. Sisko glanced up at viewscreen, taking in the sight of stars, glittering behind swirls of blue dust, only long enough to register its beauty before checking his readouts.

"Approaching grid perimeter," Dax said, and hidden in her soft voice, Sisko heard an anticipation that matched his own. On her monitor, a grid of Denorios blinked at them, showing their location on the perimeter.

"Slowing to one-quarter impulse."

Dax leaned forward to check a sensor reading and drew back in surprise. "Computer: give me visual at bearing two-three, mark two-one-seven, range thirty-one hundred kilometers."

The display wavered and changed to the requested sector. Nothing unusual; more space dust, a few errant asteroids. Sisko gazed at it, then turned, his expression questioning, to Dax.

She frowned slightly at the data on the monitor. "Sensors are picking up unusually high proton counts."

"Setting a new course to those coordinates," Sisko said, doing so without pausing to think; the runabout veered, heading for the center of the disturbance.

O'Brien's voice crackled over the comm. "Lieutenant, in that asteroid belt, you could be looking at chrondrite echoes."

Dax's frown grew deeper as she worked her panel with both hands, checking multiple readouts. "I don't think so. The neutrino disturbances are getting stronger as we approach the coordinates."

Sisko checked his own readouts. "Whatever it is, it's not affecting our systems."

Dax's eyes widened with scientific awe. "All external wave intensities are increasing exponentially, but . . . Checking . . . Confirmed. There is no corresponding increase inside the cabin." She turned to Sisko, not quite smiling in amazement. "How is that poss—"

The runabout lurched; Sisko threw up his hand to shield his eyes from the dazzling burst of light.

(Saratoga *exploding*)

Sisko blinked, clearing away the afterimage, and found his control panel. The readout screens were dark. He glanced over at Dax, who was fidgeting with the comm controls. "Sensors aren't functioning."

He was going to ask her what had happened, but it was clear enough from her expression that she knew no more than he; yet instead of showing signs of panic, she seemed to consciously relax, to grow more detached. Sisko wondered whether she was relying on the ancient symbiont for calm. He got his answer when she spoke again in the voice that reminded him of old Curzon: "We've lost all contact with the station."

At Ops, O'Brien studied his readouts and did his best not to react to the fact that the vessel bearing his new captain had just disappeared. It seemed as if space had simply opened up, developed a rip, and the *Rio Grande* had sailed right into it and been swallowed alive.

Major Kira stared up at the viewscreen, lips parted, aghast.

"Scanners are reading a major subspace disruption at their last known coordinates," O'Brien said bleakly.

Kira crossed to his station, bent over his shoulder, and looked at the monitor as if she just might throttle it. "What the hell is happening out there?"

"I don't know, sir." O'Brien drew in a breath, raised his head, and met her gaze head on. "They're just . . . gone."

In the trembling runabout, Sisko stared down at the dark, useless sensor screens and vainly tried to reactivate the controls. Beside him Dax moved her hands steadily, surely over the navigation panel. The viewscreen revealed no stars, only a flickering rainbow light show that would have been beautiful if Sisko had been of a mind to appreciate it.

"Are your navigational readings going crazy?" he called to Dax over the sounds of the ship shuddering.

Dax gave him a reassuring look and a slow,

deliberate nod. "I'll recalibrate them when I have a moment."

"Take your time," Sisko said, with more than a hint of sarcasm.

The runabout lurched again. Sisko gritted his teeth and clutched his panel, managing to stay in his seat. Slowly, easily, the craft righted herself. Screens flickered. The main viewer dimmed, then brightened . . . this time with stars.

Sisko released a sigh of relief at the sight, but the configuration was wrong: this was not the Denorios Belt. He swiveled toward Dax, who had recovered and was already checking her readouts.

"Can you get a fix on our coordinates?"

Dax stared at her now-bright screen, nodding. "There's a star just under five light-years away. No class-M planets. Computer: identify closest star system.

A pause. Sisko and Dax brightened when the computer responded as ordered: "Idran, a ternary system consisting of a central supergiant and twin type-O companions."

Sisko's lower jaw dropped. *"Idran?* That can't be right."

Dax was composed, but he caught the gleam of scientific revelation in her eye. "Computer: basis of identification."

"Identification of Idran is based on the hydrogen-alpha spectral analysis conducted in the twenty-second century by the Quadros One probe of the Gamma Quadrant."

"The Gamma Quadrant," Sisko whispered, stunned. "Seventy *thousand* light-years from Bajor. I'd say we just found our way into a wormhole."

Her expression was one of dawning wonder as she checked her readouts. "It's not like any wormhole I've ever seen. There were none of the usual resonance waves."

They stared at the stars for a few seconds, contemplating this until Sisko asked, "You think this is how the orbs found their way into the Bajoran system?"

Dax cocked her head, considering this. "Not an unreasonable hypothesis."

"If it's true, that would mean this has been here for ten thousand years. We might have discovered the first *stable* wormhole known to exist."

She finally smiled. "You may want to wait until we get safely back before you put your name in the history books, Benjamin."

"*Our* names, old man, our names." He couldn't repress a laugh; the thought of returning to Opaka with such good news made him feel giddy with accomplishment. A wormhole would save Bajor's economy, make it a thriving trade center, open up all sorts of possibilities for cultural advances. Celestial Temple of the Prophets or not, he would not go back empty-handed. "Bring us about, Lieutenant."

Yet as Dax brought the vessel around and they ventured back into the wormhole—this time with Sisko relaxed enough to appreciate the beauty of the flashing prismatic colors around them—he felt a renewed pang of regret at the thought of leaving the station.

"This is even better than finding the Celestial Temple," he mused.

Dax turned to him with a smile. "Better?"

"Think about it. A stable wormhole to the Gamma Quadrant in Bajoran space is going to solve a lot more of their problems than the Kai ever could. Expeditions from countless worlds will be coming through here now. They'll give Bajor an economic base, a way to rebuild." He turned and gazed up at the brilliantly colored lights on the viewscreen. "A perfect capstone."

Dax frowned suddenly. "What are you talking about, Benjamin?"

He tried to keep his tone and manner casual, but his cheerfulness sounded forced, even to his own ears. "I'll probably be leaving soon. Going back to Earth."

Dax digested this somberly; she did not seem as surprised as he had expected. "To do what?"

"The University at Vasteras thinks I might have something to offer its astrionics program."

She wrinkled her brow in affectionate disbelief. "A professor?"

"I'll have a beard," Sisko tried to make a joke, but it didn't come out funny. "And wear a baggy corduroy jacket with elbow patches."

"And grow old before your time." As the ship began to shudder, Dax turned sadly away from him and worked her controls. The runabout's vibrations eased. Her tone grew detached, professional. "I'm modifying the flight program to compensate for the spatial discontinuities. We should have a smoother ride this time."

Sisko frowned, sitting perfectly still, trying to tune in to his pilot's instinct. "Did you reduce impulse power?"

"No." She checked her panels.

"We're losing velocity," Sisko said, even before a glance at the readout confirmed it.

Dax shook her head at her screen. "Power output is still constant."

"Computer," he ordered, "conduct a level two diagnostic of impulse power flow downstream of the reaction chambers."

"Impulse systems are functioning within normal parameters."

Sisko checked the control panel readout. "We're down to one-twenty kph."

"Computer," Dax said, "identify cause of deceleration."

The answer was hardly reassuring: "Cause unknown."

"Increasing impulse reactor output," Sisko said, reaching for his controls as if sheer determination could power the ship. He refused to be lost, especially now, when for the first time in three years he had accomplished something that brought hope. And he could not leave Jake alone. . . .

"Velocity is still falling," Dax reported serenely,

apparently unafraid of death, of losing all the centuries of accumulated knowledge and experience.

Sisko stared back at his screen, incredulous. "Engine output is running seventy percent *above* normal."

"Down to sixty kph," Dax intoned.

"Warning," the computer interrupted. "Impulse system overload. Auto shutdown in twelve seconds."

Jake, Sisko thought, as if he could reach the boy across the starry distance with his silent call. Jake, I'm sorry. . . .

(Fingers brushing his cheek. *Breathe,* Opaka said. Her face shimmered, melted into Jennifer's . . .)

Sisko relaxed, gave up the struggle, yielded to whatever might happen. No point in damaging the engines; he reached out to press a toggle. "Disengaging engines."

"Velocity is twenty kph." Dax stiffened beside him, her gaze fixed on a readout. She faced Sisko, her eyes wide with wonder, her tone at once childlike and very, very old. "I'm picking up an *atmosphere,* Benjamin."

He stared at her, unable to comprehend what he had just heard. "Inside a *wormhole?*"

She glanced back at her screen, lips parted in amazement. "Capable of supporting life."

She and Sisko were suddenly thrown forward in their chairs by the impact; the runabout shuddered once, briefly, then grew still.

Dax checked her instruments, then turned to Sisko. "We've landed."

"On what?" Sisko asked, and was not surprised when there was no reply. He rose

(*Welcome*)

for some curious reason remembering the dream he'd had the night before he arrived at the station, remembering also the sense of mystery. The sense of coming home.

(*Welcome*)

Together he and Dax stepped out of the tiny craft.

After the Cardassians filed past, Jake walked with Nog along a row of busy food kiosks and watched with concealed amazement as the young Ferengi devoured the grayish pink glopsicle in a total of three bites, licked the stick, belched, tossed the stick over his shoulder, and sniffed the air greedily, then laughed scornfully at a human who ran to pick up the stick and put it in a wall receptacle.

Some of the aromas coming out of the kiosks smelled wonderful to Jake; some were nauseating. Nog's glop-on-a-stick had fallen into the latter category. It smelled exactly as if someone had eaten a head of garlic and then gotten sick, but watching Nog eat it had reminded the human boy that he was hungry. He'd been depressed and disgusted by the breakfast the replicator offered that morning and hadn't eaten most of it. He followed Nog's gaze as they strolled along and wondered if the Bajoran and alien shop owners knew about doughnuts.

"Does your family live here on DS Nine?" Jake asked conversationally.

Nog blinked as if he didn't understand the question, then answered finally, "My father does. And my uncle Quark." His tone was still cool and slightly condescending, as if he did not quite trust this human interloper but would tolerate him for now.

"What about your mom?" Jake almost hesitated to ask, knowing how difficult that question was for him.

Nog stopped walking and turned to him with a sneer. "My *mother?*"

Jake nodded innocently, confused by the display of contempt at the mention of mothers.

The Ferengi began walking again, shaking his head faintly at the very idea. "Males do not live with their *mothers,* hew-man."

"Why not?" Jake asked, a bit defensively. "What's wrong with it?"

"Males do not live with *fe*males."

"Why not?"

Nog emitted a growl of disgust and did not reply.

"Your loss," Jake said coolly.

Nog faced him, tiny amber eyes glittering with disdain. "I suppose *you* live with your *mother* here on the station."

"Just my dad." Jake struggled to keep the catch from his voice, to keep his tone casual, the way he always did when well-meaning strangers asked. "My mom's dead."

The Ferengi digested this silently; Jake could not

read the alien's expression well enough to interpret his reaction. Nog turned away, and they walked without speaking for a few seconds. Finally Jake asked, "How long you been here on the station?"

Nog did not seem scandalized by this question. "Forever. Too long."

Jake sighed, pouncing eagerly on their common frustration. "I know what you mean. I've been here only a couple days, but it seems like forever. I can't wait to leave. But my dad—he's with Starfleet."

"I know who your father is," Nog said in a voice that made Jake remind himself not to cringe. "Your father put me in the brig."

"I'm sorry about that, but—" the boy began quickly.

Nog interrupted with a shrug. "The bed was more comfortable than my own, and your father's plan worked. My uncle Quark says he is almost as shrewd as a Ferengi."

Jake half smiled, uncertain whether this was a compliment; reading Nog's facial expression was almost impossible, and Jake couldn't tell from the tone of his voice whether he was really angry or not. "Yeah. Well, he's smart, but he still hasn't figured out a way to get us off this stupid station."

Nog made a noise that might have been one of empathy. "Like my father. Always promising. And we almost left, until *your* father persuaded Uncle Quark to stay."

"I'm sorry," Jake said. "I really am. I don't want to be here either, but Dad keeps telling me to make the best of it."

The Ferengi nodded. "Fathers . . . They always want too much, and are never satisfied with what they get."

Jake wasn't sure what that was supposed to mean, but he said nothing. "We want to go to Earth, where my dad is from, but right now I'd rather be anyplace but here. The replicators are awful, the quarters are awful, nothing works the way it's supposed to, and the place looks like a junkyard."

"It was not so bad until the Cardassians left," the Ferengi said, his tone suddenly soft. "They destroyed everything."

"But there's nothing to *do* here," Jake complained. "I *hate* this place. I want to go to Bajor." He brightened. "Do you know how to get down to the surface?"

Nog regarded him curiously, tilting his great angular head. "You have never been to Bajor, then? You do not know . . . ?"

"Know what?"

"The destruction is far worse on the planet surface. I have been to Bajor. There is nothing there to see."

"I don't care about that. I want . . ." He lowered his voice and glanced about guiltily. "I want to find a shuttle. I want to go to Earth, but you can't tell any—"

Nog burst into raucous laughter. "Shuttle? You mean a *passenger* shuttle? You really don't know anything about Bajor, do you, hew-man? There are no regularly scheduled passenger shuttles. You would have to charter one yourself, and you do not look so rich." He looked Jake up and down.

Jake felt a surge of frustration that brought him close to tears, followed by anger at himself for acting like such a baby. "I don't *care.* I have to find a way to leave. I hate it here. There's nothing to do."

"Oh," Nog said with a sly, toothy little grimace that Jake finally realized was a smile, "but there are many, many interesting things to do here, hew-man. Are you hungry?"

Jake nodded, stifling his emotions. Maybe if he just talked to Nog, got to know him a little better, the Ferengi would trust him and show him the way down to the planet surface.

Besides, he was growing just the littlest bit anxious at the thought of actually *going* there.

"Then come. Let me get you something to eat." Nog gestured for the human to follow him to one of the kiosks, an enclosed stand with an open counter stacked with pale green-flecked round things that looked like biscuits. Jake leaned over them and inhaled their warm, fragrant steam; they smelled pretty good, sort of sweet and savory and herbal.

His mouth began to water as he looked up at the vendor, a stooped gray-haired Bajoran man, who smiled down at him. The smile turned into a scowl at the sight of Nog.

"We don't serve Ferengi here," the Bajoran said coldly to Nog. "Go on, get away."

Nog affected an air of innocence. "It's not for me. It's for my friend here—Commander Sisko's son."

The old man narrowed his eyes at Jake. "Is he with you, boy?"

Jake nodded, perplexed by the Bajoran's hostility toward the young Ferengi—until Nog slipped a nimble hand into the pan of biscuits, withdrew two, and ran laughing into the busy crowd.

"Hey!" The shopkeeper shouted. "Ferengi thief! Come back—" He broke off quickly, realizing the futility of the command, and shook his head. "Curse the Ferengi *and* the Cardassians. I had a window here to protect the goods, until they broke it. How am I supposed to make enough money to replace the window if the Ferengi keep stealing everything I bake?" He thrust a gnarled, blue-veined hand at Jake. "I hope you intend to pay for your 'friend,' Commander Sisko's son."

Jake stared wide-eyed after the vanishing Nog, then turned back to face the shopkeeper and swallowed hard. "Uh . . . do you take credits?"

The old Bajoran thrust his hand closer for emphasis. "Gold only. No credits. This is not the Starfleet commissary, lad."

"I . . . I don't have any gold. My dad could pay if you—"

"Jhakka!" the shopkeeper interrupted, shouting at the vendor next to him as he came around the stall to grasp Jake by the elbow. "Jhakka, summon Constable Odo on the pub comm for me! I dare not leave my goods unattended in the presence of this little thief. This boy's friend stole from me, and now he will not pay."

Passersby stopped on the walkway to listen with

amused expressions. Mortified, Jake squirmed in the shopkeeper's grip until he managed to pull free with a tremendous jerk that nearly caused them both to fall. He staggered, regained his balance, and ran headlong into the crowd . . .

And smack into the soft, yielding body of a woman, throwing both of them to the floor.

Out of habit and instinct, Sisko drew his phaser and set it on stun as he stepped from the runabout, but he felt little fear, only a strange excitement. He was certain that he had been to this place before, in his dream.

Yet the desert landscape was unfamiliar, brutal, anything but welcoming. A bleak expanse of rock cliffs stretched all the way to the horizon, illuminated by flashes from electrical storms in the dark, forbidding sky. Sisko narrowed his eyes against the stinging wind.

Dax followed, tricorder in hand. To Sisko's surprise, she took in the surroundings with an appreciative smile. "It's beautiful."

He glanced out at the dead horizon and back at Dax with raised eyebrows. "You have a strange notion of beauty."

Dax studied him with puzzlement. "You don't think this is one of the most idyllic settings you've ever seen?"

He shook his head, thinking he would never quite understand the Trill's odd sense of humor. "It can't beat the sulfuric mine pits of Hadas Four."

"How can you say that?" she asked, with a

confusion Sisko finally realized was genuine. "The colors . . . all the flora . . ."

He turned to her. "I don't see any flora, Dax."

She frowned, then turned to study her surroundings. "We're standing in a garden."

Sisko shook his head. "We're standing on a rock face." He pointed toward the horizon. "Do you see the storms?"

"Clear as a summer's day." She shot him an uneasy look, then turned her head sharply.

Sisko followed her gaze. Roughly seven meters away, a ball of brilliant green light sailed toward them through the stormy sky. It was identical in appearance to the orb that now rested in DS Nine's laboratory.

So we made it to the Celestial Temple after all, Sisko thought. Aloud he said, "You see it, too."

"Yes," Dax whispered.

As they spoke, the orb stopped, hesitated a few meters from them, then emitted a single beam of green light, scanning Sisko from head to foot. He remained motionless, feeling no sensation other than a gentle warmth, while Dax in turn scanned the beam with her tricorder.

"Low-level ionic pattern. It's probing us."

"Someone's idea of shaking hands, maybe," Sisko said softly, relaxing as the beam left him and turned itself on Dax. When the probe reached her abdomen, it flickered, sputtered with a burst of rainbow colors, then returned to solid green as it continued downward. Dax watched with a faint smile.

When the scan was finished, Sisko stepped forward to speak. "I am Commander Benjamin Sisko of the United Federation of Planets."

He reeled and was thrown backwards, as if someone had lifted the ground beneath his feet and shaken it like a carpet. His perspective split in two: surrounding him was the stormy rock landscape, but when he looked at Dax, he saw the garden, deep green foliage and bright flowers, collapsing around her into a spinning ball of green light.

He shouted to her, but the winds around him increased, swallowing the sound of his voice. Light surrounded him, engulfing him and the rock cliffs until nothing remained but white light and furious storms; he struggled, felt himself sink into the light as if he were drowning in quicksand.

Nearby, the green light coalesced into an orb, completely enveloping Dax. It flung itself into the dark, treacherous sky, carrying her with it. Sisko shouted again, then lunged forward, only to be pulled under and utterly consumed by the light.

CHAPTER 8

"ANOTHER NEUTRINO DISRUPTION," O'Brien reported at his station.

Kira nodded. "Scanners are picking up an object near their last known coordinates. It isn't the runabout—or a starship."

O'Brien checked his sensors and jerked his head up at the information. "Major, there's something inside it. Some kind of life-form." He squinted at the readout and drew back in surprise. "It's human!"

"Are the Cardassian sensors picking it up?" Kira asked swiftly.

O'Brien gave a nod. "They should be back on line by now. We have to assume they know everything we know."

She took a moment to consider the consequences, then made her decision. "Yellow alert. Secure Ops. Beam it aboard, Mr. O'Brien, but put it in a level one security field."

"Aye, sir. Locking on." O'Brien pressed the controls and was surprised and gratified when they responded immediately. What appeared on the transporter pad surprised him even more.

A shimmering ball of green light materialized. It hovered for a millisecond after the transporter beam dimmed, then spun away with blinding speed, revealing a slightly dazed but unharmed Lieutenant Dax.

White light. The void.

Was this death?

Breathing. Low, pulsing rhythm: the sound of his own heart. Not death. Not life as Sisko knew it. A different state altogether.

His body seemed to have disappeared. Everything had disappeared—the hellish landscape with its storms, the green orb, the runabout, Dax, himself, all of it, gone.

Nothing but white light. Breathing. Heartbeat.

Sisko waited, existing.

And then a waterfall of images cascaded over him all at once:

(Jennifer on Gilgo Beach, her oiled brown body agleam with sunlight and dusted with sand, slender hand clutching the bathing suit top to breasts as she turned toward him, frowning at the interruption)

(staring down at his own helpless hands, broad,

so much larger than hers, so much stronger and so useless, scorched and bleeding and painless)

(and wearing a catcher's mitt, feeling the solid, satisfying slap of a baseball, right in the center)

(*Commander. Come in. Welcome . . .*

Picard's face gone slack. In his eyes the smoldering ghosts of the *Saratoga.* The *Kyushu.* The *Gage.* In his eyes . . .

a protruding sensor-scope flashing red, the man's dignity, his warmth, gone, his expression utterly, terrifyingly mindless.

Resistance is futile

We will destroy you)

(The sting of smoke in his lungs, his eyes. The deck ripped asunder, flames shooting up from the level below.

Don't think. Don't feel

Beneath the twisted wreckage, Jennifer's lifeless hand)

Again the void. Heartbeat. Breathing.

"Who are you?" Sisko cried, uncertain whether the words had issued from his mouth or his mind.

Silence. And then another tide of emotion and memory overwhelmed him, like a strong ocean current pulling under an exhausted drowning man:

(The first kiss, beneath the open sky at the picnic at Szagy Park. The feel of Jennifer's lips, soft against his, the breeze cool against his skin, the stirring of desire)

(Jake's shrill cry in the delivery room, hands lifting the newborn, glistening with blood and amniotic fluid, tiny fists beating the air)

(Opaka's gentle fingertips against his face. *Breathe*)

(*Hey there, Huckleberry*

Jake's shy Jennifer-grin, fishing pole in his hand, bare feet dangling in the water)

(*Have you seen Jennifer?*

Doran, lifting her smoke-smudged face to gaze at him with mournful eyes)

(*Don't think. Don't* feel)

(Breathe)

"Who are you?" Sisko demanded, angry now. He drew in a lungful of air and tasted the sea . . . stared down at his bare feet and saw that he stood on a beach blanket. Looked up and saw that he was holding a tray of drinks. Three glasses of lemonade.

Jennifer rolled onto her side, clutching the top of her bathing suit to her breasts, dark brows knit tightly above her sunglasses. "It is corporeal," she said. "A physical entity."

Sisko blinked, stared about him, saw the sky, the white sand, the sea. Saw Jennifer and knew it was not Jennifer. "What—what did you say?"

Reality shifted so suddenly he reeled, dizzy, unable to get his bearings.

In the *Enterprise* observation lounge, Picard smiled, rose, extended a hand. "It is responding to visual and auditory stimuli," he said warmly. "Linguistic communication."

"Yes," Sisko replied with a surge of hope. "Linguistic communication. Are you capable of communicating with me?"

He reeled again.

Opaka cupped his face in her hand, gazed at him with the fondness of an old woman beholding a beloved grandchild, looked deep into his eyes. "Why do you harm us?"

His pulse quickened with excitement at the realization that he had established direct communication at last. "I don't wish to harm anyone."

On the main bridge viewscreen of the *Saratoga,* Locutus spoke in Picard's voice, but it was lifeless, grating, mechanical. "You deceive us."

"No," Sisko said and turned, distracted to find himself surrounded by the *Saratoga*'s crew: Hranok, Tamamota, Delaney, Captain Storil—yet knowing all of them were aliens. He addressed Locutus. "No, I'm telling you the truth."

The holodeck fishing pond: Jake swinging his legs above the water, turning to Sisko with a frankly curious gaze. "What are you?"

"My species is known as human," Sisko replied. "We come from a planet called Earth."

The Jake-alien tilted his head, puzzled. "Earth?"

Sisko groped for a definition, surrendered, gestured at their surroundings. "This . . . this is what my planet looks like.

The Jake-alien looked around, clearly unable to appreciate what he was seeing, and faced the human blankly.

Sisko tried again. "You and I are very different species. It will take time for us to understand each other."

"Time," Jake repeated, savoring the word. "What is this? Time . . ."

That morning, Keiko was more than a little ashamed of how sorry she'd been feeling for herself. She hated being depressed—like Miles, she was by nature an optimist—but the quarters really were gloomy and dark, the station itself was a wreck, the food was awful, and she missed her work and her friends aboard the *Enterprise.* Molly obviously missed her friends, too. She'd been fussy and uncooperative at breakfast, and Keiko felt more than a small pang of guilt for having brought her here. There had been over a thousand people aboard the *Enterprise;* in comparison, DS Nine seemed deserted.

And the people who *were* here . . . Well, Miles was the sweetest soul in the universe, the last person to say anything unkind about anyone, and he hadn't complained directly, but Keiko had learned to read between the lines and knew that he was deeply concerned about the less than professional attitude of those assigned to the station. Major Kira sounded downright belligerent, although Miles hadn't used such a harsh word, and Constable Odo was apparently a sarcastic pessimist with no respect for any authority save his own. Even Commander Sisko, who seemed to Keiko terrifically nice, was apparently desperate to find a different assignment.

At least she wasn't the only one who didn't want to be here. Small comfort.

Miles at least had something worthwhile to do. Even though he'd made a show of complaining that morning before he left for his duty shift, Keiko knew he relished the challenge of restoring the station to working order. She envied him; she had nothing to look forward to except unpacking boxes and making the quarters livable. Once that was done . . .

Well, she tried not to let herself think about it.

She kept busy for a few hours unpacking and rearranging things, but she and Molly grew restless inside the quarters. When Keiko found herself growing gloomy again, she dressed Molly, and they both went out to explore the Promenade. Miles had said that the security had improved a good deal in the last twenty-four hours, although he'd advised her to keep a safe distance away from Quark's casino and the bars. In case of trouble, Keiko wore the comm badge she'd gotten from Miles; she wasn't at all frightened for herself, but she wore it for Molly's sake.

The sight was both interesting and depressing: interesting because of the number of exotic shops; depressing because so many of them had been ravaged by the Cardassians and still lay in disrepair. But the walkways had a fair number of strollers, the casino and bars were bustling, and workers were inside many of the shops, repairing the damage. Keiko sighed. Maybe the place wouldn't be so bad once the rebuilding was completed, and at least she had more time to spend with her daughter now, something she had always wanted.

At the same time she remembered her own mother's words: *Be careful what you wish for. You just might get it . . .*

She glanced down at Molly, who toddled along clutching her mother's hand tightly. Though she was broad-faced and solidly built like her father, Molly's personality favored her mother's; she was a bold, adventurous child who loved exploring. But the bustling Promenade was an awesome place this morning, and after the sight of her first Ferengi, the girl was easily persuaded to take Keiko's hand.

Keiko smiled down at the two-year-old. "Getting tired? Ready for Mommy to carry you yet?"

Molly shook her head stubbornly, soft dark brown hair swinging, rosebud lips pursed, accentuating her chubby cheeks. Keiko sighed. They were several meters away from the food kiosks, and the smells made her want to investigate, to see if there was any food more appealing than what came out of the replicators. She would have liked to pick Molly up so as to make the going a bit faster, but Molly could be aggravatingly mulish, a trait that both her mother and her father were convinced came from the *other* side of the family.

"Okay," Keiko agreed patiently. "Let's walk this way and see if maybe there's something good to eat over here."

"Okay," Molly chirruped, her almond-shaped eyes huge as she stared up at the alien pedestrians and kiosk vendors.

They had almost approached the first of the food stands when an unseen force slammed into Keiko's midsection, knocking the air from her lungs. She fell backwards onto the deck and looked up at the stars shining down through the oval-shaped observation windows. The view was soon obliterated by Molly's tear-streaked face leaning over her.

Keiko tried to say she was all right, but she found herself unable to speak, unable even to draw a breath.

"Oh, jeez." A second face, that of a dark-skinned preteen boy, came into her field of vision. "Oh, gosh. I'm awfully sorry. Are you okay?"

Don't panic, Keiko told herself. Just relax. You'll be able to breathe soon. She sucked in air with a sudden gasp, and pushed herself up to a sitting position. "Molly?"

The little girl stood beside her, sobbing.

"It's okay." Keiko took the child's hand. "Mommy's okay, honey. I just got knocked down."

The boy knelt beside her, his expression one of alarm. "I'm really sorry."

"It's okay," Keiko said. He looked very familiar, and she realized that she had seen him earlier inside the station; Miles had pointed him out to her during a tour. "I just got the wind knocked out of me. How about you? You're the commander's son, aren't you? Jake, isn't it?"

"Yeah. I'm fine," he said shyly and glanced over his shoulder at an obviously irate Bajoran civilian, who stood behind him, arms folded.

"I thank you for apprehending this young thief," the Bajoran said.

"What?" Keiko blinked and struggled to get to her feet. Jake solicitously took an arm and helped her up. "You must be mistaken. This is Commander Sisko's son."

"So I've heard," the old man said dryly. "But he helped his Ferengi friend steal two of my drolis."

Jake hung his head. "It's not true. I didn't know Nog was going to steal the food. I offered to pay for it, but the vendor won't accept my credits."

"I'll pay." Keiko drew a gold piece from her belt pouch; Miles had warned her that credits wouldn't be of much use on the Promenade, at least, not until the economy recovered. "Is this enough?"

The Bajoran brightened immediately at the sight of the money—so much so that Keiko knew she'd overpaid him, but it was too late; the old man snatched the gold from her hand and hurried off, smiling.

"I'm really sorry," Jake moaned, with such a pathetic my-dad's-gonna-kill-me look that Keiko had to force herself not to smile. "You must be one of the officers on the station," he said.

"I'm Keiko, and this is Molly. Ensign O'Brien is my husband."

"Oh. Nice to meet you. I'll pay you back, honest. It's just that there's no one else here my age except Nog."

"The Ferengi?" Keiko asked.

He nodded.

She feigned a frown. "Why aren't you in class right now? Isn't it a little early to be out killing time?"

"What class?" Jake asked bleakly. "Look, I'm really very sorry. I'll pay you back this evening after I talk to my dad, I promise. But I think I'd better leave before I get into any more trouble." He glanced fearfully in the direction the shopkeeper had gone.

"That sounds like a good idea," Keiko said dryly. "It was nice . . . er, running into you, Jake."

"Nice meeting you, too." He grinned shyly again before running off. Keiko lifted the unprotesting Molly into her arms and watched him go. A young Ferengi—the thief in question, no doubt—approached him, and then the two disappeared into the crowd.

Keiko stood looking after them for a time. She had been so worried about her own family adjusting to life on the station that she hadn't considered what it must be like for the handful of other children here. Jake Sisko seemed very nice, but there was a sadness, a loneliness, about him that perplexed her until she remembered that Miles had said the commander was a widower.

She had been worried enough about Molly adjusting to life on the station, but to imagine her trying to adjust to it after losing a parent . . .

At long last the little girl squirmed, impatient, in her arms, and Keiko headed for the food kiosks.

* * *

At the situation table at the center of Ops, Odo listened with Kira, O'Brien, and Bashir to Lieutenant Dax's explanation of what she and Commander Sisko had encountered. As head of station security, Odo was not required to be present at such briefings, but he had a very good personal reason for paying careful attention to what Dax had to say. He was not the only one excited by Dax's report of a stable wormhole. Kira leaned forward with keen interest; next to Odo, she had the best reason to be affected by the news of the discovery. And Bashir's expression was one of almost comical enthusiasm mixed with a less than platonic appreciation of Dax. Odo found Bashir's youthful exuberance quite taxing.

"Navigational sensors will be useless. We won't be able to retrace the route to Benjamin's location," Dax was saying in her serene precise intonation. Odo admired her a great deal. The lieutenant was clearly possessed of a brilliant intelligence and a wisdom unconcerned with petty protocol. Kira had already told him the amusing story of Dax's rather intimate greeting to her commanding officer. Odo did not quite understand the Trill symbiontic relationship, but it did not bother him; he didn't quite understand himself, either, and felt a kinship with Dax because of it. After all, they were both considered oddities by the humanoids surrounding them.

O'Brien nodded. "Now that we know it's a wormhole, we can use a field density compensator." He glanced down at his sensor readouts, dividing his attention between them and the conversation.

Dax hesitated. "It's not an ordinary wormhole. My analysis suggests it isn't even a natural phenomenon."

Odo stiffened at this news. Was it possible that his own people were somehow involved?

"Not natural?" Bashir marveled. "You mean it was *constructed?*"

Dax gave a single graceful nod. "It's very possible that whoever made the orbs also created this wormhole."

"The Celestial Temple," Kira said softly, then straightened defensively when Odo shot her a curious glance. He knew that Kira had certain mystical leanings, despite her pretensions toward skepticism. He had also sensed her loyalty to Sisko ever since he returned from Opaka with the orb. Before his arrival, Kira had let fly several scathing remarks about Starfleet commanders, but she had made no further unkind comments about Sisko since the orb appeared. Odo suspected that the Bajoran major thought Sisko was somehow special, though Kira would never speak to him of such things.

And perhaps Odo himself believed it as well. Sisko was not at all what he had expected a Starfleet officer to be; and because of the commander, Odo now had the opportunity he had been waiting for all his life.

His reverie was broken by O'Brien's terse statement: "The Cardassians are leaving their position . . . on a course toward the Denorios Belt."

The group tensed at this news; Kira stood up, frowning. "What would it take to move this station to the mouth of the wormhole?"

O'Brien's mouth dropped open. Despite the seriousness of the situation, Odo felt a glimmer of amusement at his reaction. O'Brien *was* typical Starfleet, always by-the-book, always caught off guard by Kira's direct damn-the-regulations approach. "This isn't a starship, Major. We've got six working thrusters to power us and that's it. A hundred sixty million kilometer trip would take two months."

"It's got to be there tomorrow," Kira said flatly.

O'Brien shook his head. "That's not possible, sir."

"Find a way."

He released a small sigh of disbelief. "Find me a class six starship to tow us."

"Find *another* way," Kira said, implacable. "That wormhole might just reshape the future of this entire quadrant. The Bajorans have to stake a claim to it." She slapped the table with her palm, paced a few steps out of sheer frustration, and swung around to face O'Brien again. "And I have to admit that claim will be a lot stronger if there's a Federation presence there to back it up."

"I know," O'Brien admitted quietly. "I wish I knew how it could be done."

Dax, who had been watching the entire exchange with utter, detached calm, as if her close friend's life and the future of the Bajora were not at stake, finally spoke. "Couldn't you modify the subspace field output of the deflector generators just enough to create a *low*-level field around the station?"

O'Brien frowned at her, but his expression quickly metamorphosed into one of dawning revelation. "So we could lower the inertial mass."

Dax nodded, pleased. "If you can make the station lighter, those six thrusters will provide all the power we'll need."

"It just might work, Lieutenant, but—the ensign's tone darkened—"This whole station could break apart like an egg if it doesn't."

She sighed in acknowledgment. "Even if it *does* work, we're going to need help from Starfleet once we get there."

"The *Enterprise* is still the nearest starship," O'Brien said. "It would take them two days to get here."

Dax gave him a look that said, What other choice do we have? "Advise Starfleet that we will require their assistance."

O'Brien nodded and turned his attention to his panel.

Kira straightened. "You have Ops, Mr. O'Brien. I'm leading the rescue mission." She started for the corridor, looking over one shoulder at the group. "Lieutenant Dax, you're with me. You, too, Doc. Time to be a hero."

Bashir moved swiftly, eagerly, to join Dax and the major. "Yes, *sir.*"

Unbidden, Odo followed, catching up to them; he had waited too many years for this opportunity to let it slip away from him now.

Kira noticed, and began a gentler than usual rebuke, "Constable—"

Odo did not let her finish; he knew she understood why he had to come. "This is a security matter. I'm in charge of security."

"Security *here,* on the station." She stopped at the turbolift, pressed a control, folded her arms. "I can't justify taking you into this wormhole. We don't know what we're dealing with in there. It could be hostile."

Her tone was less strident than it might have been; Odo sensed her hesitation and persisted, not caring if the others heard. "Major, I was found in the Denorios Belt. I don't know where I came from. I have no idea if there are any others like me."

She began to turn away; his tone grew more emphatic, forcing her to listen. Of all of them, he trusted Kira to understand: with her, matters of the spirit superseded Starfleet protocol. She *had* to understand. "All my life I've been forced to pass myself off as one of you, always wondering who I really am. The answers to a lot of my questions may be somewhere on the other side of that wormhole."

A clank of metal; the doors parted as the lift arrived. Kira opened her mouth to continue the argument, but Odo simply walked past her into the waiting lift and said, "You coming?"

A dangerous moment passed. He saw her dark eyes narrow, saw the muscle in her jaw twitch once, twice. She glanced at Dax, at Bashir, clearly aware that Odo's insubordination made her look bad in front of the other officers.

He held her gaze with a look that said: I trust you to do what's right, Major.

And then she gave a barely audible sigh of resignation and her face relaxed. Odo smiled as she stepped onto the turbolift without another word.

CHAPTER 9

THE VOID.

Heartbeat. Breathing.

Sisko waited in pure, formless existence for the aliens to contact him again; after the mention of time to the Jake-alien, he had sensed their confused retreat.

Finally they appeared again in the form of Jean-Luc Picard, standing in the *Enterprise* observation lounge, the planet Bajor serving as backdrop behind him.

How long, Sisko wondered, had he simply . . . existed, waiting for their next appearance? He was beginning to understand the Jake-alien's bewilderment: he had no sense of the passage of minutes, hours—could not have guessed whether he had waited silently, breathing, existing, for seconds or centuries.

Picard gazed at him mistrustfully. "The creature must be destroyed before it destroys us."

Shift. The main viewscreen on the *Saratoga.* Locutus, flesh and metal, with mechanically organic mindlessness: "It is malevolent."

A blink, and the *Saratoga*'s bridge disappeared, replaced by a baseball field. Ty Cobb stood in a batter's box, dressed in the archaic white uniform of his era, and grinned puckishly as he swung at an imaginary pitch. "Aggressive. Adversarial."

Shift. The *Enterprise* observation lounge, with Deep Space Nine now appearing in the observation window. Picard dismissed the specters of the past with a blink, spoke in a voice grown infinitely cool and remote. "It must be destroyed."

"I'm not your enemy," Sisko said, and started at the sight of his body in its Starfleet uniform, at the realization that he was *physically* sitting in the observation lounge beside Picard; he touched the chair, felt fabric beneath his fingers. He leaned forward, desperate to convince the alien Picard of his sincerity. "I've been sent here by people *you* contacted."

"Contacted?" Picard said with cold disbelief. He rose, clasped his hands behind him, and walked over to the observation window as if eager to put distance between himself and the human.

"With your devices," Sisko persisted. "Your orbs."

The captain turned around and glared at him.

"We seek contact with other life-forms, not corporeal creatures who would annihilate us."

Sisko stood, breaking the pattern of the past. "I have *not* come to annihilate anyone."

Shift. A hundred flames shining in the dark stone chamber beneath the monastery. Kai Opaka, her bruised face incandescent with candle glow, tenderly withdrew her hand from Sisko's cheek and said sadly, "Can you not see the damage you have already done?"

"If I have caused you any harm, I deeply regret it," Sisko told her. "I am here only to find those who sent the orbs."

Opaka considered this, her black pupils reflecting a thousand flickering lights. "For what purpose?"

"To establish peaceful relations, as we have done with hundreds of other species."

She shrank from him mistrustfully. "Hundreds of other corporeal species?"

Shift. The *Saratoga's* bridge. Sisko sat in the chair next to Captain Storil; Tamamota swiveled from her console to face him accusingly. "This creature will lead them here."

Behind them, Delaney spoke from Ops. "They will annihilate us."

Sisko looked for help from Captain Storil. The Vulcan regarded him calmly, then turned to face the main viewscreen as the image of Locutus opened his . . . *its* mouth. A million echoing voices spoke as one: *"Destroy it now."*

Sisko propelled himself from his chair toward

the viewscreen, shouting at the Borg-human hybrid. "My species respects *life* above all else! Can you say the same? If you are going to destroy me, at least know who it is you destroy."

Storil faced him calmly and lifted a brow in mild annoyance. "We know all that we need to know."

"You endanger our domain," Delaney said.

Sisko turned back toward his dead shipmates. "I do not understand the threat I bring to you. But I am not your enemy. Allow me to prove it."

"Prove it?" Hranok swiveled from his console.

Sisko hesitated. "It can be argued that a human is ultimately the sum of his experiences. You obviously have access to mine."

Huckleberry Jake, squinting in the sun, turning his attention away from his fishing pole. "'Experiences'—what is this?"

"Memories," Sisko said, with a sense that he was once again getting through. "Events from my past. Like this one."

Jake wrinkled his forehead and broke the surface of the blue pond with one dangling toe, watching as the ripples spread outward into infinity. "Past?"

"Things that happened before now," he said, unconsciously adopting the patient, paternal tone of explanation he often used with the boy.

Jake blinked at him, absolutely stymied.

"You have absolutely no idea what I'm talking about," Sisko muttered to himself.

Jake shook his head; in a nearby tree, a bird chirruped. "What came *before* now is no different than what *is* now or what is to come. It is one's existence."

Sisko drew in a breath of amazement as he crouched beside the child, suddenly understanding. "Then, for you, there *is* no linear time."

Stretched out on the blanket, Jennifer lowered her sunglasses with a slender finger and stared at him over the rims. "'Linear time'—what is this?"

Sisko set down the tray of lemonade in the sand and leaned toward her, excited by the breakthrough, torn by the sight of Jennifer, so beautiful, so young; he was close enough now to smell the scent of oil and sun-warmed skin. "My species lives in one point in time. And once we move beyond that point, it becomes the past. The future—all that is still to come—does not exist yet for us."

She pushed herself up on her palms, alarmed, the blanket making soft squeaking noises in the fine white sand. A drop of oil had caught in a lock of her black hair, and glittered in the bright light. *"Does not exist yet?"*

"That is the nature of a linear existence," Sisko explained soothingly. "And if you examine it more closely, you will see that you do not need to fear me."

He looked into those familiar eyes, brown flecked with gold, and saw through them for an instant to the alien presence beneath, to the hesitation, the fear.

Breathing. Heartbeat. Waiting . . .

O'Brien was left at Ops with a handful of Bajoran techs, far too much recalcitrant Cardie technology, and a good deal of worry.

Since the day O'Brien had taken Commander

Sisko and his son on a tour of the station, he had been convinced the commander would not stay on Deep Space Nine. A shame, because he had instantly liked the man—and moreover he had felt a sense of immediate loyalty, which surprised him. Even more surprisingly, Major Kira and Odo seemed to feel that way toward the commander, too, especially since Sisko had returned from Kai Opaka with the orb. O'Brien doubted he and Major Kira would ever see eye to eye about anything, except the way they felt about Sisko. Despite his initial fears about accepting the Deep Space Nine assignment, O'Brien now felt as if they all fit, all belonged here; he had not expected to feel that way again after leaving the *Enterprise*—at least, not here and not so soon.

He hoped Sisko felt that way, too, now, and would decide to stay—that is, if they could help him return through the wormhole.

For some strange reason O'Brien found himself remembering the horrible moment aboard *Enterprise* when Picard had been lost to the Borg and the crew had seen him, seen what terrible mechanical and mental violations had been inflicted upon him, seen his humanity stripped away. O'Brien had thought then that the captain would never return to them.

But they had found a way. Just as they would find a way to bring Sisko home again. O'Brien was determined to do his part; then he would trust the commander to make the right decision . . .

If he could get this bloody Cardie equipment to work.

There was another, deeper worry he did not allow to entirely surface: the fear he'd felt for Keiko and Molly's sake when he awakened from the nightmare. That fear now brushed against his consciousness, but he forced it away. There was no time to be frightened for them. Not now, when he had his hands full.

O'Brien was moving quickly through Engineering, checking readouts, when the lights began to flicker and the reactor groaned with the strain.

He stopped in his tracks and swore softly; up to that moment things had been going perfectly—too perfectly, of course. O'Brien had resigned himself to the fact that the equipment simply was not going to operate as it should, but that did not lessen his frustration when it finally happened. "Dammit! Computer: analyze subspace field integrity."

A beat—too long a one for his current mood. For the thousandth time in the past few days, he found himself thinking that the *Enterprise*'s computer would never have taken this much time to respond.

"Power frequency imbalance is preventing field closure," the computer reported at last.

He grunted in disgust. "Add reactor three to the power grid."

O'Brien hurried to his monitor and watched a schematic of the station as the warp field almost enclosed it . . . then failed, dissolving.

"Partial field established," the computer said,

and O'Brien groaned. "Instability at twelve percent."

"*Partial* field," he muttered, then hesitated. "Is the station's inertial mass low enough to break orbit?"

"Procedure is not recommended at this time."

He stiffened, felt a muscle in his jaw begin to twitch, and knew, from the intimidated looks a couple of the Bajoran techs shot him, that he was beginning to look and sound like Major Kira. "Dammit, I didn't ask for an opinion! Just tell me whether or not we can get enough thrust with only a partial field established!"

"Affirmative."

He sighed and calmed himself. "All right. Initiate transit mode, three-axis stabilization. Status of aft thrusters?"

"Aft thrusters ready."

Good. O'Brien gave a slight appreciative nod. "Engage."

He checked his monitor and saw from the schematic that the thrusters were indeed firing. A low rumble, and then the deck beneath his feet began to vibrate; some of the open console panels with loose wiring and conduits began rattling noisily. The stars in the overhead observation windows began to shift slowly. They were moving, breaking orbit, O'Brien realized with an interior smile. He wished he could have seen the reaction to the surprise launch on the Promenade.

The rumbling and the vibration increased, and a low-pitched whine began. A Klaxon sounded.

O'Brien moved to his monitors and began checking readouts.

"Warning," the computer said. "Field integrity declining. Instability at twenty-one percent."

"We've got to close that gap in the field or we're going to tear ourselves into a million pieces," O'Brien called to the techs, far too busy to feel fear, to feel anything but aggravation at the limits imposed on him by the inferior machinery.

The computer again, in a dire tone: "Warning: Station is now beyond safe shutdown velocity. Subspace field collapse in sixty seconds."

The vibrations grew more intense, the whine higher in pitch; the deck rocked slightly beneath O'Brien's feet so that he had to concentrate to keep his balance. He scanned the readouts, searching for an answer, even squinting at the Cardassian hieroglyphs on the controls as if by sheer force of will he could decipher them.

The solution came, not from the hieroglyphs but from deep within O'Brien's brain.

He lifted his head and shouted over the growing rumble: "Does anyone here know if the inertial dampers can feed the deflectors?"

Blank stares. O'Brien sighed, glanced back down at his console, and said softly, "A good time to find out." He began working controls furiously. "Computer: transfer energy from the inertial dampers to reinforce the subspace field."

He watched the monitor; nothing was happening. In an almost sulky tone, the computer replied, "Procedure is not recommended."

He lost his patience. "Dammit—transfer the energy!"

"Unable to comply," the computer answered with aggravating smugness. "Level one safety protocols have canceled request."

O'Brien jerked up. *"Canceled* it!"

And then, insult to injury: "Warning. Subspace field collapse in thirty seconds."

He wasted no more time on anger but called over to the techs, "I'm going to transfer it manually!" He made eye contact with the nearest Bajoran. "On my mark, redirect the flow to the deflectors."

The Bajoran nodded. To another, O'Brien said, "Keep the power balanced."

"Field collapse in fifteen seconds," the computer reported smoothly.

"Now!" O'Brien yelled, and struggled with insane speed to work a dozen different controls, all of them inconveniently placed so that he had to move back and forth across the panel. Nearby, the two Bajoran techs worked with the same feverish alacrity.

The lights flickered, dimmed; the whine grew lower in pitch. O'Brien looked up, holding his breath, at the schematic on his monitor—Hold on, Commander, he begged silently, we're coming to bring you home—and saw the field leap completely into place around the station.

The whine ceased, the vibrations ended, and the lights brightened again.

"Field energy now within flight tolerances," the computer reported pleasantly.

O'Brien released his breath explosively and smiled weakly over at the two Bajoran techs, then returned his attention to his readouts and muttered, "Computer: you and I have to have a little talk."

Kira and Dax piloted the runabout; Odo sat behind the major and across from Bashir, who was studying his surroundings with an annoying degree of anticipation.

Odo himself was not exactly calm—after all, he had a great deal on his mind, not the least of which was the prospect of discovering something about his origins—but he had too much dignity to let his anxiety show.

Bashir, on the other hand, gazed out of the observation window and over Dax's shoulder at the controls with the frank curiosity and excitement of a child. At least the young doctor had the good sense not to try to engage Odo in conversation.

They rode together in tense silence except for Dax, who, as always, maintained an air of competent serenity. It was she who first spoke, looking down at her viewscreen.

"The Cardassian warship is in visual range."

"On screen," Major Kira ordered.

The stars on the overhead screen wavered, shifted to a view of the grim giant vessel. Kira checked her instruments, then gazed back up at the Cardassian ship, which was clearly headed for the wormhole, with an angry sigh. "They're going right to it." She drummed her fingers on the console, thinking.

Bashir put a hand on the back of Dax's chair and leaned forward eagerly, addressing Kira. "They've got to listen to reason, haven't they? When we warn them what would happen if they go in there—"

"Doctor," Odo interrupted, with blatant cynicism, "most people in my experience wouldn't know reason if it walked up and shook their hand. You can count Gul Dukat among them."

"But—" Bashir persisted.

Kira put up a hand for silence. "The question is whether or not they decide to believe us, and there's not a lot we can do about that, either way. It's up to them." As Bashir settled back into his seat with an air of frustration, she pressed a control on the comm panel. "This is the Federation ship *Yangtzee Kiang,* Major Kira Nerys in command."

The panel beeped three times in succession. The image of Gul Dukat, in all his treacherous glory, appeared on the screen. Treacherous because Dukat looked so *ordinary,* so benign, yet was, Odo knew, so capable of the most vile cruelty.

"Yes, Major," Dukat said, looking infinitely put out and impatient at having to communicate with a Bajoran underling.

Kira folded her arms as if trying to hold in her hatred. To her credit, she spoke in what was for her an almost civil tone—no small feat, to Odo's mind. He had witnessed the Cardassian atrocities firsthand, and Kira had hinted at the horrible violations suffered by her and her family. Odo was grateful, for once, that he had not had a family to lose to the Cardassians.

"Gul Dukat." Kira straightened, her expression regal, implacable, tolerating no dissension. "We know you're headed for the wormhole."

"Wormhole?" As she had expected, Dukat's lips curved in a mocking little smile that made no pretense of sincerity. "What wormhole?"

Kira began to bristle, but checked herself, held it in. "I strongly suggest you do not proceed. We encountered a hostile life-form inside."

Gul Dukat cocked his head as he listened, then drew back skeptically. "Perhaps they would be less hostile to Cardassians than to humans—"

"Dukat," Odo interrupted, with weary impatience, ignoring Kira's swift, indignant glare, "you know I won't lie to you, and I know you probably won't listen to me, but these people are trying to save you from a lot of trouble."

"Really?" Dukat's tone grew openly sarcastic. "I suppose you'd also tell me these are not the life-forms that sent the orbs and that your Commander Sisko is not negotiating for their technology." He shook his head. "Thank you for your concern, but I think we'll see for ourselves."

The viewscreen went black, then cleared to show stars, and the Cardassian warship proceeding through the Denorios Belt. Odo turned toward Bashir with a cynical sigh. "So much for reason."

Ensconced in his commander's platform on the Cardassian warship, Gul Dukat terminated the communication with a swift, imperious motion and allowed himself a contemptuous smile.

The Bajora were so amusingly stupid: all those centuries with the orbs, and all they could think to do with them was create a religion around them! And now this Major Nerys could come up with nothing more convincing than a warning that the wormhole was dangerous.

Starfleet was no better, allowing such a backward race to govern itself, spouting noble phrases about freedom and self-determination. Dukat detested Starfleet and its mealymouthed do-gooding. What was noble about self-determination for idiots? Dukat wondered. The Bajoran race would wind up exterminating itself in civil war. The squabbling had begun the instant the Cardassian forces withdrew.

Dukat understood the necessity for iron control with primitive peoples, which was why he had done such an excellent job as Bajoran prefect for so many years, despite what backbiters might have said. After all, he was, in his own estimation, as clever as he was ambitious—and he was exceedingly ambitious. He did not like losing the power and prestige associated with the office of prefect, and he'd been busy plotting a way to retrieve them. His instincts told him the orbs might just present such an opportunity. He had been right to keep an eye on the station, and especially the new Starfleet commander. His instincts were about to pay off, in the form of a wormhole inside what had been Cardassian territory for the past six decades.

His was a goal worth fighting for. But then, any maneuver that would get Sisko out of what was rightfully Dukat's office seemed justified.

His train of thought was broken when a subordinate called to him from below. "Gul Dukat, we are approaching the wormhole."

Dukat pushed himself out of his chair and paced to the edge of the platform to stare at an unrevealing mass of stellar dust swirls and stars on the viewscreen. "Very good. Inform Macet we are entering. Proceed."

The Cardassian warship eased forward. At the first burst of light Dukat did not flinch; he simply let go a laugh of sheer pleasure.

Pure existence. Timelessness. Sisko sensed a ripple in the void, a stirring, and knew instinctively the aliens approached.

And he was in Szagy Park again, in a younger, leaner body, sitting on a picnic blanket Jennifer had spread on the grass. She loved the outdoors—the park, the ocean, the mountains—with a passion he had learned to appreciate and which Jake came by naturally; and she loved old-fashioned customs. He'd thought it silly, at first, that she had dragged him out into the middle of a park on a date, until she appeared wearing a gossamer floral dress that flowed with the slightest spring breeze. He had laughed and spread out all the food he'd prepared just for her. With a sense of whimsy, he'd packed it in an old wicker basket that had belonged to his father.

Was it just the product of retrospect or had he *known,* that first time at Gilgo Beach and again at Szagy Park, with as much certainty as he did now, looking back on it as the past, that she was the one? Past and present and future were blurred now, meaningless. Sisko tried—and failed—to remember that this was nothing more than a re-creation, that the well-loved eyes he stared into now were alien, unknown.

It was a warm, cloudless day with an intensely blue sky and a cool breeze; the wind carried the reckless laughter of children. Sisko sat on the blanket beside the ruins of the recent feast. Jennifer lay cradled in his arms, breathing and warm and alive, soft skin and soft hair and soft gossamer dress pressed against his skin. For an instant he allowed himself to pretend he was holding her. *Really* holding her, holding Jennifer for one endless moment outside time . . .

She stirred in his arms, pointed to herself, and Sisko's illusion was shattered. "Jennifer," she said.

He pulled away from her, withdrew his arms quickly; the emotions took a bit longer to detach. She pushed herself up into a sitting position while he stared out at the shady, tree-lined paths, the carefully manicured expanse of flower gardens, and said grayly, "Yes. That was her name."

"She is part of your existence," the alien said, with Jennifer's voice. Sisko looked away, out at the sunny horizon.

(*Don't think. Don't* feel)

(*Feelings are irrelevant*)

"She is part of my *past.* She's no longer alive."

A pause as the alien considered this; Sisko half turned his head and caught sight of her with his peripheral vision, saw the confusion on her face. "But she is part of your existence."

Sisko released an unsteady sigh. "Yes, she *was* a most important part of my existence. But I lost her some time ago."

"'Lost' What is this?"

He turned to gaze on her directly and saw nothing but honest curiosity in her huge dark eyes. Sisko felt a keen pang of envy: a race that did not know loss. "In a linear existence . . ." He groped for the right words, trying to explain a concept he had never looked upon objectively before. "We can't go back to the past to get something we left behind. So it's lost."

She drew back in disbelief, frowning and smiling at the same time with an expression so like Jennifer's that he fully expected to hear what Jennifer would have said at a time like this: *Oh, come on, Ben, you've got to be kidding.* Instead, she said, "It is inconceivable that any species could exist in such a manner. You are deceiving us."

"No. This is the truth." He stood up, looking out at the grass, at the children playing soccer in the distance. "This day . . . this park . . ." He faltered, trying to hold back the flood of emotion and memory that threatened to overwhelm him. "It was almost . . . fifteen years ago. It was a very important day to me, a day that shaped every day that followed." He looked down at her face, tilted up toward his as she concentrated, struggling to understand his every word. He released a long, slow breath and regained his composure. "That is the essence of a linear existence. Each day affects the next."

She frowned at that, then turned her head sharply at the sound of laughter.

Sisko followed her gaze and saw . . . himself only a short distance away, lying on the ground beside Jennifer on the picnic blanket, she resting in his arms, eyes closed, giving him the opportunity to memorize each detail of her face without being seen: short sweep of a nose, coal black lashes fringing dusky eyelids, the sensual curves and planes of cheekbones, jaw, neck. . . .

Sisko the watcher turned away from the scene in pain. These were no aliens: they were Ben himself, and Jennifer, captured in memory outside time. And yet . . . He turned back, compelled to watch, unable to keep from staring at his wife, so young, so strikingly, resoundingly alive.

"Listen to it," the young Sisko whispered, smiling at his love with the pleasure of the moment.

Drowsy with food and warmth, Jennifer stirred lazily in his arms without opening her eyes. "To what?"

"The sound of children playing," the young Sisko murmured. "What could be more beautiful?"

"So . . ." A coy grin stretched her lips, revealed a white crescent of teeth. "You like children."

Young Sisko's tone grew playful. "That almost sounds like a domestic inquiry."

The grin faded; she opened her eyes and regarded him seriously. "I've heard Starfleet officers don't want families because they complicate their lives."

"Starfleet officers don't often find mates who want to raise families on a starship," young Sisko said, and held his breath during the few seconds' hesitation before she answered:

"That almost sounds like a domestic inquiry."

He smiled, suddenly aware of his increased heart rate, fighting to keep the nervousness from his voice, his eyes: "I think it was."

She did not speak, did not smile, but reached for his cheek with long, gentle fingers

(*Breathe*)

and drew his lips to hers.

Sisko the Watcher did not turn away—

(*Don't think. Don't* feel)

but instead forced himself to recover from the emotion by focusing instead on the Jennifer-alien beside him, who stared at the kissing couple in front of them with frank puzzlement.

"As corporeal entities," Sisko explained quietly, as if fearful of disturbing the young lovers, "humans find physical touch to cause pleasure."

"'Pleasure.'" She savored the word. "What is this?"

"Good feelings," Sisko began evenly enough. "Happiness—" His voice broke on the word; he fell silent, bowed his head in grief.

When he lifted it again, he found himself staring into Doran's eyes, mournful above a pale face smudged with smoke. Turned and saw Hranok, blue-skinned and muscular, beside him, felt the deck pitch beneath his feet. The corridors were limned with flame and shrouded in smoke; Sisko closed his burning eyes at the sound of survivors coughing, weeping, shouting hysterically for others.

He could not go down that corridor. Could not do what was expected of him—not this time. Not this time . . .

(*Don't think. Don't feel*)

But he could not keep from feeling now: there was no duty to be performed, no civilians to be saved, no hope, only the wraiths of those long dead. Overwhelmed, he began to lean against the bulkhead, but pulled back swiftly from its heat, turning away from Doran as if to return to the questionable safety of the turbolift.

He would not go. Would *not.*

Behind him, Doran spoke, her tone questioning. "But this is your existence . . ."

"Yes," Sisko admitted hoarsely, feeling dizzy, overwhelmed by heat and smoke. He drew a hand across his perspiring brow. "But it is difficult to return here. More difficult than any other memory."

"Why?" Hranok asked gently. There was no hostility in the question, only sympathetic curiosity.

"Because," Sisko began, fighting hard to get the words out, to keep his voice from quaking, "this was the day . . . I lost Jennifer." He leaned against the bulkhead, suddenly exhausted, no longer caring if the hot metal was capable of inflicting real or imaginary burns. "And I don't want to be here."

A form emerged from the thick haze of smoke, one incongruous with his memory of the event: Jennifer, in her Gilgo Beach bathing suit and sunglasses, calmly walking barefoot through the flames, oblivious of the limping survivors beside her, of the vision of hell surrounding her.

She stepped up to him, so close the smell of her sun-warmed, oiled flesh mingled with that of the smoke, and held him with her hidden, inquisitive stare. "Then why do you exist here?"

"I—I don't understand," Sisko stammered. He glanced over his shoulder at the empty lift with the wild thought that perhaps he could retreat to its safety . . . but where could he go on the *Saratoga* except to the bridge, where the bodies of his dead shipmates lay?

Jennifer tilted her head; a small frown formed above the bridge of her sunglasses. Sisko saw himself twice reflected in the lenses: two small frightened men in burgundy and black uniforms, backlit by flame. "You exist here."

Uncomprehending, he stared at her, overwhelmed by fear, grief, confusion. He pushed himself away from the bulkhead, opened his mouth to plead for help in escaping.

The words died in his throat as all movement and sound abruptly ceased. The scene in the *Saratoga* corridor became as static as a still life. Flames froze in mid-leap, fleeing survivors in mid-stride;

smoke hung motionless, suspended in the air. Jennifer, Hranok, and Doran stood still, breathless, lifeless reproductions.

Sisko looked about him, panicked; as much as he had wanted to flee this memory, its sudden suspension seemed desperately *wrong.*

He watched as the burning corridor and those within it began to melt away. A shrill, piercing whine filled Sisko's skull; he raised his hands to his ears to blot it out, but it increased to agonizing levels as he watched Doran, Hranok, and Jennifer dissolve.

"What's wrong?" Sisko shouted, unable to hear his own words over the deafening sound. "What's happening?"

The void. Breathing. Heartbeat. Pain . . .

With a sense of triumph, Dukat relaxed back in his chair and enjoyed the flickering circus of light surrounding the warship. The Cardassian Empire would name this wormhole after him, would find a way to suitably reward him. No matter that Sisko would try to claim it. Let him try. Let him try to outgun two Cardassian warships with the pathetic weaponry on the station.

The light cleared and gave way to stars.

"Gul Dukat," the navigator reported excitedly from his station. "We have reached"—he glanced back down to verify their position as if he couldn't believe it—"the Gamma Quadrant."

Dukat smiled. "Very good. Come about and prepare to reenter the wormhole."

He watched the stars shift slowly as the great vessel turned one hundred eighty degrees to face the wormhole once again, its entrance still illuminated with soft, flickering rainbow light. Dukat could barely contain his exultation, could hardly remain in his chair, but the ride had been a bumpy one, and so he contented himself with sitting still and gloating silently.

"Approaching the worm—" the navigator began, then broke off with a gasp.

Dukat followed his gaze. Before them, the wormhole shattered into a million points of light.

"The wormhole . . ." Dax turned to Kira, her voice soft with amazement. "It's gone!"

CHAPTER 10

"WHY DID YOU do that to me?" Jake asked bitterly, when he and Nog were out of Keiko's earshot. He strode so rapidly that the Ferengi was gasping in an effort to keep pace with him. "Is that your idea of a joke?"

A deep crease formed between Nog's hairless brow ridges; his eyes widened with confusion. "I thought you would know when to run. I was clearly mistaken."

Jake stopped in the middle of the walkway and stiffened, hands clenched into fists. "How was I supposed to know you were going to *steal* them?"

"I'm a Ferengi," Nog replied with an air of wounded dignity, which quickly changed to glee. He glanced surreptitiously over his shoulder, then drew a green-flecked roll from his pocket. "Here. I saved this for you. Hungry?"

Jake groaned and started walking again.

Nog followed, and took a large bite of the stolen droli. "I do not understand humans," he said with his mouth full. "Why are you angry? You were caught because of your own stupidity. A Ferengi would have known when to flee."

"Well, a human wouldn't," Jake countered, not even watching where he was going, just walking fast as if he could put distance between himself and the humiliation of what had just happened. Things had been bad enough, but now Keiko would say something to Ensign O'Brien, and Ensign O'Brien would say something to Dad, and Dad was going to be furious and probably tell him never to see Nog again—which right now didn't seem like such a bad idea. "Because humans don't steal. At least, not most humans. It's . . . it's dis*honest.*"

"You humans and your honesty!" Nog took a second savage bite of the droli, then another, until Jake could barely comprehend his words. "I have never understood it. How can it make sense to be honest when there is clearly more profit in deceit?"

"Because . . . because that's a crummy way to live, that's why, always having to worry that someone's going to steal everything you own the minute you turn your back."

"You have no sense of adventure," Nog said, jabbing a sharp-nailed, stubby digit at him. "You do not understand the thrill of outwitting a foe, of living by your wits. Your race has a very boring view of life." He finished off the bun with a flourish and licked his fingers.

Jake felt heat rise to his cheeks. "We understand adventure! We'd just rather explore the universe than other people's pockets!"

"Hmph." Nog sniffed. "Have you ever stolen anything, Jake Sisko?"

He tilted his chin up at the suggestion. "No! Have you ever tried to be honest?"

"If I said yes, you would know I was lying," Nog replied, grinning. "Then how can we understand each other if we do not make an attempt to experience each other's world?"

Jake fell silent, unable to think of a rebuttal.

"Come." Nog tugged his elbow and gestured. Jake looked to his right to see that they had arrived in front of Quark's casino again. "Let me help you experience *my* culture, hew-man."

"You'll just get me in trouble again," Jake said darkly. "Besides, if I go in there"—he jerked his head in the direction of the busy casino—"they'll just tell me to leave 'cause I'm a kid."

"I know a secret passage." Nog lowered his voice and gestured enticingly. "No one will see us. I promise I will do nothing without telling you first. And I will not get you into trouble this time."

Jake frowned as he stared into the busy casino. "You promise?"

"On my honor as a Ferengi," Nog said somberly, then let go a low, braying laugh.

* * *

Nog led Jake around to the casino's secluded rear entrance, where the Ferengi swiftly keyed a code into a lock pad. The low door slid open; Nog gestured, palms out, shooing the human inside.

"Quickly, quickly," he whispered and stepped in behind Jake so gingerly that the boy held his breath for fear of making too much noise.

They entered what seemed to be a storage area filled with boxes, a broken-down servitor, and spiderwebs. Jake could hear the hubbub of the casino through the interior wall and marveled that the structure was not soundproofed.

Nog moved with exaggerated stealth toward a ventilation grate and soundlessly removed it, then dropped to his hands and knees and started crawling in. He stopped, turned, and motioned for the human to follow.

Jake swallowed hard, then dropped to his knees and crawled in behind the Ferengi. He was no longer so sure why he was doing this, and had to remind himself that he was bored out of his skull and mad at Dad because he *still* hadn't figured out a way to get them out of this crummy place and back to Earth.

They crawled through the pitch-dark duct for what seemed like forever. The shouts and groans and laughter of the casino grew so loud Jake felt he was no more than an arm's length away from the customers and decided they were separated only by a thin wall.

In front of him, Nog suddenly stopped. Jake collided with him and suppressed a moan as the

Ferengi leaned close enough for the boy to smell the strange, sour scent of his skin and breath.

"Look," Nog said into Jake's ear, then shifted so that Jake could lean down and forward and peer through the grate in front of the Ferengi.

Jake squinted. He couldn't see anything for a lot of dusty boots and some bags on a dirty floor.

"Dabo!" a Ferengi voice cried.

The boots shifted position slightly as their owners leaned forward and back, the movements accompanied by sounds of disappointment and victory; apparently they were standing around a gaming table.

"Gold," Nog breathed. Jake strained in the darkness to follow the Ferengi's gaze to the grimy bags sitting on the floor.

With painstaking stealth, Nog slowly began to remove the vent. Jake turned to him with a tiny, terrified gasp as he realized what the Ferengi was about to do. Nog turned angrily and made a swift gesture for silence.

"Nog . . . no! Don't leave me!"

But the Ferengi had already removed the grate and wriggled halfway through the opening. Jake watched in soundless horror, settling back on his heels in the darkness so that he remained out of sight while able to keep an eye on Nog.

Crouched down, moving silently on oversized feet, Nog made a beeline for the sacks on the floor. Jake couldn't see the faces of those at the table, only boots and one pair of huge splayed webbed feet. Nog moved in until he was only a hand's width away from the nearest boot—the sight made Jake grimace with anxiety—then scooped up the two largest bags, one in each hand.

The bags must have been terrifically heavy, because the Ferengi nearly lost his balance and toppled toward the heavier one. Nog had to rise almost to his full height to keep the sacks from dragging on the floor. He managed to regain momentum, but the effort made him stagger in an oscillating path toward the open ventilation duct.

"Dabo!" the Ferengi pit boss cried again, and a gleeful roar came from the wearer of one pair of boots. Someone had just struck it rich.

Nog arrived at last at the opening and handed the smaller sack, with difficulty, to Jake, who gasped at its weight—probably half his own, more than twice that of the young Ferengi. Unable to rise with it in his lap, Jake shoved it onto the duct floor and rose to a half-crouched position, stretching his arms out, ready to receive the second bag, then help Nog inside.

Another roar came from the winner—one of outrage rather than victory this time as he discovered his cache of winnings had disappeared.

Nog turned, wide-eyed, at the sound, and stopped in mid-swing; the momentum threw him off-balance. He staggered as the bag slipped from his grasp and slammed to the floor with a loud *whump* that made the boots—and the webbed feet—turn in the direction of the sound.

Jake clamped his hands over his eyes in dismay.

Nog released a squeal and dived for the open

vent—only to be caught in mid-leap by a pair of large hands. Jake whirled, thinking to flee the way he had come, but a sense of guilt and responsibility and the heavy sack of gold blocking his way made him hesitate a second, no more.

Just long enough for the Ferengi pit boss to shove his hideous face in the vent opening and demand: "You there! Hew-man! Where do you think *you're* going?"

Aboard the runabout, O'Brien's voice filtered through the comm panel. "Are you sure the wormhole collapsed? It could have withdrawn deeper into subspace."

In his voice Dax clearly heard the desperation all of them felt—she perhaps most of all, because she was closest to Benjamin. Outwardly she showed no sign of her distress, but worked swiftly to take sensor readings of the area. She had always known that she would someday lose Benjamin, just as she had lost so many other close friends over the centuries; but she had not expected to lose him quite so soon.

"We haven't found any indication of that," she told O'Brien smoothly. "But we're still checking."

A pause, and then O'Brien's voice replied: "Should I turn this thing around and go back?"

Major Kira leaned forward over the control panel, her short auburn hair falling forward against her cheeks, her eyes burning with intensity. Dax knew that she, too, was struggling to suppress her despair over the loss of Benjamin . . . and more.

The wormhole meant the economic salvation of Kira's people. Yet Kira's tone was even, her question to the point; Dax watched her with admiration. Despite her temper, she was a born commander, like Benjamin.

"What's your position?" Kira asked.

O'Brien again: "I'll be at your coordinates in less than three hours."

Kira paused and drew a breath. Uncertainty flickered in her dark eyes for a millisecond, then was replaced by utter determination as the major made her decision. "Maintain your course. We'll rendezvous here. By then our scans should be complete."

O'Brien's tone revealed his relief at her decision; none of them wanted to yield to hopelessness, to give up on Benjamin, on the wormhole, this soon. "Aye, sir." He paused. "By the way, we've been getting queries from the Cardassians since their ship disappeared from the sensor field."

Kira's lips thinned. Wryly she said, "I'm sure you have."

Odo spoke, his tone colorless, humorless. "They'll see Gul Dukat in sixty or seventy years if he starts back right away."

Dax glanced at him over her shoulder and favored the security constable with a faint reassuring smile. Odo tried to return it, failed, and turned his gaze away, toward the stars. Dax took no offense; she had overheard his conversation with the major, of course, and knew that he had much to lose from the wormhole's disappearance . . . as they all did.

She returned to checking her instruments with a silent sigh.

The void. Heartbeat. Breathing.

The pain had grown to insane, unbearable levels and then abruptly ceased. Sisko allowed himself to linger in the void, to rest, until at last he was able to speak. Despite the horror of returning to the dying *Saratoga*, he felt a deep loneliness at the aliens' withdrawal.

"Talk to me," he called. "Are you still there? What just happened?"

Jennifer appeared, clad again in bathing suit and sunglasses; to his utter relief, Sisko saw that she was strolling, not along *Saratoga*'s flaming corridors but along the seashore, tiny green waves cresting around her ankles. She approached Sisko solemnly.

"More of your kind." Her tone held a faint accusation.

He struggled to understand. "Another ship? In the wormhole?"

She tipped the sunglasses down with a finger and stared over the rim at him. "'Wormhole . . .' What is this?"

"It is how we describe the kind of passage that brought me here."

Jennifer and the beach vanished. Sisko blinked at the transformation and saw that he stood once again in the *Enterprise* observation lounge. Arms clasped behind his back, Captain Picard turned away from the window, from the sight of the Gothic space station, his expression tight and disapproving.

"It has been terminated," Picard said coldly.

Sisko shuddered with a sudden chill. "Terminated?"

The bridge of the *Saratoga*: Sisko looked down at himself and saw that he wore a lieutenant commander's uniform. Beside him, Storil sat in the captain's chair and gazed impassively at the sight on the main viewscreen.

Locutus. The Borg-human hybrid's red sensor beam flashed and began to scan Sisko, then retracted from what it found. Locutus stared at him mindlessly. "Our existence is disrupted whenever one of you enters the passage."

Tamamota turned from her console and faced Sisko. "Your linear nature is inherently destructive."

Delaney now, her pale face taut with accusation. "You have no regard for the consequences of your acts."

"That's not true," Sisko protested. "We're aware that every choice we make has a consequence."

Storil swiveled toward him, hands steepled, his tone quiet, reflective, so like the dead Vulcan's that Sisko felt a pang of grief. "But you claim you do not know what it will be," Storil said.

"We don't . . ." He began.

The fishing pond. The trees, the shade, Jake dangling his legs in the water. "Then how can you take responsibility for your actions?" the boy asked, frowning.

Sisko sighed, weary of explaining, but unwilling to surrender. "We use past experience to guide us." He paused, his tone softening at the sight of his son; it was difficult to believe that this was not really Jake sitting before him. "For Jennifer and me, all the experiences in our lives prepared us for the day we met on the beach . . . and helped us recognize that we had a future together. When we married, we accepted all the consequences of that act, whatever they might be . . . including the consequence of *you.*"

The boy drew back, puzzled. The red and white cork bobbed atop the water, suddenly disappeared beneath the surface, then reappeared again. "Me?"

"My son, Jake," Sisko answered softly.

Sickbay. The newborn Jake, swaddled in a blanket, nestled in his father's arms. Sisko grinned from ear to ear, unable to resist the memory of gazing down at that tiny red wrinkled creature and overwhelmed by desperate, depthless love. He turned and looked over to see Jennifer, flushed and exhausted, surrounded by medics, gazing up at her husband and son with pure adoration.

"The child with Jennifer," she whispered.

"Yes." Sisko looked down at his son and blinked back tears.

"Linear . . . procreation?"

"Yes." He contained himself, nodded excitedly. She was beginning to understand. "Jake is the continuation of our family."

"The sound of children playing," the Jennifer-alien murmured thoughtfully.

A pitcher's mound. Sisko wound up gracefully and hurled a perfect fastball at the batter, who swung at the air; the ball smacked into the catcher's mitt—Jake's baseball glove.

The batter, Ty Cobb, lowered the old-fashioned wooden bat and shook his head, sighing. "Aggressive. Adversarial."

"Competition," Sisko corrected, from his place on the mound. "For fun. It's a game that Jake and I play on the holodeck. It's called baseball."

Jake rose out of his crouch behind home plate, took off the catcher's mask, and stared at it curiously, then walked over to his father, studying the baseball diamond on his way to the mound.

"'Baseball,'" Jake said in a low voice, as if afraid Cobb might overhear the discussion, and tossed the ball to Sisko. "What is this?"

Sisko caught the ball in his glove, at the same time releasing a sigh that was almost a groan. "I was afraid you'd ask that." He paused, wondering how in the hell to explain baseball to an alien who had no concept of linear time. He drew a deep breath. "I throw the ball to you. And this other player stands between us with a stick, a bat, and tries to hit the ball in between these two white lines." He pointed.

Jake stared at him blankly.

Sisko regrouped. "The rules aren't important. What's important is . . . it's *linear.*" He held the ball up in his ungloved hand. "Every time you throw this ball a hundred different things can happen in the game." He pointed at Ty Cobb. "He might swing and miss, he might hit it. . . . The point is, you never know. You try to anticipate, set a strategy for all the possibilities as best you can. But in the end, it all comes down to throwing one pitch after another and seeing what happens. With each new consequence, the game begins to take shape."

Cobb stepped toward them from the plate, his expression one of sudden comprehension. "And you have no idea what that shape will be until it is completed."

"That's right," Sisko said, with increasing excitement. "In fact, the game wouldn't be worth playing if we knew what was going to happen."

Jake squinted at them both in disbelief. "You *value* your ignorance of what is to come?"

Sisko nodded, driving home his point. "That may be the most important thing to understand about humans. It is the unknown that defines our existence. We are constantly searching—not just for answers to our questions but also for new *questions.* We are explorers. We explore our lives day by day, and we explore the galaxy, trying to expand the boundaries of our knowledge. And that is why I'm here. Not to conquer you either with weapons or with ideas. But to coexist and to learn."

Jake ran the back of his hand across his forehead, wiping away perspiration, and studied Sisko intently, digesting all this. Sisko waited, hoping for a response, and glanced back down at the baseball in his grasp.

The ball had disappeared. Sisko gasped and recoiled from the sight of his hands, scorched and bloody. Panicked, he looked around him to see not the baseball diamond from the holodeck but his quarters aboard the *Saratoga:* Hranok beside him; the deck ripped asunder, flames shooting up from below; the twisted, scorched bulkhead collapsed atop furniture and belongings; and

Jake, unconscious; and just visible among the rubble,

Jennifer's lifeless hand. . . .

Sisko squeezed his eyes shut and screamed silently.

Nooooooo . . .

"If all you say is true," Hranok asked, over the crackling of the flames, "why do you exist *here?*"

Sisko stared at him wildly, beyond understanding.

Minutes after the space station arrived at the wormhole site, Major Kira stood at Master in Ops watching three Cardassian warships approach on the viewscreen.

She was not surprised; she knew the Cardassian mind well. She had grown up under their rule in a refugee camp after seeing her home, her family, destroyed. She had known this would happen the instant Gul Dukat's ship appeared.

Outwardly Kira allowed herself no reaction at the sight other than to curl her hand into a fist and dig her fingernails into her palm. Inwardly she was consumed by frustrated rage and confusion. If Sisko was indeed the one who could save her people, if Kai Opaka had had faith in him, if the wormhole was a gift of the prophets, then why did the universe seem to conspire against the commander now?

She did not surrender to the confusion or anger. She had not stubbornly survived childhood in the camps only to give up now. As always, she would find a way to survive. And she had a plan.

Surrounding her, at their stations, O'Brien, Dax, Odo, and Bashir waited for direction.

Still staring at the viewscreen, Kira addressed O'Brien calmly. She had a good deal of faith that he would find a way to do whatever she commanded; she had asked the impossible of him in bringing the station here, and he had found a way.

She wished now she could ask him to blow the warships into oblivion.

"Mr. O'Brien, can you establish a high-energy Thoron field before they get into sensor range? I don't want them to be able to scan our defense systems."

"Aye, sir."

She glanced over at the ensign's station to see him staring at the screen with an expression very like her own: one of carefully controlled hatred.

"They're hailing us," Dax said.

Kira turned her attention back to the warships. "On screen."

The image before her flickered, became that of a Cardassian commander in his ready room. She straightened and with cool formality said, "This is First Officer Kira Nerys."

The commander—balding, slightly plump—studied his nails, then glanced at Kira with unmasked contempt. "May I speak with the Starfleet commander?"

"He's not available," Kira said.

The Cardassian's full upper lip curled slightly, and the thick ridges on his forehead and beneath his eyes creased; he leaned toward the screen. "I'm not used to talking to Bajoran majors."

"I'm all you've got." She dug her nails deeper into her palm.

He studied her for a beat, then gave a sigh of infinite aggravation. "I am Gul Jasad of the Cardassian Guard, Seventh Order. Where is our warship?"

"With any luck," she said, "they're in the Gamma Quadrant. At the other end of the wormhole."

Jasad half rose out of his chair, his face contorted with the rage Kira felt. "What wormhole?" he shouted. "Our sensors show no indication of a wormhole in this sector!"

Nice try, Kira thought, but she played the game. "That's because it just collapsed."

Dax spoke up from her station and stepped forward so Jasad could see her. "We believe it was artificially created," she said in the same pleasant, instructional tone she might have used with her fellow officers. "That may be why our sensors never picked up any of the usual quantum fluctuation patterns."

Mouth open in angry disbelief, brows knit in a scowl, Jasad shook his head. "You expect me to believe that someone created a wormhole and has now conveniently disassembled it?"

Kira opened her mouth to reply and closed it again when Jasad's image disappeared abruptly, replaced by that of his warship.

"They're flooding subspace with anti-lepton interference," Dax called. "It will cut off our communications with Starfleet."

"They're powering up their forward phasers," O'Brien reported tersely.

"Red alert," Kira ordered automatically. "Shields up."

"*What* shields?" O'Brien asked.

"They're hailing us again," Dax said suddenly, cutting off her curt reply to O'Brien.

Kira waited a moment and then issued her order. "Open the channel." The Cardassian Jasad appeared on the screen. He spoke immediately.

"We do not accept your explanation. Somehow you have destroyed our warship . . ."

"Gul Jasad, I assure you . . ." Kira responded, but she knew that Jasad would not listen to reason.

"We demand the unconditional surrender of this station. Or we will open fire."

Kira knew that was coming. She shot O'Brien a last warning glance about the shields and turned her attention back to the screen.

"I'll need at least a day to make the necessary preparations . . ."

Jasad's response didn't surprise her. "You have an hour," he said curtly.

His face vanished, to be replaced by his ship on the screen. Kira leveled her gaze at O'Brien. She knew that once again she was asking the impossible and didn't care to hear the arguments against it this time.

For a handful of seconds, no one spoke. And then O'Brien said, "I can transfer all available power to establish partial shields around critical areas. But if they hit the docking ring, we'll sustain heavy damage."

Kira gave him a grateful look that said, Do it. O'Brien nodded, and returned to his work.

"Constable," she said quietly to Odo, "if you would coordinate moving all personnel to safer locations . . ."

Odo responded by moving swiftly toward the Promenade.

Kira turned to Dax. "Lieutenant, what was the last reported position of the *Enterprise?*"

"At least twenty hours away," Dax said, with such serene professionalism that Kira felt a deep surge of gratitude toward her despite the bad news.

Twenty hours. Impossible for the virtually unarmed station to last even ten minutes against three Cardassian warships, but Kira had been up against impossible odds her entire life. "We've got to hold out until it gets here."

Most times she had no faith in the prophets—she had seen too many of her people killed for that—although she respected their religion. Yet she had believed in them on the nights she'd had the dream about Sisko, and now she was moved to desperation. It was not right, was not fair, that the commander should try so hard to help, should risk his life on behalf of her people, only to fail, to die.

She had heard rumors of the Kai's great powers and thought surely they were only a myth, but she sent a silent message now to Opaka: *Kai, do you not sense what is happening? Do you not see? Is there nothing you can do to help?*

And if the Kai had chosen Sisko as the messenger of the prophets, why did they abandon him now? *Help him,* Kira pleaded silently. *Help us. If you can hear me, if you can sense what is going on, if you exist at all . . . help.*

Dr. Bashir's normal enthusiasm had turned to quiet shock; he stared at the screen, his handsome olive-skinned face devoid of expression. "I can't believe the Cardassians would attack a Federation outpost."

Kira wheeled on him, intending to lash out, but O'Brien spoke first, his tone heavy. "Doctor, have you ever studied the military history of the border wars? Ever heard of the Setlik Three massacre?" Something in his voice said that he spoke from firsthand experience.

Kira met his gaze, and they shared a look only survivors would understand. "I assume, Mr. O'Brien," she said softly, "you would agree that surrender is not an acceptable option."

O'Brien lifted his chin. "You know what they do to their prisoners, sir."

Yes, Kira thought, and I'm sorry to learn that you do, too. She nodded thoughtfully at the ensign, then turned her attention to Bashir, who stared, still in shock, at the warships looming on the screen.

So much for the adventure of the frontier.

"Did I mention, Doctor," she asked, "that heroes often die young?"

The Ferengi pit boss grabbed Jake, heaved him out of the ventilation duct, and set him down beside a downcast Nog, then retrieved the second bag of gold and handed it to its indignant owner. The group surrounding the gaming table—mostly humanoid and Bajoran miners, covered with soot and sweat and several days' growth of beard—studied the two boys menacingly. The owner of the second bag made a move toward his belt as if to reach for a weapon. Jake was overwhelmed by the sudden urgent conviction that the Ferengi pit boss's presence was the only thing between him and a swift and tragic end.

"Gentlemen, gentlemen . . ." The Ferengi lifted his hands in a mollifying gesture. "My deepest apologies. Drak"—he jerked his head at another Ferengi pit boss—"resume the game. I'm personally taking these young thieves to the security constable's office."

Jake's heart sank. Dad was *sure* to hear about this. If Jake didn't wind up in the brig, at the very least he'd be sentenced to months, maybe even years, inside the dismal living quarters with nothing but holos of Dr. Lamerson to keep him company.

The older Ferengi gave Jake a decidedly hostile nudge and dragged the two culprits out of the casino and onto the Promenade walkway, moving quickly until they reached a secluded alcove, well out of earshot and sight of the casino.

The pit boss stopped abruptly and rounded on his two tender victims, then proceeded to scream at the top of his lungs in Ferengi. He kept repeating one word over and over—the only word in Ferengi that Jake recognized: "Nog."

He glanced over at Nog, who was staring down at the deck with a sullen expression that Jake understood very well—he wore it himself every time Dad started in on one of his lectures. He gazed back at the older Ferengi and said, with innocent surprise, "You're Nog's father." The realization brought with it some small sense of relief; perhaps they weren't going to the security constable's office, after all. It occurred to him that Nog's dad was probably chewing him out for hanging around with a no-good human.

The pit boss turned on him with a vengeance, shoving his huge square face close to Jake's. The boy cowered, partly from the paternal fury, partly from the same strange sour, garlicky smell he'd noticed around Nog. "And you're Commander Sisko's son! Tell me, did your father send you here to find a way to further humiliate me? Or do I owe all this to Nog, who cannot manage even the simplest of tasks without getting caught?" He turned his fury back on his son, finishing the rest of his diatribe in Ferengi.

Jake waited humbly until Nog's father finished, then asked timidly, "Are you going to tell my father?"

The pit boss jabbed at the air in front of Jake's

face, spreading his sharp-nailed fingers like a cat revealing its claws to a foe. "Not only will I tell your father, I will insist that he—"

He was interrupted by a loud voice behind him. Jake looked up, startled, at the strange flat face of the security constable. He'd seen him only once, from a distance, and had asked Dad what sort of alien he was. A shapeshifter, Dad had said—it seemed this body wasn't his real form—but when Jake asked what planet the constable was from, Dad just shook his head. If he really *was* a shapeshifter, Jake decided he wasn't a very good one; he was trying to look like a humanoid, but the nose was too smooth, and he had very thin lips, just a slit for a mouth, and his ears were too smooth, looking like modeling clay that had not been detailed yet.

"Everyone is to evacuate this area," the constable said to Nog's father, in a voice loud enough for passersby to hear, "and proceed to the central market area. Stay away from the buildings."

"Can't you see I'm having a private family discussion here, Odo?" the older Ferengi snarled. "What's going on?"

"Trouble," Odo began, and paused as a computer voice came on the intercom system.

"All civilians and personnel are to proceed immediately to the central market area," the voice said calmly. "This is a red alert. Proceed immediately to the central market area and await further instructions."

"Cardassians," Odo said. "I don't have time to stand here and argue with you. There might be other people on this Promenade more interested than you in surviving an attack." He turned and began to move swiftly away.

"Wait!" Jake cried, with a surge of panic. The constable turned and frowned impatiently at him. "My dad . . . is he back yet with the runabout?"

A glimmer of discomfort crossed the shapeshifter's face. "I don't have time for this."

A memory surfaced unbidden in Jake's mind: him, three years younger and glancing up that last day aboard the *Saratoga* to see the wall burst into flames and come hurtling down toward him. He felt suddenly near tears. "Please, Constable, has my dad come back?"

Odo hesitated, his expression unreadable. "No," he said at last, softly. "The runabout has disappeared inside the wormhole."

"Disappeared?" Jake whispered, unable to comprehend, to make sense of anything except the clutching fear.

"Lost. I have to go warn the others," Odo said, not unkindly. "Please move to the evacuation area." He hurried off before Jake could ask any more questions.

Jake stood, numbed by the news: Dad was lost. That meant he might not ever be found, and Jake might never see his father again.

It had happened the same way with Mom. One minute Jake was in her arms, and the next he was waking up in a strange sickbay and Dad couldn't talk to him about it, except to tell him his mom was gone. Lost, he had said: "We lost your mother." As if they might be able to find her if they all looked hard enough.

He had known this was going to happen. He should never have let Dad come here; he should have run away to Earth long ago, from Planitia when Dad first told him about the transfer to Deep Space Nine. But now it was too late.

He glanced up at a tug on his sleeve; Nog was looking at him with an odd mixture of impatience and compassion.

"Come on, Jake. We have to go."

Inside his quarters aboard the dying *Saratoga,* Sisko coughed and fanned billowing smoke away in an effort to breathe, shrank from the unbearable heat on his exposed face, neck, hands, shrank from the unbearable sight of Jennifer and Jake crushed beneath the bulkhead. Overwhelmed by grief and anger, he shouted at the Hranok-alien beside him.

"I told you I didn't want to be here!"

Hranok's pale blue face undulated in the heat waves thrown off by the fire. "You exist here," he said simply.

"What's the point of bringing me back again to this?"

"We do not bring you here."

Sisko wheeled at the sound of his son's voice behind him, saw a second Jake, three years older and unharmed, dressed in his fishing costume; beside him stood Jennifer, fifteen years younger and wearing the dress she had worn the day he had proposed in Szagy Park.

"We do not bring you here," Jake repeated.

"You bring us here," young Jennifer said.

Hranok gave a single sympathetic nod. "You exist here."

Sisko raised a trembling hand to his warm, sweat-beaded forehead, exhausted by grief and fear and rage, exhausted from trying to understand and be understood. "Just be done with it. Whatever it is we're trying to do here, let's get it over with. *Enough!*"

"Look for solutions from within, Commander," Opaka said, smiling at him through the veil of smoke and flame as she leaned forward on her cane.

Sisko started at the sight of her, and again at the sound of his own voice: "Just help me get her free."

He looked up to see himself, in his fiery quarters aboard the *Saratoga* as it had actually happened three years before. Watched as, a short distance away, a second Hranok looked on as Sisko paced uselessly beside the collapsed bulkhead.

The Bolian scooped the unconscious Jake up in his muscular arms, then gazed with pity at his commander.

"She's gone," Hranok said. "There's nothing we can do."

Sisko watched himself, wanting to close his eyes at the painful scene, wanting to turn away from the past, but compelled to look on the horror.

The past Sisko stared numbly at his charred hands, at his dead wife, at the collapsed, scorched bulkhead, and did not let himself understand. "Transporters," he murmured.

Hranok shook his head. "None of them are functional, sir. We have to go."

The computer's voice, strident over the sounds of chaos: "Warning. Damage to warp core. Containment failure in two minutes."

The past Sisko knelt beside his wife and took her hand. Sisko the watcher remembered the horror of that utterly lifeless, cool touch, gasped at the pain of it.

The past Sisko's voice, rational, reassuring, numbed by the insanity of grief: "You go ahead, Lieutenant. Take the boy."

A security officer appeared in the doorway. Hranok handed the boy off to him.

"I was ready to die," Sisko the watcher whispered as he gazed on his past, aware of others watching beside him: Jake, Jennifer, Opaka, the first Hranok.

"'Die,'" the first Hranok murmured as he watched his double. "What is this?"

Sisko opened his mouth, prepared once again to explain, but it was the Jennifer-alien who answered: "The termination of their linear existence."

He glanced at her in amazement; she reached out toward him and placed a comforting hand on his shoulder, and he looked deep into eyes that were at once familiar and alien, but no longer as alien as they once had seemed. They were now filled with new understanding.

Beyond them, in the fiery scene aboard the *Saratoga,* the second Hranok grabbed Sisko by the arm and yanked him to his feet, speaking with the absolute authority born of desperation: *"Now,* sir."

(*Don't think. Don't* feel . . .)

"No," the past Sisko said, and Sisko the watcher heard the madness beneath the calm. "I can't leave without her."

Hranok pulled, pushed, and propelled his commander toward the door.

"Dammit," the past Sisko said, as the Bolian shoved him through the door and out into the corridor, beyond Sisko the watcher's line of sight. "We can't leave her here."

The words echoed in the corridor and in Sisko the watcher's memory. His gaze swept over the twisted wreckage of what had been his life aboard *Saratoga,* the flames leaping up through the ripped deck, the body of his wife pinned beneath the collapsed bulkhead . . . and a simple realization struck him so forcefully, so resoundingly, that he wondered at his own blindness.

"I've never left this ship," Sisko murmured.

Jennifer nodded soberly, her warm hand still lightly on his shoulder. "You exist here."

Sisko looked with dawning wonder at the hellish scene. "I . . . exist here."

Before him, Hranok led the Sisko from the past gently out of his flaming quarters, away from Jennifer, trapped beneath the wreckage. Sisko the observer stepped forward, taking the place of his double to kneel beside his dead wife and lift her hand. "I don't know if you can understand," he said hollowly. "I see her like this every time I close my eyes. In the darkness, in the blink of an eye, she's there . . . like this."

Jennifer's alien voice came from behind him. "None of your past experiences helped prepare you for this consequence."

Sisko shook his head slowly; his voice dropped to a whisper. "And I've never figured out how to live without her."

"So you chose to live here."

He nodded and drew in a gasping breath, overwhelmed, unable to speak, as the Jennifer-alien moved beside him.

"It is not linear," the alien said.

"No," Sisko whispered harshly, his voice breaking. "It's not . . . linear."

(*Don't think. Don't feel*)

But the wave of emotion swept over him and at last broke. Gently Sisko let go of his dead wife's hand and wept amid the flames.

The alien figures stood quietly as he grieved. When he was finished, Sisko rose and turned to find the Jennifer-alien gone, but Opaka, Jake, and Hranok were waiting for him.

There were no questions left, no longer any need for words. The Jake alien graced him with a faint smile and a look of compassionate understanding; Sisko wiped the tears from his cheeks and returned the smile with gratitude.

CHAPTER 11

"THEIR LEAD SHIP is hailing us." Lieutenant Dax looked up from her Ops station with the singular grace and detachment of a Bajoran Kai—a resounding contrast to Bashir, who fidgeted impatiently nearby. "Gul Jasad wants an answer."

Kira acknowledged with a swift nod and turned toward the engineering station. She forced her breathing to slow, her voice to steady itself; the lives of Sisko and everyone on the station depended now on whether they were able to pull the deception off. "Are you ready, Mr. O'Brien?"

"Yes, sir." O'Brien pressed a final control, then drew back and hovered, poised and intent, over his console. "When they penetrate our Thoron field, the results should raise a few eyebrows over there."

She gave him an approving look—she and O'Brien disagreed on many things, but he had earned her trust—and stared back at the warships as she tried to ignore her quickening pulse. "Then let's give them our answer. Fire six photons across Jasad's bow."

O'Brien released a faint noise of surprise. "We only *have* six photons, Major."

She kept her gaze on the screen. "We're not going to win this battle with torpedoes, Ensign."

His response was almost a sigh of resignation: "Aye, sir."

Kira watched with anxious exhilaration as the torpedoes streaked through the starlit blackness and exploded in dazzling bursts just off the lead warship's starboard bow.

"An urgent hail from Jasad," O'Brien said as the last torpedo was detonating.

Bashir was smiling toothily, with noticeably shaky relief. "I guess we got his attention."

"On screen," Kira said.

Jasad was not shouting now; he was composed, but there was a clear note of incredulity in his tone. "*This* is your answer?"

Kira tilted her chin at him, her stance defiant as she placed a palm firmly on the situation table beside her. She knew that outwardly she exuded confidence; inwardly, though, she wanted to clutch the table desperately to keep from sinking, trembling, to her knees.

But damned if she would kneel, cowering, before any Cardassian. Never again . . .

To Jasad she replied haughtily, "You don't think Starfleet took command of this space station without the ability to defend it, do you?"

His full lips twisted into a sneer. Lucky for him, Kira thought, that the void of space separates us. "Defend it?" Jasad chuckled at the notion. "Your space station could not defend itself against *one* Cardassian warship."

She drew herself up to her full height and took a menacing step toward the screen. "You're probably right, Jasad. And if you were dealing with a Starfleet officer, she'd probably admit we have a hopeless case here." She let her tone grow impassioned, let some of the venomous hatred she felt emerge as she leaned closer to the screen, and was gratified to see the Cardassian shrink back ever so slightly. "But I'm just a Bajoran who's been fighting for a hopeless cause against Cardassians all her life. So if you want a war, I'll give you one."

She drew back, her chest heaving with honest rage; she had meant every word with the whole of her being, and Jasad knew it. The Cardassian shook his head, speechless at her impudence. The screen darkened abruptly and Jasad's image was replaced by that of ships and stars.

"Major," O'Brien said softly from his station, and she wheeled toward him, still angry, auburn hair swinging. The human was studying her with frank admiration, smiling without quite smiling. She blinked at him, taken aback by the sudden shift in emotional intensity.

"Remind me never to get into a game of Roladan

wild draw with you," O'Brien told her earnestly, and Kira almost—*almost*—smiled.

Aboard the bridge of the Cardassian warship, Jasad stared at the space station on his viewscreen with frank puzzlement, index finger to his lips, then glanced up as his second-in-command, Majut, approached. Jasad had no idea what to make of the Bajoran major's threat. He assumed that she was ranting, of course, and throwing out idle threats in her desperation, as all Bajora were wont to do. But how could he be sure her threats were idle, now that Starfleet had command of the base?

Majut gave a slight bow and waited for Jasad to signal with a nod before beginning to speak. "They were using a Thoron field to block our sensors, Gul, but we were able to penetrate it."

"Hmmm . . ." Jasad ran his finger across his lips and down to his chin. "What are their defenses?"

Majut handed his commander a datapadd; Jasad studied it while his second-in-command spoke: "According to our scans, they have an estimated five thousand photons and integrated phaser banks on all levels."

Jasad frowned in amazement at the information before his eyes. "When did they transport all these armaments? How did they install them without our knowledge?"

Majut hesitated, then gestured at the padd in Jasad's hands. "The analysis clearly shows—"

Jasad hurled the padd across the room. Majut

stiffened but remained silent, waiting for his commander to speak first.

Jasad shook his head. "Somehow they've created a massive illusion out of duranium shadows."

"But if it is not an illusion—"

"It *is!*" Jasad roared.

Majut leaned toward him, adopting a soothing, let's-be-reasonable tone. "Why risk a confrontation, Gul? The Fourth Order can be here in a day."

Jasad sighed in utter frustration. "And so can Starfleet." He raised a hand to his forehead and struggled to think.

"They went for it!" Bashir said exultantly, turning toward Dax as if to hug her in his joy. She remained motionless at her station, leaving Bashir to look to the others for support. "We've done it!" he cried.

"Not yet," O'Brien warned tersely. "They're still thinking about it."

Frowning faintly at her console, Dax addressed Kira. "Major, the lead ship is sending out a subspace message asking for reinforcements."

"Yes!" Bashir shoved a fist gleefully in the air.

Unmoved, Kira stared at the screen. She had dealt too long with Cardassians to trust them. "Too soon for a victory celebration, Doctor. . . . Mr. O'Brien?"

The ensign checked his readouts, recoiling slightly at what he saw. "The ships are being deployed into a standard attack formation, sir."

Bashir dropped his arm and fell silent; Kira exchanged grim glances with O'Brien and Dax. As resentful as she had been to learn that Starfleet would be sending personnel to operate the station, she was now even more grateful that these people had come, that she had had the opportunity to work with them, come to know them. And she felt sorry now that they would have to die.

At the very least, she would have the cold comfort of dying in good company. If Bashir could just manage to keep his mouth shut . . .

"Battle stations," Kira told them all quietly, and fought the despair that seized her at the thought that the dreams of the Kai and Sisko, the dreams of the prophets, had all been just that: dreams. Prophets, she asked silently, where are you and your Celestial Temple now that we need you?

Numbed by grief, Jake let the two Ferengi lead him back down the walkway toward the casino.

There was hardly anyone out walking now; most had already made their way to the central market area, and those who hadn't—mostly merchants who were unwilling to leave without first securing their goods—were moving past them at a steady jog.

"Red alert," the computer kept repeating on the overhead intercoms. "Proceed to the central market area *now.*"

At the casino, Nog's father paused. "Go ahead. There are some things I need to attend to."

"I'll help," Nog volunteered, clearly eager to get back in his father's good graces.

"You shouldn't go in there," Jake said dully. "We should all go straight to the market area."

"You go on." Nog gave him a little push.

Jake staggered, but stood his ground. He felt no fear for himself; he could think only of Dad, lost in the wormhole, and of how he had stroked Jake's hair the night before, thinking the boy was asleep.

I was just thinking how much you look like your mom . . .

At the same time, he knew that if there was trouble—if the Cardassians opened fire on the station—it would probably be dangerous to be inside the buildings.

He watched Nog and his father disappear inside the casino.

"Please don't," Jake said, with no one but himself left to hear, and then he heard the deep rumble, like an earthquake, as the deck lurched beneath him and knocked him off his feet.

The Ops deck shuddered beneath the heels of Kira's boots; she shifted her weight, managing to keep her balance. That was not a direct hit, thank the prophets; she keyed up a schematic of the station on her console and saw that the charges had exploded off the docking ring.

As the station rocked under the impact, O'Brien called out to her: "They may just be testing us. I could run a pulse compression wave through the phaser banks, put out a blast that'll make them think twice."

"Do it," Kira ordered, and clutched the console with one hand as the deck shook again.

She watched along with the others as the phaser blast streaked toward the Cardassian warship and made contact with vessel. No yelps of victory from Bashir now; he stood in somber silence beside Dax as the afterimage of the blast faded, revealing damage to the warship's hull.

But the Cardassians' fire showed no sign of easing. Kira held on with both hands this time as the station rocked.

"Damage report," Kira shouted, but even before O'Brien could reply, she knew that the habitat ring had been struck.

"Direct hit," he called out. "Level fourteen. Empty storage bays . . . no casualties."

Her relief was short-lived.

"Shields are down to twenty-seven percent," Dax called, just before Kira's world heaved to one side with a deafening roar, slamming her facedown onto the deck.

The shaking got worse before it eased a bit; Jake lay on the dirty metal deck, pawing it with his fingertips as if to somehow grip it, to hold on. He drew in deep breaths and shook off the panicked thought that he was back on the *Saratoga* and they were all about to die. It was going to be all right, he told himself. He was on the space station, and the

Cardassians had fired on them, but they had stopped now, and he was okay.

So long as he didn't let himself think about Dad. If the Cardassians had used their weapons on the station, what had they done to the small runabout?

It's okay. The runabout's lost in the wormhole, remember? The Cardassians probably can't find him, either . . .

Small comfort. *If you ever make it out, Dad, I swear I'll never complain about this space station again. And I'll never ask about Earth. Just make it out . . . please . . .*

Jake forced himself to stop thinking and scrambled to his feet. The Promenade shuddered again, but this time he was ready for it and managed to keep his balance by extending his arms; he was afraid to support himself against the rickety-looking shopfront.

"Nog?" he yelled into the casino. "Nog, we've got to hurry!"

No reply, but Jake could hear movement and the clank of metal inside the structure. He felt oddly guilty deserting Nog and his father, although they certainly hadn't done him any favors; he reassured himself with the thought that Dad would want him to leave and get to safety. If Nog and his father wanted to ignore Constable Odo, that was their business; Jake had done what he could. "I'm going now!" he shouted as he turned and loped down the walkway.

Without warning, the floor beneath him shuddered, then heaved straight up into the air, as if a giant had grabbed hold of the station and shaken it like a rug. Jake sailed upward a good quarter-meter, then plummeted face forward, striking the metal floor painfully, first with his elbows, then with his chin, causing his teeth to clamp down on his tongue.

The movement was accompanied by an earsplitting roar. Jake lay where he fell, tasting blood as he burrowed his face into his arms and covered his head with his hands to protect it from the rain of metal fragments.

He lay motionless for a few seconds until he was sure the rain of metal and the shaking had stopped, and then he rolled onto his side and sat up with a groan, gingerly pressing his fingertips to his bruised chin.

Several meters to his right, fire tore up through the deck; as he watched, a second burst of flame made its way along the left side of the deck. He stumbled to his feet, ran back to the casino, and peered inside, only to be horrified at the sight of flames shooting through smoke near the bar. It was a small fire that could easily be quenched by an automatic extinguishing system—assuming it worked better than the other systems on the station—but Jake was not reassured.

"Nog!" he screamed.

The Ferengi emerged from the center of the haze and ran gasping into the walkway.

"My father," Nog croaked, waving back at the

center of the flames before he doubled over coughing. The Promenade rocked under the impact of another blast. He and Jake clung to each other in an effort to stay on their feet.

Jake stared back at the flames for an instant, then ran across the walkway and pounded on the nearest public comm panel. "Constable Odo—anyone!"

He broke off at the sound of static coming through the grid. Farther down the walkway, toward the central market area, he could see flames spurting up through the deck; the fires looked worse down at that end of the Promenade. Help would be some time in coming.

Moans began to emanate from the casino's interior. Without thinking, Jake drew in a lungful of oxygen and dashed inside toward the fire. It was small and contained; the smoke was worse than the flames. Jake fanned the air with his hands, straining to see through stinging tear-filled eyes.

Nog's father lay writhing on his side between the staircase and the bar, alternating moans with coughs. The heavy metal railing had fallen across his legs. Flames shot up from beneath the deck near the bar, precariously close to the older Ferengi; heat waves glimmered near his feet. At the sight of Jake, he said in a wavering voice, "Help me," then covered his face with his arms and yielded to a coughing fit.

Jake reached for the railing and let go almost instantly, yelping as the hot metal blistered his fingers and palms.

He thought suddenly of Dad aboard the *Saratoga,* finding his wife and son trapped beneath the burning bulkhead, and he recalled, with a sense of revelation, that Dad's hands had been bandaged that first awful day when Jake woke up in the starbase sickbay. He had seen them, but never really registered them before. He had been too full of his own pain to think of Dad's. . . .

Hearing a bleat beside him, almost in his ear, he looked around to see Nog, fearful, hovering beside him, wringing his hands.

"We can't stay!" the young Ferengi cried. "The system's not working! The fire's—"

"Then you go!" Jake shouted angrily. "I'm just a stupid human and I can't leave him here like—"

The lights dimmed as the floor pitched under the impact of another blast, causing him to stagger toward the fire, waving his arms in an effort to keep his balance; his hands and forearms brushed the flames. He closed his eyes at the heat on his face. A surprisingly strong grip caught him and yanked him back. He stood, dazed and coughing, as Nog swiftly patted out a glowing cinder on his sleeve. The older Ferengi's moaning redoubled, as if the motion had caused him great pain.

There was a tinkling crash at the bar; bottles had fallen over, and some were cracked and leaking. Some of the contents dripped onto the floor. They watched in horror as the puddle burst into flame with a soft *whoosh.*

* * *

When the alert sounded, Keiko's first impulse was to return to her quarters. She was too well trained in Starfleet procedure to even consider trying to contact Miles, though she wanted to desperately. He would be far too busy, and speaking to him now would only distract him from his efforts to defend the station.

And so Keiko scooped Molly up in her arms and hurried back toward the turbolift. She stopped, frightened people streaming past, when she realized the lifts might no longer be safe.

She turned and headed with the fleeing crowd toward the open area, not quite able to believe the station was really under attack. The Cardassians were probably violating their peace treaty with the Federation, but why?

She did not allow herself to yield to fear. She had been on the *Enterprise* when it was attacked, and she had survived, even when they faced the worst of all enemies, the Borg. Of course, that had been before Molly was born; it was easier, then, when she risked only her own life. But for Molly's sake, she dared not panic.

But the girl sensed the fear of the others and began to cry, wriggling so violently in her mother's arms that Keiko could scarcely hold on to her.

"Not now, Molly! We have to hurry. Just let Mommy carry you."

Molly began wailing like a little Klaxon and redoubled her wriggling; Keiko gritted her teeth and held on tight, almost running to try to keep pace with the swarm of escapees. She had no idea where the central market area was, but she trusted the crowd, most of whom were Bajoran, to lead her to the right place.

A loud rumble, like thunder; the floor shuddered and pitched to Keiko's right. She stumbled into the Bajoran woman in front of her, almost falling, squeezing Molly so hard that the child cried out, elbows and knees struck her back and sides as others around her staggered, trying to keep their balance. Soft cries of fear rippled through the crowd. Molly began to whimper.

"It's okay," Keiko gasped. "Hold on to Mommy, sweetheart. Hold on *tight.*"

Wide-eyed and silent now, the girl clung to her mother as they began moving again, more slowly this time. Despite the explosion, the crowd quieted as a Bajoran man moved through, speaking in a voice both commanding and comforting:

"Remain calm, please, and don't run. Your chances of reaching the evacuation site safely will be much better." He reached out and put a restraining hand on a young man running past; the man immediately slowed down.

It was the security constable, Keiko realized, the one Miles had told her about, and as he approached, she could see what Miles had meant about his not being able to "pull off a proper Bajoran." She had never seen a shapeshifter before, but as Constable Odo passed, she lowered her eyes and fought the impulse to stare. Miles had described Odo as a cynical curmudgeon who was

was none too pleasant to be around, but at the moment, Keiko was grateful for the effect his presence had on the crowd.

They had almost reached the evacuation site when the deck lurched again. Keiko fell to one knee, was helped up by another Bajoran, and kept going. Molly was too terrified to make a sound.

Another explosion, and another. Keiko gave up trying to move forward and simply concentrated on keeping her footing. "It's all right," she repeated softly, kissing the top of Molly's head and jiggling her as she had done when the girl was an infant. "Mommy's right here. It'll all be over soon."

"Daddy," Molly wailed, and buried her face in Keiko's neck.

"Daddy's all right," she said, swallowing sudden tears. "He's at Ops, sweetheart, taking care of everything. He's making sure we're all right. We'll see him tonight at dinner." Oh, how easy it was now to think it had been a mistake to come here.

"Want *Daddy,"* Molly murmured into her mother's neck. Keiko blinked hard and tried to distract herself from the tears by looking up through the observation windows.

Beyond the farthest one, she could make out the forward hull of a Cardassian warship, and saw the phaser beam streak through the starlit darkness before it struck.

The world tilted on end; the sound of rending metal shrieked in her eardrums. Keiko was thrown hard onto her side, unable to think, to breathe, to hold on to her child. She covered her head against a hail of shrapnel from the nearest building. A burst of orange-red flared in her line of vision.

She pushed herself to a sitting position, then scrambled to her feet along with others beside her. Only a few meters away, fire blazed up through a rip in the metal deck. As she watched, a second, smaller blaze erupted nearby, then a third.

The blast had struck a fuel conduit, Keiko realized. And if they didn't contain it fast, the entire Promenade would go up in flames. The others around her scattered and ran away.

Keiko looked on the deck beside her. "Molly?"

No sign of the girl, only of panicked Bajora and Ferengi and humans fleeing as they cried out to their lost companions. Constable Odo seemed to have vanished. Keiko stood in the center of the confusion and began to scream as the crowd swelled past her like a tide, jostling her, forcing her to move backwards with it or be pulled under and crushed in the stampede.

"Molly!"

O'Brien reached for his console and pulled himself to his feet. Below him, at Master, Kira had just struggled up and had opened her mouth to issue an order when Dax called over the chaos, "A fuel conduit has ruptured on the Promenade."

O'Brien felt a sudden chill of fear and remembered the dream he'd had about the Setlik massacre and Captain Maxwell . . . and the odd, clutching conviction that Keiko and Molly were in mortal danger from the Cardassians.

Ridiculous, of course. They were probably in their quarters, safe but frightened . . . but O'Brien's fear refused to yield to logic.

He forced it aside, forced himself to concentrate on the question Major Kira addressed to him: "Can you divert the main power flow?"

His fingers began working his panel before she could get the words out, but the result made him grimace in frustration. "Controls are locked."

A voice emanating from the comm grid interrupted. "Odo to Ops."

O'Brien could hear the clear ring of barely suppressed panic in the constable's tone. Kira pressed the comm control, her expression grim; she knew, as did O'Brien, why Odo had called. "Go ahead."

"I've got wounded people down here! Have you seen that doctor of yours anywhere?"

Dear God, O'Brien prayed as he continued to struggle with the controls, let Keiko and Molly have stayed in their quarters. Don't let them be down there.

Kira turned toward Bashir, but he was already moving for the turbolift. "On my way," he called, without pausing to look at her, and for the first time, the major looked honestly glad to have the young doctor on the station.

Not that it mattered that much, really, O'Brien thought, yielding to a surge of despair: Bashir could only ease the discomfort of the wounded. They were all dying, now; it was just a matter of time before the Cardassians ruptured another fuel line, and another, and another, until the station went up in a blaze that would light up the Bajoran sky like a small sun.

Just the way they had killed on Setlik, showing no mercy to the young or the aged, killing until they forced men like Captain Maxwell and O'Brien himself to become murderers. O'Brien thought of Maxwell, driven to the brink of insanity after the loss of his family. How easy it would be, if Keiko and Molly were gone, to take his revenge on them, to kill and kill and kill. . . .

The turbolift had just descended out of sight when the station reeled again. And again. And again.

O'Brien's expression hardened as he hung on to his console through the shaking. He'd be damned if he would let the Cardies win this one, damned if he would give in to fear and despair. Before he let anything happen to Molly and Keiko, he would fight the Cardassians off with his bare hands.

O'Brien set his jaw, stepped down from Engineering and staggered across Master, muttering as much to himself as to Kira. "I'm going to have to shut down the primary power flow or the whole Promenade will go up." He crossed over to the pit, swung his legs into the hole, and crawled down. "Bloody Cardies . . . We just fixed the damn thing."

* * *

In the casino Nog cried out in alarm as a new blaze started in the spilled liquor. Jake remained silent and tried to think. He knew the second the fire would spread to the other bottles, the entire place would go up quickly, and there would be no time to save Nog's father. Billowing smoke engulfed the older Ferengi as the blaze moved closer to his feet, but he was in more immediate danger from smoke inhalation, Jake realized, than from burns.

The lights flickered again, then went out entirely, reducing Nog and his father to hazy silhouettes backlit by fire glow.

Dad must have felt like this, Jake thought—helpless and scared and overwhelmed—but he had found a way to help, had found a way to face the smoke and the fire and the fear, and had saved Jake's life. . . .

"We've got to put it out," he shouted. "Are there any manual fire extinguishers? Any backup systems?"

Nog shook his head.

"Is there any water behind the bar?"

Nog released a whine of fear and backed away from the increasing flames.

"Is there water?" Jake demanded, grabbing his shoulder.

Nog moved so suddenly and swiftly that Jake at first thought he was running away, but the younger Ferengi skirted the flames, brushing against them, and ran behind the bar. He returned with water-soaked cloths and gave one to his father, who placed it over his mouth and nose, and one to Jake, who began slapping out the flames with it. Nog joined him.

The floor and walls continued to rattle with the impact of continued explosions, causing the two of them to stagger drunkenly to keep their balance. Even so, within a minute they had reduced the small fire to a pile of steaming cinders.

Gasping and coughing, his throat and eyes burning, Jake nevertheless felt a surge of exhilaration. He looked over at his friend as Nog flicked his cloth and extinguished the last small tongue of flame. Perspiration rolled down the young Ferengi's smudged face, mingling with the tears streaming from the corners of his eyes. The smoke, heat, adrenaline, and effort had left them exhausted, but there was no time to rest.

Still holding the damp cloth to his nose, the older Ferengi had calmed down somewhat, but he remained glassy-eyed with pain. Jake called for some thick, dry cloths. Nog nodded and hurried back behind the bar.

Nog was okay, Jake decided, as he watched the Ferengi gather the cloths. Maybe he was a thief and sometimes a bit of a coward, but he could be counted on in a crisis. And he certainly wasn't dumb.

Nog scurried back and gave Jake a dry cloth, then took one of his own and wrapped it around one end of the metal railing that pinned his father to the floor. Jake wrapped his cloth around the other end of the hot metal and nodded at Nog when he had both hands in place.

Jake pulled up with all his might, letting his thigh muscles push up against the burden until they ached.

As he tugged, he remembered the Bolian lieutenant, Hranok, who had served with Dad on the *Saratoga.* Hranok had come to the starbase sickbay to talk to Jake when Dad was not there. He had not told him everything, Jake suspected, but he had told how Dad had struggled so hard trying to free his wife and child. . . . Struggled, but nothing had happened. The bulkhead was too heavy. . . .

Across from him, Nog gritted his teeth and released a low, hoarse groan as he strained.

Slowly, slowly, they lifted the heavy railing . . . one millimeter, then two. With a shriek, Nog pulled even harder, beyond all possibility, and Jake pulled with him, every muscle crying out with effort. The railing trembled, then rose farther upward.

The station rocked. Through a miracle of chance, Jake managed to keep his balance and hold on, able now to feel the metal's heat passing through the cloth, but the railing dropped precariously close to the older Ferengi's chest.

Awful. It must have been so awful for Dad, to have tried and tried and been without help, to have had to leave her lying there. . . . If it had been Jake trying to lift the bulkhead alone, he would have stayed with her, would not have been able to leave her there, but Dad had left, not because he was weaker but because he was so strong. He had left out of love for his living son. . . .

Jake cried out and strained against the railing;

Nog followed suit. At last the railing rose far enough for the older Ferengi to pull himself free, dragging the wounded leg behind him. Both boys let go at the same time, flinching as the metal struck the floor with a loud clank.

"Under his shoulder," Jake said, and went into a paroxysm of coughing. When it passed, he and Nog slipped under the older Ferengi's arms. It was awkward, and Nog's father grimaced at the pain, but it worked well enough to get them out of the casino and onto the walkway, where Jake drew a deep, sighing breath.

They moved down the walkway like a halting, wounded six-legged beast, heading toward the central market area. Jake could see streams of black smoke rising from other recently extinguished blazes. Nog's father began to speak in Ferengi to his son, in a hoarse but surprisingly brisk lecturing tone.

They had made it to the fringes of the crowd gathered in the marketplace before Jake got up the nerve to ask his friend, "What'd he say?"

Nog's eyes narrowed slyly. "He says you set a very bad example for me, hew-man. He says it was very stupid to risk our lives by saving him. No self-respecting Ferengi would have done so."

Jake rolled his eyes and sighed with disgust.

Nog favored him with a toothy expression that could have been a smile or a grimace of pain. "He also says to thank you."

Jake turned to the adult Ferengi with a grin and said, "You're welcome," but his words were drowned out by the roar of another direct hit on the station.

"Molly!" Keiko screamed, as she was pulled backwards by those fleeing the fire. The flames from the broken fuel line leapt higher; she could feel the heat on her face. She desperately scanned the crowd for any sign of Molly, but the toddler seemed to have been swallowed up. Keiko surrendered to panic; Molly was so tiny, she could easily have been crushed in the stampede. "Oh, gods, Molly!"

This is all your fault. You should never have talked Miles into accepting this promotion. . . .

Stop it. Calm. Try to stay calm. If she was hurt, she'll be lying back closer to the fire.

Keiko fought her way against the tide and broke free. Station fire fighters, all of them Bajoran, had managed to get past the crowd and were already starting to control the blaze with portable extinguishers; apparently the damage to the station had knocked out the automatic systems.

"Have you seen a little girl? A little human girl?" Keiko cried out to them, but they were preoccupied with the fire and only one noticed her and responded with a shrug. She swept her gaze over the deserted deck: no Molly. If the child *had* been crushed, she would have been lying there. . . .

Don't think about it, she warned herself. Just don't think about it.

Fighting tears, Keiko turned and jogged back toward the group, which had slowed its insane rush and was reassembling farther down the walkway.

"Molly?" Keiko shouted the instant she reached the edges of the crowd. This morning's depression and self-pity seemed a million light-years distant, utterly ridiculous, meaningless in the face of losing her child. "Has anyone seen a little girl? A two-year-old human girl?"

Most were too frantic, or too busy murmuring to others, to hear her question; but a few, mostly Bajora, looked on her with pity. One of them, a young male, opened his mouth to say something, but his words were lost in the deep rumble of another explosion.

Keiko lost her footing and fell on her rump. She made no attempt to get up once the shaking stopped, but sat, peering through people's legs in hopes of spotting Molly from a child's perspective.

An outstretched hand made her look up.

Constable Odo stood over her. His odd, crudely formed features were difficult for Keiko to read—the lack of eyebrows and lips gave his face the look of an expressionless mask—but she clearly saw the concern in his eyes.

"Are you injured?" he asked. His tone was brusque, almost uncaring; an act, Keiko decided. She clasped his hand—a little surprised that his hand felt like normal, warm flesh—and let him pull her to her feet.

"No," she answered, embarrassed at her tearful, wavering tone; she fought to keep her voice steady. "But my little girl, Molly—Chief O'Brien's daughter—I can't find her. We were separated during an explosion when everyone started running." She scanned the crowd as she spoke.

"Well, she couldn't have gotten very far," Odo said impatiently, as if eager to solve this problem and continue his patrol. He turned and followed her gaze, then shouted loudly in Bajoran. The assembly immediately hushed and listened as Odo continued, apparently inquiring after Molly.

When he finished, a murmur rippled through the crowd; from its farthest edges, a female voice shouted a reply in Bajoran. There was a thin, familiar wail that made Keiko put a hand to her heart and step forward, and then Molly appeared, crying and kicking, held aloft by alien hands, which passed her overhead from one pair of arms to another.

"Molly!" Keiko cried, no longer restraining the tears, and spun around toward Odo, who was already trying to make good his escape. She clutched his arm. "Oh, Constable, *thank* you!"

Odo recoiled in distaste and pulled himself free from Keiko's grip. *"Please,* madam. There isn't time." He had taken only step away from her when one of the fire fighters, his expression urgent, approached and dragged him away.

"Thank you anyway," Keiko said to his receding back, and pushed her way through the crowd to her sobbing child.

On the Promenade, the lights flickered once, then went out entirely, but the explosions did not ease.

Odo knelt over the unconscious Bajoran woman and was afraid. Not for his life—he was not frightened of dying at the hands of Cardassians; he had lived with that threat all of his remembered life, since the Bajora had taken him in—but he had never felt so utterly, completely helpless. He had no instinct, no understanding for humanoid bodies at all, which was why he was capable of reproducing only the crudest semblance of one. And he had not the slightest inkling of what to do when one was injured, which was one of the reasons he insisted so strongly on the Promenade's no-weapons rule.

The wounded woman stirred slightly and groaned. She was young, attractive, one of the shopkeepers; Odo had seen her many times on the Promenade, often enough to have a nodding acquaintance with her. The worst explosion had shattered a shopfront. The flying shrapnel had struck the woman's neck; a puddle of blood was collecting beside her head.

She was bleeding to death, and Odo had not the faintest idea what to do.

She sighed and opened dark, frightened eyes, to stare up into his face.

"It's all right," he reassured her gently in Bajoran. "You're going to be all right. The doctor is coming."

She parted her lips as if to speak, but he could only hear the sound of her rapid breathing. Her eyes remained entirely blank and uncomprehending for an instant, then slowly closed.

Desperate, Odo pressed his hand against her wound—he felt he should try to do *something* to stop the bleeding—and shuddered at the warm, sticky feel of blood on his fingers, at the sickening metallic-organic smell. The sensation made him dizzy, and he took in a deep breath and closed his eyes.

Movement beside him made him open them. For the first time since the young human's arrival, Odo was truly glad to see Dr. Bashir.

The doctor knelt beside them and quickly swept a tricorder over the woman, his movements as confident and practiced as if he had been doing this for a hundred years. Odo felt a nearly overwhelming surge of relief.

Bashir narrowed his eyes at the readout, set the tricorder aside, and, without warning, grabbed Odo's hand.

Odo made a noise of surprise and drew back, but Bashir's movements were firm and tolerated no resistance. He guided Odo's finger to a precise spot on the woman's neck.

"Press there," Bashir said brusquely. *"Hard."*

Odo pressed hard, realized with a shock that he was pressing on the woman's artery, *inside* the wound, and felt his head swim in another wave of dizziness. He began to pull away. "Look, Doctor, maybe I should find you someone—"

More skilled in the medical arts, he was going to say, but Bashir grasped his hand again and said, in a tone so commanding it would have rendered Major Kira docile: *"Hold it there."*

Odo blinked. Mastered his dizziness. Pressed with his finger, hard, in the precise spot. The bleeding stopped, giving Bashir time to retrieve a surgical laser from his medikit and cradle the woman's head firmly in his free hand. The young doctor leaned over his patient with an intensity of concentration Odo had never seen and began to wield the laser.

Odo was still motionless, still pressing hard, still marveling over Bashir's skill when the lights came back on.

"That should do it for a while," O'Brien said, starting to climb out of the pit just as another blast struck the station. He reeled, almost lost his balance, but managed to hang on to the edge of the pit until the shuddering eased. He pulled himself out and ran, crouched in anticipation of another hit, to his station.

"Shields at eighteen percent and falling," Dax called calmly, as if she were not heralding her own doom.

Kira gripped the edge of the console as if to dig her fingers into the metal and stared at the warships with a bitter sense of failure and depthless rage at herself for having trusted the prophets and her own foolish dreams. Her whole life had been one protracted struggle against this enemy, and now she had lost.

Just as her people, her planet, would ultimately lose.

O'Brien must have sensed her desperation, for he said, "I might still be able to give you one more round, Major."

Kira pulled her hand away from the console and

stood without support. "No," she said evenly, ignoring the pain that pierced her; there was nothing to be done now except to die with honor, without fear. "Signal the lead Cardassian ship that we will proceed with the—"

"Major," Dax interrupted, her normally even tone filled with an excitement that made Kira swivel her head to stare at her. "I'm reading a neutrino disturbance fifteen kilometers off the forward docking ring." She looked up at Kira with a dazzling smile. "It's the wormhole!"

Kira inhaled sharply, somehow managing to expel the words during the intake of breath: "On screen."

The wormhole exploded into view, shattering the darkness with a shimmering rainbow blaze of light. The Celestial Temple, Kira thought. To her mind, it was the most beautiful sight she had ever seen. She grinned back at Dax, whose beatific expression was softly illuminated with reflected glow, then returned her gaze to the screen.

In the mouth of the wormhole, the tiny runabout appeared, followed by a gigantic Cardassian warship some fifty times its size.

Sisko's voice, loud and triumphant, came over the comm: "*Rio Grande* to DS Nine."

Kira felt overwhelmed to the point of tears; the emotion was quickly replaced by disgust at her own weakness. "On screen," she repeated brusquely, but could not quite keep herself from grinning at the sight of Sisko, perfectly unharmed and grinning himself, in the runabout's cockpit. "Go ahead, Commander."

"Sorry to be so late," Sisko apologized, with a casualness that the brightness in his eyes belied. "I didn't know we were having company. Clear me for docking, Mr. O'Brien."

"Aye, sir," O'Brien replied with gusto. "Cleared for pad C."

Thank you, Kira thought, no longer caring whether the entities to whom she addressed her gratitude existed or not. *Thank you . . .*

And laughed as, for the first time, she realized the firing had stopped.

Sisko stepped through the airlock onto the Promenade feeling like a man reborn. For the first time in three years, he felt freed of his grief, freed of the past, able to look at the future. He could see how holding on to his own grief had harmed Jake, but that had changed now; things could only improve between them.

He knew what he wanted: the clouds of guilt and self-pity had lifted, leaving him with clear vision. He wanted to remain on DS Nine, wanted to continue to help the Bajorans. He felt a kinship with these people; they, like him, had been given another chance, a fresh beginning.

But turning down the position at Vasteras University was not a decision he could make alone; he would have to talk about it with Jake. The boy's feelings had to be considered. . . .

Sisko's attention drifted to the Promenade. One of the shopfronts had been heavily damaged, and he could see where one of the buried fuel lines had erupted, scorching the deck. A crowd had gathered out on the walkway, already helping to clean up the rubble, and a short distance away, Odo and Bashir were crouched over a wounded Bajoran and talking in such a decidedly amicable fashion that Sisko blinked and did a double take.

"Dad!" Jake ran out of the crowd and threw himself into his father's arms with such force that Sisko staggered backwards. He recovered and hugged the boy with a surge of love so fierce he blinked back tears.

"Dad . . ." Jake choked, gripping his father as if afraid to ever let go. "I was so scared you . . . you wouldn't come back."

"It's okay," Sisko soothed, patting the boy's back as he would an infant's. "It's okay. I'm home." He held his son until he felt Jake relax in his arms, then gently moved him to an arm's distance and studied him closely. "My God, Jake . . ." Sisko sniffed the air. "You smell like smoke! Are you okay?"

"Yeah. There was a fire in the casino, but we put it out." Jake grinned crookedly, his soot-smudged face animated, his eyes glittering with held-back tears and enthusiasm. "I knew you'd come back, even after Odo said the runabout had disappeared in the wormhole. You shoulda seen it, Dad, it was really scary for a while. The Cardassians were firing on us, and the whole Promenade was shaking, but Nog and I put out the fire and helped his father because the metal railing fell on him. He broke his leg but he's gonna be okay, Dr. Bashir said, and—"

"Whoa, whoa, whoa, there, partner," Sisko said, crouching down to Jake's eye level and smiling at the boy's warp-speed chatter. "You and *Nog?"*

"Yeah. He's really not so bad, even though he's a Ferengi. He got really scared when the Cardassians were firing on us—he hates the Cardassians—and I swear I didn't steal anything, Dad, honest, no matter what anyone says. And then there was a really bad explosion and the deck caught on fire, and Nog's dad was hurt, but I think he's going to be okay." Jake stopped and blinked as though the thought had finally occurred to him. "Are *you* okay, Dad? What *happened* out there?"

"I've never been better," Sisko said softly, rising. "I'll tell you all about it when we get back to our quarters. And maybe I'll talk to you a little bit about the Ferengi and this, uh, not-stealing-anything business. But I need to take care of a few things first." He slipped an arm around the boy's shoulders and together they walked over to Odo and Bashir. The Bajoran woman they were tending smiled up at Sisko in faint recognition.

"Casualties?" Sisko asked.

Bashir looked up at him, his expression serious, his demeanor confident. He seemed decades older than the young doctor Sisko had met that first day. "Thirteen injured, Commander. None seriously." As the doctor spoke, Odo listened quietly with something that looked suspiciously like respect.

Sisko nodded and moved with Jake toward a turbolift. "There's something I need to talk to you about tonight," he told the boy. "A decision I need you to help me make. I got a job offer earlier today, as a professor at a university."

"A university?" Jake wrinkled his nose at the thought. "You mean you'd be a teacher?"

"Yes."

"Well . . . is that really what you want to do, Dad? It doesn't sound very exciting."

Sisko took a deep breath and tried to keep his tone as neutral as possible. "It's at Vasteras University, Jake. On Earth."

He braced himself for an excited outburst, for Jake to fling himself into his father's arms again, but instead, the boy frowned at the decks passing by the open turbolift door and said, in an oddly subdued voice: "Oh."

"I thought you'd be happy," Sisko said.

"Well . . ." Jake hesitated, then straightened his small shoulders as if determinedly confronting an unpleasant task. When he spoke again, his tone was so mature that Sisko felt a welling-up of love and pride. "I guess I'm happy if you're happy. I just . . . I just don't care where we live anymore, Dad. I want you to do what you want to do."

The tiny catch in his voice made Sisko ask, "But . . . ?"

"Well . . ." Jake hung his head and stared at the turbolift floor. "I'd have to leave Nog." He looked back up at his father. "I mean, I've hardly had any time to get to know him." Hastily he added, "But it would be okay, Dad, if that's what you want to do."

A slow smile spread over Sisko's face; he patted

the boy's shoulder gently. "I think we can manage to give you that time, Jake." Before he could say more, the lift came to a stop at Ops.

As the two of them stepped out, Dax called: "The Cardassians are waiting to speak to you, Benjamin."

Sisko let go of Jake and strode over to Master beside Kira, who greeted him with a broad smile. "On screen," Sisko said.

The images of Gul Jasad and Dukat appeared before him.

Sisko graced them with a tight little smile. "Welcome back, Gul Dukat."

"Commander." Dukat revealed a white sliver of teeth. "I'm pleased that we were able to escort you safely home."

Sisko exchanged a faintly amused look with Kira. "Gentlemen," he said formally, "I've made contact with the life-forms that created this wormhole."

Jasad leaned forward with a bit more eagerness than Sisko suspected he'd meant to reveal. "We look forward to your arranging appropriate introductions."

Sisko continued, ignoring the interruption. "They have agreed to allow us to use it to explore the Gamma Quadrant."

Jasad straightened his back and began in a threatening tone: "Then I must state our position that this phenomenon is clearly in territory that has been controlled by the Cardassian Empire for six decades, and as such—"

Sisko cut him off. *"I've* made an agreement with

these beings *on behalf of the planet Bajor* that allows for safe passage through the wormhole." In the periphery of his vision, Kira turned her head sharply to stare at him. "Those who violate that agreement will find themselves lost between here and the Gamma Quadrant. If you care to challenge what I am saying, I suggest you fly back into the wormhole and see for yourselves."

A long silence passed as the Cardassians scowled at him. And then Dukat asked, with no small amount of bitterness, "Just who *are* these beings?"

Sisko opened his mouth to begin a long explanation . . . then stopped and smiled faintly as a simpler, truer answer occurred to him. "The prophets of the Celestial Temple."

He turned to find Kira gazing at him with unmasked wonder.

"Good morning," Jean-Luc Picard said pleasantly, but there was a hesitancy, a barely perceptible hint of defensiveness in his manner as he lingered in the doorway to the station commander's office.

Sisko glanced up from his monitor, where he had just terminated the comm link with Opaka, and rose. "Captain."

He extended his hand and crossed to where Picard stood. This time Sisko smelled no smoke, heard no wailing, saw no red flash of a sensorscope, no monstrous hybrid of metal and skin. This time he saw only a man, a very human man made of flesh and blood, who had been deeply scarred by the Borg.

Sisko forgot his own pain and considered Picard's, and felt ashamed of his earlier behavior; he had succeeded in easing none of his own grief, only in adding to the captain's. He could not imagine what demons his words had evoked. He wanted to explain, to apologize, but could find no words.

He clasped Picard's hand firmly, as he would an old friend's, and was relieved when the captain returned the pressure. Picard narrowed his eyes slightly, curious about this sudden warmth, as he studied Sisko.

Forgive me, Sisko wanted to say, but the words died in his throat. Instead he smiled, very faintly, in apology.

Picard caught the smile and returned it, very faintly, and in it Sisko thought he saw a trace of gratitude.

He released Picard's hand and motioned for the captain to sit. Picard sat, and Sisko returned to his chair behind the desk.

Picard spoke first. "So, Commander. Apparently your transfer to DS Nine has already borne fruit. I'm most curious to hear how you managed to locate the wormhole."

Sisko grinned and told him, explaining about Kai Opaka and the orb, about Dax's use of Bajoran mythology to help locate the entrance, about the Celestial Temple, about the Cardassian attack and Kira and O'Brien's valiant efforts to save both Sisko and the station.

Picard listened with great interest, nodding with

approval at Sisko's praise for his officers, and at his optimistic outlook on the effect the wormhole would have on the Bajoran economy.

". . . And the Cardassians have made it clear they are prepared to cooperate," Sisko finished, realizing with a twinge of sheepishness that he had been prattling on, nonstop and at warp speed, for some time, just as Jake had when he'd met his father coming out of the airlock. "At least for now."

Picard wore a small smile, knuckles to his chin, index finger resting against his cheek, apparently enjoying the commander's show of enthusiasm. "It seems you've put Bajor on the map, Commander. This should become a leading center of commerce and scientific exploration." He shifted his weight in the chair and leaned forward. "And for Starfleet, one of our most important ports."

"Captain," Sisko said awkwardly, and hesitated; Picard looked at him questioningly. "Regarding our conversation about someone to replace me . . ."

"I'm sorry. I haven't had the time to communicate it to Command." Picard's expression grew opaque, unreadable.

Sisko relaxed in relief. "I would prefer that you ignore it, sir."

Picard tilted his lean, angular face, eyeing Sisko in a manner that said this was not going to be so easy. "I'm not sure I can, Commander. Are you certain this is what you want? Because we can't afford to have someone in command here who—"

"I'm certain, sir," Sisko interrupted firmly.

Picard regarded him in silence for some time. Then he stood up and extended his open hand across the commander's desk. "Good luck, Sisko."

"Good luck to *you,* sir," Sisko responded as he shook the captain's hand. Picard blinked in surprise at first, but then his expression shifted, grew somber, and Sisko had no doubt that the captain understood perfectly well what was meant.

"Thank you," Picard said softly.

CHAPTER 12

KEIKO SAT in their quarters, legs curled beneath her, on the overstuffed Cardassian settee and watched her husband and child at play. Miles lay on the floor and hoisted Molly into the air, jiggling her until she cackled ecstatically. It was late, more than two hours past Molly's bedtime, but Keiko didn't have the heart to put her to bed. The child didn't seem at all drowsy, and Keiko knew it would be hours before her parents calmed down enough to fall asleep themselves, despite the fact that they were all emotionally and physically exhausted.

The events of that afternoon seemed terrifyingly near. Keiko had merely to close her eyes to see the flames and smoke, see the panicked crowd around her, pressing in, pulling her along, away from Molly. As frightening as it was, Keiko hoped the memory stayed fresh; she did not want to forget what the fear had taught her.

When she had found Molly again and the two of them had clung to each other through the last of the Cardassians' phaser blasts, everything in Keiko's life had been reduced to its purest elements. In the crucible of the Promenade, everything became so simple, so clean, so breathtakingly clear.

She loved Miles. She loved her daughter. The three of them were human, mortal, and there would come a time when two of them would lose the other. As cruel as that fact was, Keiko could not control it.

But she could control her own happiness. And she could keep self-pity from dimming the joy she shared with Miles and Molly.

She and Molly had returned from the Promenade bruised and shaken but unhurt. The quarters had seemed no longer gloomy and desolate, but numinous, alive with possibility. Miles had returned from duty, and she had told him everything. Then the three of them had held each other a long, long time.

Now Keiko sat and watched Miles and Molly in the soft evening lighting and the starshine and hoped that the deep gratitude would never fade.

She had been so foolish. Instead of being depressed about the amount of time on her hands, she had decided to take advantage of it. After all, she'd felt guilty while aboard the *Enterprise* that she wasn't spending enough time with Molly, that she was working too much. Well, here was the time.

And here was the time to read all the botanical journals she'd never quite had the time for aboard the *Enterprise,* especially after Molly was born, and here was the chance to attend a postgraduate course and symposium or two via holo.

"I've been thinking . . ." Keiko began softly.

Miles lowered his daughter onto his chest, not before planting a noisy kiss on her cheek. Molly squealed, then reached out and grabbed a handful of golden brown curls with a dimpled fist.

"Ouch!" Miles gently extricated himself with a grimace. "Molly, me love, you don't know your own strength! Someday you'll be the world's arm-wrestling champion!" He turned a smiling face toward his wife. "You were thinking what, honey?"

"I was thinking about starting a botanical research project here at the station. I can order everything I need—"

"Especially now that a lot of shuttles will be coming through these parts because of the wormhole." He pushed himself to a sitting position, Molly in his lap.

"I'll ask Commander Sisko's permission, of course."

"I don't see why he wouldn't approve."

Keiko sighed suddenly at the memory of Jake Sisko and the Ferengi boy on the Promenade.

"What is it, honey?" Miles asked, concerned.

"Oh. Nothing really. I was just thinking about Commander Sisko's son. He was on the Promenade. I wish I could do something to help him. He seems so lonely."

"I'm not surprised. It must be tough, being on this station with no kids his own age, and only one parent." Miles glanced down at his lap and lowered his voice. "Ah. Look."

Molly lay curled up asleep, her delicate brow furrowed as if in deep concentration, pink rosebud lips parted. Miles carefully lifted her into his arms, then waited for her mother to take her so that he could rise to his feet.

Keiko carried her into her room and tenderly set her on the small bed they had brought over from the *Enterprise.* Miles followed, and the two of them stood in the darkness watching their sleeping daughter.

"When the Cardassians began firing," Miles whispered at last, reaching forward to place a hand on Keiko's shoulder, "I was so frightened for you both."

"We're all right," Keiko answered softly, turning toward him.

He kept talking as if he had not heard her. "I felt so terribly guilty for bringing you here, for putting you through this—"

"Was this any worse than being on the *Enterprise* when we faced the Borg?" Keiko interrupted, laying gentle fingers on his shoulder.

Miles paused, remembering. "It was a miracle we survived then . . . So many didn't."

"We were lucky," she said simply. "And we were lucky again today. Why worry about blame? Why not just be grateful? I'm just so glad we're all here."

"So am I," Miles said, and hugged her.

Keiko smiled in the darkness and slipped a hand around his waist. "Come on. Let's go to bed."

Sisko transported planetside alone save for a very special burden, carefully hidden from sight in its receptacle. This time as he walked down Bajor's streets his attention was drawn not to the destroyed buildings, the scorched ground, the dead vegetation, but to the signs of rebuilding, of new life. Workers had begun reconstruction on the salvageable buildings, and the streets bustled with a midmorning crowd. Shopkeepers had set up an open-air market in the square near the temple, and the air was filled with the voices of haggling merchants and buyers. In the distance stood the aubergine mountains, so serene and breathtakingly lovely as to seem unreal, like an artist's rendering.

Sisko found himself imagining how lovely the city must have been before the destruction—and how much more so it would be in the near future.

He came to the entrance of the great stone temple, and paused before stepping from the bright sunlight into the cool shadows. A young monk appeared almost immediately and bowed.

"Commander. Welcome."

Sisko smiled, returned the bow—a little awkwardly, because of the size of the receptacle in his hands, although it weighed virtually nothing. The monk turned and strode briskly through the great echoing chamber.

Sisko followed, hurrying to keep pace, noting the improvements. The exterior walls had been patched, and monks were now restoring the interior ones; the rubble had been cleared away, the shattered windows replaced, the broken statues removed, presumably taken to be repaired.

"Commander Sisko."

Kai Opaka stepped forward out of the darkness. She now looked precisely like the woman in his dream; the bruises had faded, and though she still carried the cane, she scarcely limped as she crossed the stone floor toward him. Her smile was as radiant as Sisko's own. "So. I see you have brought us yet another gift."

Sisko laughed aloud and realized with a small start that he was feeling genuine *happiness,* an emotion he had not experienced in more than three years. "No, Opaka. Just returning one you gave me."

"Come," she said, and turned. He followed her to the reflecting pool hologram, and together they went downstairs into the secret chamber.

Opaka gently took the ark from him and placed it on the shelf.

Sisko smiled faintly. "Fourteen planets have already contacted us about opening trade routes through Bajoran space."

Opaka nodded as she turned to him. "The prophets have been generous."

He moved toward her, eager to tell her about the amazing, timeless beings within the wormhole. "I have a lot to tell you about your prophets, Opaka."

She silenced him with a wave; her expression grew apologetic. "Does it surprise you that I do not wish to hear?"

He drew back, disappointed at not being able to share all that he had learned . . . but then he considered her point of view and gave her an understanding smile.

She returned it with relief. "Perhaps that is why an unbeliever was destined to seek them. One should never look into the eyes of her own gods."

Sisko nodded and sighed at the memory. "It was . . . quite a journey."

She took a step toward him and held his jaw with gentle fingers, tracing her way up to his ear. This time he relaxed and did not recoil from her touch, and he felt no pain.

"Interesting," she murmured after a time, then said aloud, "It was only the beginning of your journey, Commander. . . ."